3 4028 09247 8552
HARRIS COUNTY PUBLIC LIBRARY
W9-AOS-371

Savage Country

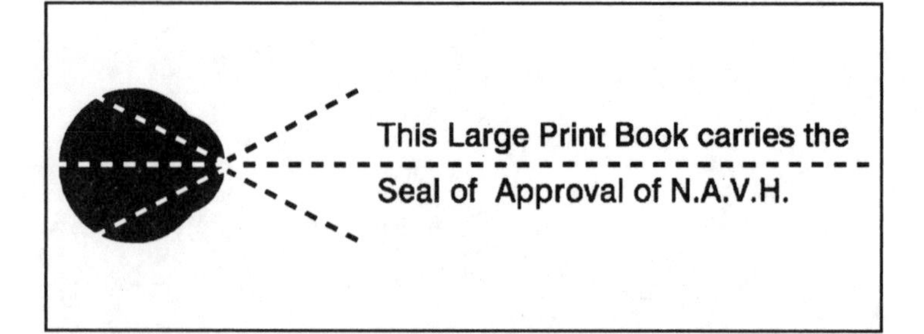
This Large Print Book carries the
Seal of Approval of N.A.V.H.

Savage Country

Robert Olmstead

THORNDIKE PRESS
A part of Gale, a Cengage Company

Farmington Hills, Mich • San Francisco • New York • Waterville, Maine
Meriden, Conn • Mason, Ohio • Chicago

This is a work of fiction. While, as in fiction, the literary perceptions and insights are based on experience, all names, characters, places, and incidents are either products of the author's imagination or are used fictitiously.

Thorndike Press® Large Print Historical Fiction.
The text of this Large Print edition is unabridged.
Other aspects of the book may vary from the original edition.
Set in 16 pt. Plantin.

**LIBRARY OF CONGRESS CIP DATA ON FILE.
CATALOGUING IN PUBLICATION FOR THIS BOOK
IS AVAILABLE FROM THE LIBRARY OF CONGRESS.**

ISBN-13: 978-1-4328-4375-5 (hardcover)
ISBN-10: 1-4328-4375-3 (hardcover)

Published in 2017 by arrangement with Algonquin Books of Chapel Hill, a division of Workman Publishing

Printed in the United States of America
1 2 3 4 5 6 7 21 20 19 18 17

See now that I, even I am he, and there is no god with me, I kill and I make alive, I wound and I heal, neither is there any can deliver out of my hand.

— DEUTERONOMY 32:39

Therefore rejoice, ye heavens, and ye that dwell in them. Woe to the inhabiters of the earth and of the sea! for the devil is come down unto you, having great wrath, because he knoweth that he hath but a short time.

— REVELATION 12:12

CHAPTER 1

Some distance from town he was met with the smell of raw sewage and creosote, the stink of lye and kerosene oil, the carrion of dead and slaughtered animals unfit for human consumption. He struck the mapped, vacant streets where there was a world of abandoned construction, plank shacks with dirt floors and flat-pitched roofs hedged with brambles and waste. Two cur dogs snarled at each other over a bone. Dead locust strewed the ground three inches deep.

The year was 1873 and all about was the evidence of boom and bust, shattered dreams, foolish ambition, depredation, shame, greed, and cruelty. Notes were being called in for pennies on the dollar. Money was scarce and whole families were pauperized.

For weeks countless swarms of locusts, brown-black and brick-yellow, darkened the air like ash from a great conflagration, their jaws biting all things for what could be eaten. They fed on the wheat and corn, the lint of seasoned fence planks, dry leaves, paper, cotton, the wool on the backs of sheep. Their crushed bodies slicked the rails and stopped the trains.

Michael rode light in the saddle, his left hand steady on the reins. His trousers were tucked inside the shafts of his stovepipe boots, and the buckhorn haft of a long knife protruding above the top was decorated with plates of silver. His black hair was long and plaited into a queue, which hung down his back. A shotgun was cradled in his free arm and on the saddle before him sat a setter dog and behind his right leg hung a string of game birds. The red dog had fallen out a mile ago and he thought that was perhaps for the best.

Farther on was a ravine of tents and dugouts where gambling, drinking, dog fights, and cockfights were taking place. Dingy flaps of canvas were flung back and barefoot women swept their dirt floors into the road. From a tent advertising Turkish baths came the bleating sound of a hurdy-gurdy. Men lay sleeping on the ground undisturbed, a paste of dirt and saliva on their bruised faces.

Ahead was the darker line marking the

railroad grade and the looming warehouses lining the tracks, the bone pickers and hair scavengers converging and departing from across the open land. Along the right-of-way was a rick of bones twelve feet high, segmented in the shape of boxcars, and a half mile long. This was the last of the Kansas buffalo.

Soon he could hear the hammering and banging of the blacksmith. There was a fine dust in the air that remained suspended. An eastbound train chuffed to a stop to take on bones, water, and the broke families bankrupted by the plague of locust.

A portly man in fawn-colored trousers and black overcoat came off the platform in a hurry. He stepped into a two-horse fringed-top surrey parked at one end. The man reached for the whip and gave the team a smart cut across the flanks. The drays stepped out and in tandem, their broken tails lifting in cadence.

At the post office Michael asked after mail for himself or anyone at Meadowlark. There was a letter for him from Mr. Salt.

"Michael Coughlin," the postmaster read, handing him the envelope.

"This letter has been opened," he said.

"It must not have been adequately sealed," the postmaster said.

He handed the postmaster the sealed envelope he carried. He paid the postage to London and inquired when the mail would be sent. The stamp affixed, he took back the envelope.

"I will be happy to take care of that for you," the postmaster said, his hand out.

"You can take care of this one," he said, handing him another.

"You can do that?" he said.

"Yessir," the postmaster said.

There was a plaza in town and a collection of shops on the four sides of it: saddler, watchmaker, gunsmith, mercantile, hotel, barroom, two druggists. Michael stopped at each one, explaining that his brother, David Coughlin, had passed and Michael would settle outstanding balances. From the druggists he purchased their supply of quinine and asked that they order more and make delivery to Meadowlark. The first had nothing to say, but the second one did.

"Malaria?" the druggist said.

"I was very ill for several weeks," Michael said, switching his shotgun from the cradle of one elbow to the other.

"It will be here tomorrow. Your brother, he was a never-give-up man. He will be missed."

Stalls were erected in the plaza and men

and women were raising money to leave by selling what little they owned to immigrants newly arrived. From one, a tatterdemalion boy was selling honey and beeswax candles. Michael paid for a mixture of nuts, candies, figs, and four oranges. He stood about, drinking gently a cored orange.

The postmaster stepped out and went down the street where he entered another building that represented itself as the Kansas Land Office. Young boys of a hard nature loitered in front, posing and strutting. They wore shiny revolvers and knives. Their neckerchiefs were as if brilliant plumage. The black runner and a big raw-boned sorrel were hitched at the rail.

"Mister," the tatterdemalion boy said, offering him an envelope of gold stars to put in the night sky. He'd cut them with scissors out of tissue paper. Michael paid for the stars as the postmaster was setting off again in the direction of the church steeple, carrying Elizabeth's letter in his hand.

Beneath a tarpaulin roof an old man with a brick-red face and deep-set eyes was selling bread drenched in sweet molasses, wolf pelts, and broken pinchbeck timepieces he displayed on a three-legged stool. The old man had a walleye and his cheeks were deeply pitted by smallpox. He carried the heavy scar of an edged weapon. The stroke was vertical and cut through his forehead, his nose, lips, and chin. The halves of his face were sewn together in a ridged seam, stitch holes scarring both sides. He wore a fur hat decorated with two stuffed blue jays. He smoked a pipe with a red clay-stone bowl and a cane-joint shank and labored with each weary breath.

From somewhere off came the slurred harmonizing of men singing. A strange languor settled in the space between Michael and the old man as they watched two little girls play marbles in the dust.

"What happened to yo'r pony?" the old man said, asking after the scars on Khyber's flanks.

"A lion," Michael said.

"A big big lion," the old man said, inclining his head as if to hear better.

"Big enough," Michael said. "Nine feet seven inches from tooth to tail and near four hundred pounds."

"Where are you from," the old man said, "they have such lions?"

"I am from away," Michael said.

The old man told him his name was Bonaire and he was a wolfer and he was also from away. His mother was Lakota and his father French. He fished inside his shirt for the medallion he wore around his neck, Agnus Dei, the lamb of God.

"What is it you are wanting?" the old man said, letting the medallion drop. "A woman or a drink?"

"I do not want neither nor."

"What man from away does not want neither nor?"

The old man dragged off his fur hat and rubbed at his forehead. He had no ears. The auricles had been cut away, and left were the receptacles of his ear holes. He then slyly lifted a cloth and invited Michael to look. Beneath was a collection of six skulls he said were Kiowa.

"Make me an offer," he said, but Michael declined.

At a street corner a man in a derby hat let down the leg in his barrel organ. His companion, a capuchin monkey with cup in hand, bounced from his shoulder to the organ to the street. The man had fixed mechanized birds to the top, and when he played, the birds bobbed their heads and flared their tail feathers. The little girls gathered their marbles and ran in his direction.

Michael asked after Whitechurch, the man he was looking for.

"He would be one of the evil kings of the

earth," the old man said.

"Be that as it may, I have business with him."

"He'd eat his own gut for money," the old man said.

"It takes all sorts to make a world," Michael said.

The old man took the bowl of his pipe in his right hand and pointed with the stem at the Kansas Land Office.

Chapter 2

Michael crossed the street with Khyber behind him, the setter perched in the saddle. The boys watched as he came on. He hoisted the saddlebag onto his shoulder and with the shotgun tucked beneath his arm he climbed the steps.

One of the loitering boys stepped up to bar his way. He was a hard boy, they all were. He wore hobnailed lace-up boots with leather gaiters. He carried revolvers and a knife. On his right hand the little finger had been chopped off and his face was as if permanently bruised.

"I need to pass by," Michael said.

"What are you going to do about it?" the boy said.

"If you fight, try to kill," Michael whispered.

"He thinks he's got brass balls," one of the other boys said, and they all began to laugh.

"I have a good mind to kill you right now," the boy said, squeezing his eye at Khyber.

"I have died before," Michael said.

"I ain't afraid of you, mister," the boy said, but his nerve was fading.

"If I were you, I'd mind my own business," Michael said.

"Is that a warning?"

"I do not give warnings."

The boy looked away to where hogs wallowed in a mud hole in the street.

"You go to the devil," the boy said, and with a wave of his hand he stepped aside. Michael went through the door, and once inside, his attention was alive to the men who sat before him.

Whitechurch was at his desk reading a newspaper. He looked at Michael over the top, a silver toothpick in his mouth. He was a little blue under the eyes and purple about the end of his nose. He wore fawn-colored trousers and a black vest. There were studs in his white shirt and his sleeve buttons were set with blue stones.

There were two others. The taller one had a shotgun athwart his lap and a battered slouch hat down over his brow. When he looked up Michael could see scars radiating from his right eye. The other was shorter with a heavy paunch and bull neck. His hat in his lap; he had a large head with long, strawlike hair. His chin was square and his cheeks tallowy. He sat with his chair leaned back and his heels hooked in the front spindle.

The tall one stared at him, his heavy eyebrows wrinkled as he struggled to awaken memory, while the other sat contentedly, chewing tobacco and blowing his nose with his fingers.

"What is it you want?" Whitechurch said, dry-washing the backs of his hands.

"I don't want anything," Michael said.

"Take a seat. Make yourself a cigarette," Whitechurch said. "I have first-rate tobacco."

"I am here to buy the paper you hold on David Coughlin's property, the Meadowlark. It is my understanding he rented money from you."

"Who are you?"

"I would recognize him in the blackest night," the tall man said.

"I'd know him in hell," the heavy man said, tobacco juice leaking from the corner of his mouth.

"I know you too," Michael said, "and I will kill you."

"I know that," the tall man said. "You've already killed a good many."

"Shut your mouth," Whitechurch said to the taller one. He stirred the papers before him in an idle, absent manner, letting the moment settle. The man controlled any number of deeds, notes, mortgages, and private accounts.

"I am his brother. I am Michael Coughlin."

"I did not know he had a brother," Whitechurch said.

"I tol' you he had a brother," the tall man said.

"And I told you to shut your g.d. mouth."

"I have a passport," Michael said, "as well as letters of credit and introduction."

Michael handed over a leather bifold wallet with printed endpapers. There was a fold-out sheet pasted inside with his name, purpose, destination of voyage, and date of issue.

"You are a Britisher," Whitechurch said, admiring the office of the papers.

"I am a citizen of England."

"There's a likeness," Whitechurch said, staring across the desk, "but how do I know who you are?"

"I have no interest in this little charade," Michael said.

"You fought in the Southern army," Whitechurch said, drumming on the desktop with his fingertips.

"Anybody is welcome to know my past," Michael said.

"When did you arrive?"

"Yesterday."

"When was the last time you saw your brother?"

"A long time ago."

"You are younger by?"

"Fifteen years."

"And what is it you do Mr. Coughlin?"

"I am a traveler."

"I have a lively interest in travel. Where have you been?"

"I am not here to waste my time."

"Sounds like a man whose pockets are full," Whitechurch said to the tall man, and he and the heavyset man smiled.

"What do you require?" Michael said.

"A good price takes longer than a bad one," Whitechurch said. He then looked to the ceiling as if in calculation. He referenced a faint scrawl of numbers on the cuff of his sleeve and then the ceiling again. The door opened, and when Michael turned, there were a scared-looking old grandfather and his grandson.

"Not now," Whitechurch barked, and they backed out the door. He then wrote a figure on a piece of paper and slid it forward across the desktop.

"You make capital out of another's tragedy?" Michael said after looking at the paper.

"Everything has its price."

Michael reached in his vest pocket and threw the loose change from his day's trading on the table. "What I'd give for your life," he said.

"Caveat emptor," Whitechurch said.

"I'll not pay that," Michael said, leaving the paper where it was.

"There was a loan and there was an investment. There was the promise of a profit on that investment," Whitechurch said.

It was strange to Michael how embittered a man could be over the loss of what he never possessed. Here was one of those mysterious people of very little conscience who would rule the world and yet he was fooled by the deception of unrealized gain.

"I am not wanting to dicker with you," Michael said. "The loan was secured by Meadowlark, but what you call the investment was not. I will pay on the rented money, but as to the speculative money, you are owed nothing."

"What is it you are saying?"

"You cannot get blood out of a stone."

"I am owed, sir," Whitechurch said.

"It isn't money until it's money."

"What, then, do you propose?"

"I am here to pay not what you think you are owed but what you will take."

"You do not feel bound by the rules that govern most men, Mr. Coughlin?"

"Lex talionis," Michael said as he held the man's gaze.

Whitechurch picked up a sharper pencil and began to cipher on his shirt cuff. His mouth opened and closed like a fish. He dropped his pencil after writing a figure on the paper and sat blinking at Michael. He pushed forward the paper and Michael pushed it back.

"Does it go well between you and the widow?" Whitechurch said. "Not so young anymore, but still a handsome woman."

"You will not talk that way," Michael said, feeling the twitch of reflex.

"Keep your seat!" Whitechurch said to the tall man as he leaped up. The tall man shifted the revolver on his hip, fed a quid of tobacco into his mouth, and sat down.

"In the war I killed better men than you," Michael said to the tall man. This moment he expected and he was prepared to have and even provoke. He was not afraid of the banker and his gunmen, not in the light of day, not in the middle of town, not ever. He let down his shotgun.

"The war is over," Whitechurch said, pounding his desk. "Eight years over."

"Is it?" Michael said as the moment of danger passed.

"I'll tell you what, throw in that horse you ride and we will close the account in no time. I'll bet she's a goer."

"I suggest you do not covet that horse."

"Fair enough," Whitechurch said, and the paper slid back and forth across the desktop several more times until there was a number Michael found acceptable. Whitechurch, having gotten all he could, sank back in his chair.

"A bird in the hand," he said to the air.

"Draft the papers," Michael said, lifting the saddlebag onto the table.

"Call in the penman," Whitechurch said.

The old grandfather returned with his grandson. In his case were steel pens, paper, blotting paper, ink, and a chamois pen wiper. He set to work with a flourish, and when the document was complete with the language of their agreement, Michael began counting out twenty-dollar gold pieces. Whitechurch fixed his eyes upon the gold, his lips moving as Michael counted.

Chapter 3

When Michael finally took up the road, the hour of twilight had come. He did not want to be in this town any longer and knew to move on as quickly as possible.

He'd made the depot the moment the mail sacks were being loaded and the engineer was getting up his steam. There were so many people who were broken and buying their tickets out. They possessed the clothes on their backs and whatever fit into the carpetbags they clutched.

He left behind the littered streets and miserable shacks and rode into the gloom. Behind him was the clang and cough of the boiler, the successive exhausts of the high-pressure engine, the smokestack pouring out soot and ash, the steam whistle resounding. He turned in the saddle to see a column of sparks burst from the stack. Jets of lightning flashed over the town. He knew Whitechurch would take what hard money he could get. He knew he'd be caught out by the darkness.

He rode into the red sky of the westering sun. He kept to no single beaten way but rode by many turns of lane and crossed streams and traveled through thickets and over rough hills, his eyes ever turning in the direction of his back trail.

He let down the setter to run alongside and rode with the shotgun across the saddle before him. He looked about for the red dog but could not find him. He knew the value of the signed documents he carried and the number of double eagles still in the saddlebag.

He topped the crest of a hill where he could look off in every direction. He pushed back his brim and stood in the stirrups. He scanned the darker line of the horizon. He ran his eye along a line of timber and came off the hill just as quickly.

He called in the setter and she came running. His right foot was clear of the stirrup and he swung it idly. His left hand held the shotgun perched upright on his thigh and with his right he gripped the cantle at his back.

"What now, Sabi?" he said to her.

The setter uttered a low whimper and once or twice wagged her tail. He slung the shotgun over his shoulder. He said her name again and she leaped up to him where he caught her in his arms.

In that same instant he saw its gray mottled coil and upraised head, lifted and steady. Without warning, the deadly rattlesnake struck from where it lay poised in the grass. It threw itself thrice its length and hit the stirrup iron, its fangs pumping their venom into his boot heel before falling away.

The horse bounced and jinked sideways from where the snake coiled in the grass to strike again. She flung round her head and her ears pricked. A tremble shivered through her body. She champed at the bit, pawed the ground, and collected.

He unclenched himself and caught his breath and felt suddenly the sadness of his brother's death.

"Damn your eyes," he said.

He uncurled his whip, a sjambok made of hippopotamus hide. The sound broke off as short and sharp and with a single stroke he took off the snake's triangular head. No, there was something more to come, more than this snake and more than David's death, and its experience could not be avoided.

The setter shivered and whined softly as he pulled the thistles and cockleburs from her long hair. She was footsore and cut by the hard sun-burned stubble of the old grass. He rummaged in his saddlebag until he found small leather moccasins to cover her feet.

He urged the horse another mile. They crossed the road and in some trees he reined up. He threw his leg over the saddle horn, slipped to the ground, and let drop the reins. He took a position in a small glade with the shotgun tucked under his arm. The night was chill, damp, and dark. It'd begun to vapor a little and the dank grass was bending under dewdrops. He petted the setter and told her to stay quiet.

He waited in the trees beside the road, scrutinizing the darkness, and then Khyber signaled by throwing up her head and snorting and it was not long before he saw the band of horsemen, one dark figure after another looming out of the darkness, bending low in their saddles, lashing their horses, and galloping ahead with noiseless rapidity two hundred yards away, one hundred yards, and then the ruck of their hoof tracks telling plainly. The tall man was in the lead, riding the black runner, and strung out behind him were the hard boys.

There were six of them and their dark and fleeting forms were going at a slashing rate.

A force inside him came surging back.

He stepped into the unoccupied road after the last one had passed, and waited. He stood motionless, watching, and soon enough, lagging behind the others, the big raw-boned sorrel with the heavyset man was bearing down on him.

Now is a good time, he thought as he raised the shotgun to his shoulder.

There was a moment of breathless pause as the horse and rider came down on him and then from the roadside was the red dog, sharp, agile, hard-biting, and on a dead run. The red dog leaped into the air and flew straight at the horse's head and struck full with its massive jaws. So sudden was the shock, both horse and rider turned in a somersault, and still the red dog held on.

Michael stepped aside as they skidded by at great speed over the rough road. The horse, so violently hurled to the ground, was shaken and trembled as it stood. The heavyset man made no effort to rise. The heart side of his chest had been crushed by the fall. His left shoulder was separated and wedged behind his back.

Michael reached down and grasped the man by his tallowy cheeks. There was no breath, no death rattle, to be heard. He lit a match to his eyes, but there was no reaction.

The man stared glassily, his chest crushed and his neck broken. In one second he was alive and in the next he was experiencing the awfulness of sudden death.

The red dog came to Michael and sat at his feet. There was a flap of skin where he was torn at the shoulder. From deep in his throat came a murmur, a sound more like words than a growl.

"May the devil come take your soul," Michael said to the man.

He gathered the man's long greasy hair in his left hand and twisted it in his fist. With his knife he slashed once and twice, a circle around the top of the man's head. He slid the blade beneath the skin and with a quick jerk he took the scalp. He held it up and then left it on the man's chest where it could be found.

He swung into the saddle, made a nicking sound, and Khyber reached along in a brisk, swinging walk and then jumped into a lope. The red dog came into her moon shadow. He ambled along as the country unfolded itself in undulations of grass and fallow land, trees in islands and ribbons, wheat fields and cornfields picked clean.

Michael eased on the reins and Khyber responded with stride and speed. She lowered her head and flattened her back and the world pressed against him as she built to full speed. The black ground flew beneath them as they traveled on by the moonlight.

Soon, carried on the wind, came the faint smell of wood smoke, and the road they picked up was dirtied with cow manure and beneath the darkness he found the lights of Meadowlark.

At the top of the lane he thought they'd be waiting for him, but they weren't. Overhead was a squanking sound. Geese had lifted off the water and were flying south for the winter. He watched as they made their arrowed passage across the moon.

In the valley below, beside the barn was a long shed filled with farm implements and the three big wagons painted blue. The grass-plotted yard was fenced in white pickets twined about with honeysuckle vine. He'd known the house from David's letter, its red shutters, green door, and gilded vane and on the verandah the wicker-back rockers and a glider painted white.

He let down his neckerchief to spit into the dust. He sat perched in the saddle, with a leg curled round the horn, the shotgun cradled in his lap. From his case, he lit a cigarette he'd rolled.

Fence country, he thought, and spanning out before him were thousands of feet of strong and high board fences enclosing the gardens, cattle yards, and horse pastures, and beyond that were four-strand fences of double-twisted and barbed wire that ran straight as a die as far as the eye could see where the cattle grazed. To the windward grew a permanent fence, a prickly hedge of Osage orange ten years planted.

There was a granary, chicken coop, hog yard, a cow barn crowned with cupolas, and stables for twenty horses. The corncrib was full of cobs, and in the coops and pens, chickens, geese, and hogs were asleep. There was a bake house, bunkhouse, cottages, and quarters for the laundress traced by the swinging clotheslines in front.

Rising in his stirrups, he surveyed the horizon, its suggestion of the dark infinity beyond and then again the direction ahead.

How strange to him the abstract theories of finance that so much could be worth so little.

CHAPTER 4

Elizabeth was sitting by the light of a small lamp. The on-sweeping darkness had condensed and closed on the windows. The veil-fold of another somber night had come to her in her terrible solitude and she could not quiet the aching in her heart, the trembling balance inside her body. She was so tired, but in recent days she'd rarely slept for more than a few hours at a time and when she awoke her body ached. If her heavy eyes closed, she opened them again with a start. She felt to be some coasting vessel adrift on a stormy sea and the shore ever receding.

That day she had washed David and dressed him and with the help of Aubuchon they settled him inside his coffin. How many accidents had brought her to this place so many miles from the bay and Nova Scotia? Where now were those promiseful days she trusted and thought she knew so well?

A big intractable stallion had lashed out wildly with its furious heels. The horse had struck David on the forehead and buried a small piece of hoof in his head. He went down and when they picked him up he was in convulsions. They removed the scrap of hoof from his forehead and bathed his head in cold water. He asked for his pipe and then lay down and not again did he utter a sound or a groan.

For days she'd been living in painful suspense, longing for David to recover, struck by panics and spasms as she passed her time in the middle of a half-waking dream. How palpable the feeling of disquietude, the loss and emptiness she felt without him, the void that could not be filled.

He had no business being alone with that wild horse. And now she'd come to learn their prosperity was not real. Whitechurch, the banker, told her David had bought foolishly. He bought without sense or forethought. Everyone had and now they all had to pay up. Whitechurch shamed her and badgered her and she'd fought her tears to maintain her dignity, and then she watched helplessly as a hundred head of cattle were driven off the farm to service the debt and in the morning a hundred more would be driven off.

They'd always done a busy trade with the railroad: contracts for wood, milk, eggs, meat, produce, and labor. Her husband had always told her to make money you had to spend money and however much he spent on land, livestock, buildings, implements, the prospect of money was always in the future. Wages and income had already declined, but then the locusts came ruining farmers with even the smallest of debt.

How much was owed she was still learning. As a woman she was removed from the world of money. He'd spared her the truth. Could love survive such concealment come to light? There would be a small settlement from the American Life Insurance Company, but it wouldn't be near enough. She was afraid and angry. She'd fooled herself and no longer expected to return to the happiness she'd experienced every day of their life together. It'd all been a bright and beautiful hallucination.

On this night, her heart like stone, not a tear, not a sigh, she fussed with her wedding ring. She thought of the things she did not want to think about, his dark moods, her longing to reach him in those awful bouts that could last for days. She tried to chase these memories from her mind even as she conjured them. None of that mattered now. She wanted to close her eyes and sleep in the heavy silence, but she was afraid to.

A commotion outside brought her from her solemn loneliness, brought her from her chair across the dark floor and to the window.

It was Michael returned from town. The setter dog rode in his lap and the long-nosed dog, as red and rough coated as a wolf, loped behind. His flat back, the erectness of his carriage in the saddle, the square set of his shoulders — these were the characteristics of military training. When he left for town that morning she wished he'd not come back but keep going and return to wherever he'd come from. He was a stranger and yet he was hauntingly familiar to her. He was David's brother, but she'd not met him before and had not known he was coming and did not know his intentions and did not trust him, his arrival coincident with such tragedy. What rights were hers and what rights were his, the brother of the deceased?

Aubuchon came from the kitchen with tea and honey to tell her Michael had arrived and when he saw her at the window he quietly set down the tray and went back to the kitchen.

Elizabeth watched as Michael let the setter to the ground, dismounted, and dropped the reins. He unlashed a lanyard, the game loops full with a dozen birds. He entered the gate down the flagstone path, pushing his hat back onto his shoulders. Then she could hear the heels of his boots on the steps, on the floorboards of the verandah. She buttoned her dress at the throat. She held a hand to quiet her beating heart as she waited for the knock at the door.

When she opened the door he beheld her sorrowful face, thin and heart-shaped, and her cheekbones were high and her hair was a mass of blue black, with the greater part pulled into a loose chignon at the top of her head and encircled by a black velvet ribbon.

The setter dog slipped in behind him. She was a swirl of long-coated dog as lithe as a cat, and he said, "Sabi," as she dashed about the room.

Elizabeth looked fixedly at him, her tremulous lips parted as if to speak. His bearded face was naturally melancholy. His eyes were faded and pale and held a sort of dark spell. She had the vague thought the sadness was one he always carried.

"You have been gone all day," she said, making herself stand straight and sturdy and strong, her blue eyes fixed intently. She studied him with intense concentration. His eye seemed indifferent and he appeared to look neither to the right nor left. He was here and not here at the same time. He was so strange, silent and alert. He was a fine-enough-looking young man, but she could not escape the idea she distrusted him. He arrived yesterday, unannounced, and was if he'd been to a place and had yet to find his return. All day long she wished he'd ride on and not come back.

Michael felt her watchful eyes upon him. He wanted to say something, but there was nothing he could think to say. It was lodged in his chest, the ache and murder he felt.

"Michael," she said.

"I have to stitch the dog," he said.

While he washed and stitched the red dog's wound, Aubuchon removed the breasts from the birds. He wrapped them in strips of bacon secured with a sliver of wood and sautéed them. He toasted bread and there was wine, coffee, and cream.

"I am so tired," Elizabeth said, her hands resting in the lap of her mourning dress, "the sort of tired that can't be helped by sleeping."

She watched as Michael pinched close the dog's hide and worked the needle.

Aubuchon was standing in the doorway to the kitchen.

"Madame," he said faintly, raising his eyes. The manner in which the old servant treated Elizabeth had in it far more than respect. As a much younger man he'd been educated for the priesthood but had never taken holy orders, never married, never had children of his own.

"Yes," she said. "Thank you." Aubuchon nodded once and returned to the kitchen. When Michael finished stitching the red dog, she asked that he sit and their supper would be served.

"If only we knew you were coming," she said. "David might have held on a little longer."

He held out his left hand, a gesture, he did not know what to say. He'd written from England, New York City, Chicago, and St. Louis, but they'd not received his letters.

"On devrait souffrir comme le Christ," Aubuchon whispered, setting the plate between them.

"Aubuchon made coffee," she said, "and I am wondering if you'd like some."

He shook his head no. Where she was stricken by grief, he harbored a resentment for how cruel and unjust life can be, for the black seam that ran through it. It burned inside him. He wanted to say how bitter his heart was, but he did not.

"You should know his death arrived quietly," she said, her anxiety for the future a mere breath away.

"I am sorry," he said.

"Please, no pity."

"I am sorry for myself," he whispered.

"Oh, yes," she said, how secret his feelings, how severe his detachment. "You've seen many dead people?"

"Quite a few," he said, and then, "You also."

"The slaughterous American war," she nodded, recalling her days as a nurse. "Quite a few of the men and boys did not recover from their wounds."

He searched for his grief. His brother's death was the death of an idea more than a man, the death of family, and something he was not ready to consider. He'd done what he could. He'd paid off his brother's creditors and soon he would be moving on. But for now he changed his mind and decided upon a cup of coffee.

"You are not a believer?" she said.

"Yes, I am," he said. "Life has taught me to believe in the one but not the other."

She sat erect, her eyes flashing, her cheeks spotted with crimson, her expression strangely imposing. She drew in her lower lip. Who was she to judge? What truth could she lay claim to? Her husband was dead and she was poor.

"I am very tired," she said, her voice shaking a little. "I would like to rest."

Her eyes were fixed on the fire. She drew her shawl closer about her. She turned her head to him.

"You sleep at night?" she said. "I can offer you a sleeping powder."

"I will sleep."

"Do you walk in your sleep?" She'd steadied her voice.

"No."

"Then you won't bother me."

She stood and when he stood before her she extended her hand and he accepted it.

"I'll say good night now," she said, leaving him to the dog.

When he finally lay down to sleep that night the coyotes made a fearful howling and gibbering down by the river and his dream was the rattlesnake striking the stirrup iron. Again, he uncurled the whip and took off its head, and in the morning when he awoke, he found a broken fang embedded in his boot heel.

Chapter 5

The sun had risen and the shadows driven from the land. On the stovetop were kettles of stew and in the ovens were roasts.

The simple coffin was made of pine and lined with cambric. Under the head was placed a black velvet pillow trimmed with gold thread, and gilt tassels were at the four corners. The exterior of the coffin was covered with black velvet and set in the cover was a pane of glass above the face. The shield of flowers was made of paper.

Carriages filled the lane as the people arrived carrying hampers of food for the table of David Coughlin's always hospitable house. The people gathered from town and the surrounding countryside to stand by the grave, the surviving farmers and stock raisers, merchants, homesteaders, businessmen, and their families. They lived on top of the land in houses and they lived beneath it in dugouts. They were dressed in ready-made and homemade, the garb of spun butternut, the cloth of handlooms. Some wore new suits bought in stores and others their old army uniforms of sky-blue trousers and navy-blue blouses with brass buttons with the American eagle upon them, blue overcoats with the long cape of the cavalryman. The women and girls were as if dressed in a single black garment shaped and sized for fit. Among them was Bonaire the wolfer whose hat was decorated with two stuffed blue jays. He rode a mule and walking some distance behind him was an olive-faced woman dressed in buckskins and moccasins and whose nose had been cut off.

Their heads bowed to the ground in sorrow, they understood the strange and terrible in life. They were believing people, and in their lives the men were watched over and they in turn watched over the women. In their lives there was no chaos and there was no coincidence. There was only the pattern of providence, the cycle of loss and restoration.

The pallbearers who carried the flag-draped coffin to the little hillside cemetery that morning were Alvin Lee, Darby, Ransom, Daragh, and the Miller brothers — Story and Temple — all men who had devotedly followed David Coughlin into battle after battle and after the war came west with him to Kansas to break the land. They respected him in life and revered him in death. Their hair was washed and combed and plastered behind their ears.

The sun rose that morning in brilliant reds and oranges and yellows. A more beautiful day could not have been asked for.

Elizabeth stood bravely and silently by the grave with Michael beside her. Behind her veil her eyes were swollen from weeping. Her mourning was fearful to her for how hollow she felt. Grief seemed as if something she could not afford. She was too haunted by the memory of Whitechurch's hard boys, the ones who drove off the cattle to pay debt interest, their eyes like burn holes in their young faces. She would pray for them, but not today.

She'd met David in Washington, where she was a nurse and he was recuperating from a gunshot, the ball having passed through both his thighs. When he proposed she fled back to Halifax and he followed and persuaded her to marry him. They were married in New York City and from there they traveled to Key West, Jamaica, and Panama, where he loved the flowers, and then here, to Kansas. He'd been a great dreamer from the very start and she always felt that she was with an old friend living an eventful life.

Because of the locusts, there were no flowers to place on David's grave. She stepped closer to Michael so that should she fall he might catch her.

The Reverend Doctor Purefoy conducted the service. He was tall and strikingly handsome and spoke in a singularly clear and pleasing style. He did not maunder. He read from the Psalms and the old soldiers bent their heads forward and their eyes wetted with tears.

Michael scanned the hillsides before he bowed his head. He wore his brother's long mourning coat and beneath it he wore his revolver.

The Reverend Doctor Purefoy then closed the little volume bound in leather and spoke extemporaneously. He spoke of life as a day: the graying, the pale blue, the sun, the greatness of the coming light. He said David Coughlin was a courageous man and was worshiped by his men, who would have followed him anywhere he asked them to go.

He shot out his tongue and licked his lips. He smiled. He said, "There is a divinity that shapes our ends, rough-hew them how we will. In times like this we must do our best to come to life."

Michael listened to what the reverend doctor had to say until his mind began to wander. He held no anticipation of punishment or reward after death. He experienced no terror of the underworld, of the afterlife. He had no dread of suffering upon perishing. He believed in the transition of souls into horses and in the second sight of dogs and their ability to see invisible spirits and witches. He believed in omens and dreams and warnings and instinct. He believed, contrary to the Gospels, the meek, however blessed, would not inherit the earth.

When they took up their rifles to fire the salute, Michael could hear in his mind the bygone bray of drums, the melancholy bugler, the rasp of swords unsheathed. The rifles reported and there was a hush and from high an adjacent hillside, his shoulder roughly stitched, the red dog began to howl.

People milled about before starting down the hill, but not for long. They were hungry.

Aubuchon had set the big dining table and two more tables made of planks and sawhorses to receive the roasted geese, the boiled hams, meat loaves, and curled links of sausage. From the bake house the Miller girls brought doughnuts, coffee cakes, pies, and large loaves of wheat bread. There were baked beans, potpies warmed in the oven, a great tureen of oxtail soup, lamb stew. There were pickles, gravies, preserves, coffee, milk, and buttermilk.

Elizabeth welcomed everyone into her house. She stood erect, her left hand resting lightly on the table and then more heavily on a chair back. Her other hand hung by her side to be clasped again and again in condolence. Now and then she caught her breath and reset her feet. She had never felt so alone in the company of so many people. She felt damaged and their sympathy for her felt like pity. Soon enough there would be evening chores to do and the men and women would begin to depart and journey to their homes that they should arrive before dark. Until then there was nothing she could do to speed them on their way.

Chapter 6

Michael went to the stable to be with Khyber and Sabi. He touched Sabi curled up in the straw and rubbed her smooth and then Khyber. The night Khyber was foaled a crowd gathered and he'd caught her in his hands and there was a great noise of exaltation. "Amen!" they cried. "May Allah bless thee! He has sent thee a child." He then fed her three eggs before setting her to her mother.

In the stall next to Khyber's was an iron-gray hunter named Granby. Eyes full and large, nostrils wide, and mouth deep, his neck was long and straight with a firm thin crest. He was broad-breasted and stood about sixteen hands in height.

"Mr. Granby was a gift from the major to the missus," came a voice.

Michael turned to the speaker. It was a Negro, about his own age, who wore dark blue wool trousers with a yellow leg stripe.

His shirt was white with a placket front and his boots were cavalry.

"The major was very good to me," he said, extending his hand.

"You rode with him in the war."

"He took me under his wing at a very young age."

"What's your name?"

"Darby."

"Who do you answer to?"

"I am my own master."

"It is good to be your own master," Michael said.

The man was silent for a thoughtful moment. He seemed to be thinking of something else and changed his mind before he spoke again.

"It was a pleasure to meet you," he said, and without another word he walked away.

Michael moved a chair into Khyber's stall, his back against the wall and Sabi settled between his legs. Through the boards he could hear the hired help migrating with their plates of food into an empty stall. Elizabeth made them to know they were welcome in the house, but here was where they worked and where they felt most comfortable. They sat on cracker boxes and nail kegs and drank their hot coffee and ate hungrily from the plates they'd filled. When they stood they groaned and limbered their bodies and hesitated before they sat down because they knew they'd eventually have to stand back up.

After a time he could hear them talking. He had little interest in what they might say. He found his reading book in his saddlebag and tobacco and left the stables. He passed under a bower of thorns and entered Elizabeth's garden.

He sat smoking in silence. From inside his shirt he withdrew a gold chain with a locket. Inside the small folding case was a photographic portrait of a young woman. Her hair was long and fell in waves and curls about her shoulders. He closed the locket and let it inside his shirt. He opened the novel he carried and found the page he'd bookmarked with a quill.

When the reverend doctor stepped into the garden he saw Michael in the arbor, deeply engrossed in his reading.

"Good afternoon, young man," he said. "Don't rise. Keep your seat."

The reverend doctor slipped into a chair opposite him where he hummed and nodded his head.

"You have found a good spot here," he said.

Scraping at the bowl of his pipe, knocking

the sparks onto the ground, he asked Michael what he was reading, and before he could answer, the reverend doctor said he liked a good book too and was especially fond of Fenimore Cooper, met him when a boy and read him with great pleasure.

Michael finished the passage he was reading, inserted the quill, and closed the book.

"Your brother was to build a little chapel over there," the reverend doctor said, pointing to a hillside caught in pretty sunlight. He shaded his eyes and looked at the sunlit hill. He seemed to study it as closely and as long as he could.

"I'm clean out of tobacco," he announced, and Michael handed over his pouch. The reverend doctor repacked his pipe, scratched a match, and lit it again. He had a habit of clacking the stem against his teeth.

"I am grieved at your loss. Your brother and I were dearest friends. Intimates," the reverend doctor said. He was a man who spoke in declarations.

"You arrived yesterday," he said. "I understand you have traveled to the strangest lands."

"I have been around the world."

"I guess you have some fine stories. I should like to know them sometime."

Without pausing, the reverend doctor told

Michael how he loved to plant and the husbanding of animals. He was by nature a homebody. He loved the sun. He loved Kansas and had come here before the war with the Massachusetts Emigrant Aid Society.

"How do you find Kansas?" he asked.

"Rattlesnakes," Michael said, then shrugged.

"We don't mind them. I have killed three hundred on my place alone."

"You just want to mind where you step and walk and sleep and where you put your hand, that's all."

Michael knew no matter what he said the reverend doctor would continue down the path of his own interests. As with all religious men, he was a man of many ideas but only one conclusion.

"I have worked hard in my life and roughed it," the reverend doctor said. "Hardship is God's gift for self-improvement."

"Then you must be much improved by the many snakes," Michael said. He had little interest in this conversation.

"Were you baptized?" the reverend doctor asked.

"I do not know," Michael said, building a cigarette and lighting it.

"Are you a believer?"

"Sometimes I have wished I were, but no," he said.

"You were in the Southern army."

"Yes, I was," Michael said. "At the time, David was in Massachusetts and I was in Texas with my mother's people. I rode with the Eighth Texas Cavalry, Colonel Terry's Rangers. We fought from Bull Run to Appomattox and as you know we lost."

"You were just a boy," the reverend doctor said.

"A lot of men were boys."

"You've had a hard life."

"I don't think of it that way," Michael said.

"David said you were ten when last he saw you."

"I always wondered if one day we would meet on the battlefield, but it wasn't meant to be."

"What would you have done?"

"I do not believe I could have killed him if that is what you are wondering," Michael said.

"And then?"

"I went abroad."

"Why not come home?"

"There was no amnesty," he said. "It was for the better good."

"God's judgment," the reverend doctor

said with cool sympathy.

"Both sides prayed to the same God," Michael said.

"And he made his decision," the reverend doctor said, smiling thoughtfully.

Going-away crows hoarsely cawed over the corncrib and went silent. A calf bleated inside the barn and a cow bawled in return. The windmill pumped lazily.

"Where did you go afterward?"

"I shipped out to Vera Cruz, and when the French left Mexico, I went back with them. From there to Egypt, where I served the khedive in the Abyssinian campaign."

The two men could not help themselves and turned from each other toward the westering sun.

"Nature is a miracle," the reverend doctor said, and then turning back to Michael, he said, "Do you like it here?"

"Like it?"

"This beautiful farm," he said with a magisterial wave of his hand.

"Yes, I like it," Michael said, understanding that the reverend doctor would conclude him to be prodigal and grasping.

"It's the liberal use of Peruvian guano that gets such results. Wheat, corn fodder, beans, peas, cabbages, squash, strawberries, fruit trees — it is indispensable. It provides for roses' and flowering plants' color and brilliancy. With good guano, three hundred pounds per acre is considered a very fair manuring."

Michael had nothing more to say. He'd judged the man insincere and hypocritical. He was like talking to a drunk.

"Where have you been lately?"

"Africa, primarily," Michael said.

"How did you find it there?"

"I was not overawed by the brutality."

"What does one do in Africa?" the reverend doctor said.

"I thought to get rich in the ivory trade."

"And how did that fare?"

"The trade in slaves is inextricably tied to that of ivory. Slaves are needed to carry tusks to the coast. Lately I work for a man named Mr. Salt," he said, "shooting large mammalia and preserving and collecting their skins and skeletons." Mr. Salt had standing orders for museums and private collections. Michael explained that he'd shot tigers in India, bears in the Balkans and Tibet, elephants in Ceylon and Abyssinia. He also captured wild animals, a male and a female were needed, and these were sold to zoos or private menageries in New York City, Berlin, Hamburg, Cologne, Vienna, London, Amsterdam, Paris.

"Sometimes they require one of each, but more often two of each, four of each, sometimes six," Michael said, thinking that just as the reverend doctor was in the pursuit of souls, men such as Mr. Salt were in pursuit of all the phenomena of nature. They would possess the flora and fauna of the earth, its machines and art, its minerals, water, fire, and air. They would own the rising and setting sun, the moon and the planets, the shining stars and the meteors, the seasons and the change of season, the clouds, the wind, the rain and snow. They would possess the created and the uncreated. They would own history.

"Like Noah," the reverend doctor said.

"Without an ark," Michael said.

"Why did you never come visit sooner?"

He shrugged his shoulders as if to say it could not be helped.

"You could have come home," the reverend doctor said, more adamantly than he intended. There was reproach in his words.

"Home," Michael said. The word, it seemed strange to him and his thoughts sank more deeply into the motionless past. His face altered and darkened. He released his lower lip from his teeth where he held it.

"May I ask what finally brought you

here?" the reverend doctor said.

"David wrote to me."

"He wrote you?" the reverend doctor said. He could not help himself, his surprise.

"He asked that I should come see him and I had a strong feeling to do so."

"And the horse? You journeyed here with the horse and the dogs. She is perhaps the finest I have ever seen. What happened to her?"

Michael told the story of the lion attack and then said, "Dr. Livingstone claimed the lion's bite is painless, but I can vouch that is not true."

"You've been leading the wandering life for so many years. You must miss it."

"I have had no other calling."

"I wish I could say the same. I envy you your lot. I am sure I could enjoy such beautiful scenes forever and ever. But are you alone? Without companions? Without even a roof to shelter you?"

Michael was suddenly tired of talking.

"Yes, you have surely come from another world," the reverend doctor said, looking off.

"I have my experience."

"Do you think you will be staying long?"

"Only another day," Michael said, and satisfied with that answer the reverend doctor drew his watch by its chain, looked down at it, and declared it was time for him to go.

"Young man," he said, "I have enjoyed our conversation. Feel free anytime to unburden yourself."

Michael turned his gaze on the man, the stub end of his cigarette smoldering between his fingers. He despised such as the reverend doctor, their worlds of righteousness and reward, punishment and damnation.

The reverend doctor stood and stretched his limbs. His eyes were clear and untroubled. His face was smooth and peaceful. Michael opened the book he was reading and found his place. The reverend doctor drew a breath and took his leave.

Chapter 7

All afternoon she'd listened to the stories of her husband's many kindnesses. Apparently, there was livestock throughout the countryside maintained on his behalf, animals these farmers and stockmen could not afford to own. They grazed his beeves in return for the calves. They pastured his milk cows for their butter, milk, and cheese. Because of him, one old woman had the finest flock of Barred Rocks that gave her so many eggs. For these, the old woman squeezed into Elizabeth's hand a few dozen coins wrapped in a knotted cloth, and yet every condolence was a reminder of the tragedy. She wondered what weight of agony the human heart could bear. There was a sob in her throat and another and she was instantly sickened by the illness of her sorrow. She knew she had to be patient, she had to collect herself, she had to will it away.

David must have thought about it constantly, but not once did he intimate the precariousness of their situation and not once did he take her into his confidence. He'd taken such chances with their future and she thought angrily how improvident he'd been. Then she turned her anger upon herself. She too was responsible. He was the provider and a promiser and she took everything he gave her. Whatever he did he always said he was doing it for her and how wonderful it had been to hear such expressions of love. To receive his kindness and solicitation was always a glory. His pride was in her delight, but his failings were his secrets alone. That is until now. Her dependence upon him had been complete and because of that, she would now lose the very ground in which he was interred.

And what of these good men and women who built and maintained Meadowlark? Where would they go? What would they do? They'd finish their lives in the poorhouse living on charity. It was all a shambles. She'd end up a widow living in the old home, a madwoman spending her days rocking and sewing in someone's attic. She steadied herself as if come from a hospital bed after a long illness. She brushed out her hair and braided it, then changed from her mourning dress into a linen shift and wool stockings and one of David's old chambray shirts with long tails, and over this she threw on a shawl.

When she found Michael he was sitting in her garden asleep in the shadows, the sleeves of his flannel shirt rolled to his elbows. The windows of the house cast bright squares of light that fell at his feet. She approached noiselessly in the gray and cold twilight and draped a blanket over him and when she sat beside him he stirred awake.

"Did I startle you?" she said, putting a hand on his shoulder. She let Sabi into her lap and took her muzzle in her hands.

"Everyone has gone back to their homes?" he said.

"May I get you anything?" she asked. "There's enough food left over to feed an army."

He told her he was fine and then apologized for his afternoon's absence and she said she understood. They were all strangers to him and she knew how awkward that could be.

"This came for you," she said, handing him the package from the druggist and another letter from Mr. Salt. He marked his place with the letter and closed the book. He thanked her and set the book and the package at his feet.

"My busy day," she said, her hands resting on the long-coated dog and her eyes staring out into the dim formless evening.

"Maybe sleep will be part of your future," he said.

"Nothing wakes me up more than lying down to go to sleep," she said. "Once I close my eyes I wake out of some devil's nightmare and live it again." There were tears in her eyes and she began to weep quietly. "When I close my eyes he keeps coming to me." She told him she anticipated sadness, but today she confessed there were moments when she was angry and hated David for dying and leaving her.

He had nothing to say to this.

"Forget my anger," she said. There was still a lump in her throat.

"I do not want to wear a widow's cap and die an old lady alone in some single room. It's a great thing to be a man. Men are born free and equal. A man's security is in his being."

She turned her face toward him, the rushing thoughts filling her mind. A rising moon in the east drenched the night with its light. The yard smelled of cool smoke and animal dung. The evening was eerily still. She looked off intently before speaking again.

"David hadn't been well. He'd been possessed by a sadness he could not explain, but as the planned expedition south neared, his spirits began to return. He threw himself into it. Whatever may have ailed him work was his cure. His vision was to go south and hunt the buffalo and make a great fortune. He was so happy at the prospect of the hunt."

Her eyes were cast down and in shadow where they could not be read. There was something she wanted to ask him. He was afraid he knew what it was.

"I was there," he said, interrupting her. "Before the war. When a boy I rode with the regulators."

"What kind of country is it?"

"Violent."

"I'm not afraid," she said.

"What are you saying?"

"Will you take us there? I would like to go."

"What do you plan to do down there?"

"I would like to employ you to carry out the hunt."

"How long do you plan on being out?" he said, the idea so incredible.

"We will stay until we have enough."

"How much is enough?"

"Enough."

She could not possibly know what she was proposing to do. His brother was one man. He rode in and he rode out and with some luck that could be done, but she was talking about staying for months south of the dead line and west of the Indian meridian and that was foolhardy.

"Am I so funny?" she said, angry for what must be passing in his mind.

"Perhaps less ambition and more judgment," he said.

"I am prepared to take the risk."

"Elizabeth, it's not possible."

"Everything is possible."

"Please think what you are saying."

"I have no choice."

"Do you think there will be torches to light the way?" he said. He had the idea his brother had been her moderation and not the other way around.

"I am afraid," she said, "and I am not ashamed of saying it. This hunt was to pay off our debts."

"You still have your life."

"Life is small property," she said, and she looked to the stars as her fears for the future flared inside her.

"I have been to Whitechurch," he said.

"Whitechurch?" she said. "You have no idea what a thief he is." She filled with the memory of the hard boys Whitechurch brought with him and how while David lay dying they cut out the beeves, opened the gates, and started them down the road.

"He is paid."

"Paid?"

"I have purchased the paper he held."

"You would ride in here and take everything?"

"It is yours. I am giving it to you."

"You are giving me what I own? By what right do you assume? Now I owe you when I would owe no man."

"Jesus, God. You do not owe me anything."

"You say that, but I am now in your debt. You have done me a kindness and I am grateful, but you have not done me a favor. And what of the next hard times? You will ride in from nowhere at the last second? I won't take it," she said. "The money is not mine. It's yours and I will not ever be in this position again."

"There is no use talking. These men of yours are hearty enough, but the work requires killers and butchers. It's dirty work and monotonous and every day it turns the land into an abattoir."

"Do you think the troubles are over?" she asked.

"Troubles?"

"With Whitechurch."

"Yes," he said, but he knew that was not the case and knew that she knew it as well. Sabi lifted her head. Michael looked off in the direction she indicated. He waited to see what she saw and as if on command the red dog appeared.

"I intend trying," she said, "even if it costs me my life."

"It just might."

"That means what? That you do not care to consider it further?"

"No," he said.

"People change their minds," she said, her face blued by starlight. She quietly stood up and crossed her hands behind her back. "I have his maps and his journals if you are interested."

"If I try harder, can I change yours?" he said.

"There are things," she said, "I do not worry about anymore. If you change your mind, the rifles are in your brother's gun cabinet in the room where you sleep," and she led him to the room.

Inside, he turned the key in the lock to the gun cabinet. The first two pieces were identical big-bore, single-shot rifles made by Sharps Rifle Manufacturing Company of Hartford, Connecticut. Their oil-finished stocks and forearms were made of walnut with steel butt plates. They carried side hammers and double-set triggers. Each was equipped with a 20× German-made telescopic sight. They were brand new and as yet unfired.

He selected one and half-cocked the hammer. The lever operated down and forward opening the breech where it would receive the cartridge. He brought the lever back and up and the breechblock closed. He lifted it to his shoulder. It must've weighed sixteen pounds.

As he lay in bed that night he knew she would go whether he went or not. He read again the most recent letter from Mr. Salt. There'd been a delay of several months in mounting the expedition he was to lead. Michael would have ample time, but it was more than that. His brother wanted this place to go on. She was now his only family. She'd have her excursion south. She'd get a taste of the bloody business. The journey would be its own hardship. She'd come to her senses eventually and return to Meadowlark.

CHAPTER 8

In the following days Michael and Elizabeth made their final preparations. The blue wagons David had bought for the expedition were immense vehicles with beds of steel plate and steel wheels with nine-inch rims. Each required eight yoke of the long-horned oxen and were capable of hauling four tons, and each towed behind it a lighter trailer. The camp wagons, half as large, also had nine-inch steel wheels and steel boxes, and each needed four yoke of oxen. Under the rough work and dry air, the steel would hold up better than wood.

Another large wagon was outfitted for Elizabeth, an ambulance with a half tent at the hinder part for dressing and sleeping. Inside was a light, thin mattress on a bedstead consisting of four boards that lay lengthwise on two strong trestles twenty inches high, and over the whole was stretched a large canvas sheet.

Into the cumbrous wagons went all manner of supplies. They loaded flour, coffee, salt, and beans. There was sugar to cure buffalo hams and canvas to sew them up. There were large cheeses, pickles, sauerkraut, peaches, canned tomatoes, cucumber pickles, yeast powder, molasses, crackers, tea, and lard. There were tents; stoves; camp stools; skillets; coffeepots; cooking utensils; a wrought-iron camp kettle large enough for boiling meat and making soup; tin cups and plates; frying and bake pans of wrought iron, the latter for baking bread and roasting coffee beans; wax candles; lanterns and kerosene; bottles of matches corked tight.

For Aubuchon's kitchen a wagon was fitted up with side chests, water casks, a sheet-iron cooking stove, and a sufficient variety of cooking utensils and an assortment of canned fruit and vegetables. Bacon was packed in strong sacks a hundred pounds each and placed in the bottom of the wagons to keep it cool. The sugar was secured in gutta-percha sacks to keep from getting wet. There were dried and compressed vegetables. They freighted enough shelled corn in sacks to feed the horses and oxen until they could become accustomed to the hard work and a grass diet.

In another wagon, flying a red pennant,

there were ten thousand primers, 440 pounds of Du Pont powder in 25-pound cans, and 1,600 pounds of St. Louis shot-tower lead in bars done up in 25-pound sacks, enough for twenty-five thousand rounds. There were two thousand shell casings and a thousand loaded cartridges. There was strychnine and arsenic.

And still another wagon carried chicken coops with a dozen hens that laid an egg daily. There were hogs and a drove of six milk cows.

Elizabeth told the men there'd be no gambling or whiskey, but they could have their tobacco. She told them they'd wash themselves every day and their clothes every week, and for this purpose there was an ample supply of brown soap.

"You will make use of the washboard," she said, "and you will work hard and there will always be plenty of food to eat whenever you are hungry."

She paused and then she said, with all depth of conviction, "Mark my words. The work will be productive. You will make money. For that to happen we will need to work together." She paused. "I'll need your prayers."

New men had been hired when many of David Coughlin's chosen men decided against going without him, but still there would be Darby, the Miller brothers, Daragh, and Aubuchon, whose wages would be paid monthly, as well as the skinners who'd be paid twenty-five cents per hide for skinning. They were still in need of haulers, a reloader, peggers, and butchers and these men they'd pick up on the trail.

Michael looked hard at the men. In these times of crop failure there were so many encumbered with mortgages they could not pay and yet they would not agree to venture south and cross the dead line into the Comanche territory. In their stead, these were the men she hired and each of them had a story, and not a very good one. These men were landless and homeless and blown by the wind of circumstance. When they could find work they chored for twelve dollars a month and room and board. They were men of no home, no house, no place, no romance, no longing for something that never was. They would never again die for land.

They had no idea of what lay ahead. They'd keep their rifles within reach and they were determined to never be off their guard, but they didn't know. Whether the fault of the times or the fault of their own, he had the painful feeling he could place no reliance on them and assumed them to be no better than murderers, liars, drunks, horse thieves, robbers, failures.

The old man who wore blue jays in his hat was hired and with him came his woman without a nose. He rode a mule and she drove a team pulling a small cart with all that they would need. It would be his job to poison every carcass and let the wolves and coyotes eat their fill and die and then he'd collect the pelts. For this purpose he carried knives and would use the bottles of strychnine crystals and Elizabeth would pay him so much per pelt. The arsenic would be used to kill the bugs that infested the hides.

Attached to the old man's wagon were his collection of skulls and three brass crucifixes and between two of them there hung a black scalp a full yard in length.

Among the skinners there was a boy Willy and his life-bitten grandfather William Penniman. The old man was showing the boy how to pack the bowl and light the pipe. The grandfather's teeth were badly abscessed and he treated them with cotton soaked in brandy to which Elizabeth consented. The boy's voice was high and rather shrill. He wore silver-rimmed spectacles and he was nervous.

"I know you," Michael wanted to say, but

he did not. This was the same grandfather and grandson he remembered from Whitechurch's office who'd drawn up the debt agreement. He seemed a gentle man, with a purple nose, black hair, and blue eyes, humble, intelligent, and a bit devilish.

The man told Michael their home was in Wisconsin and they came to Kansas to teach penmanship, but they'd fallen on hard times.

"You have beautiful penmanship," Michael said. "I have some of it."

"Yes. Yes, you," the grandfather said, then turning to his grandson he said, "He has some of our penmanship he does, doesn't he."

Two of the men were Meadows and Cochran, both in their forties and come off the railroad where they claimed to have been employed as track walkers and fired for drinking too much at the wrong time. When younger they were with the British at Lucknow during the great Indian Mutiny. Meadows had lost an eye to a powder explosion and wore a black patch over his eyehole. Cochran carried three coins that grape shot had driven deep into his external thigh. They showed him their campaign medals as proof of experience.

Trusting they knew something about

discipline, hardship, and danger, he assigned them to the butcher wagon to turn the horses and oxen that couldn't keep up into fresh meat, to collect the game he shot for the cook pot.

Two others were the Gough brothers, Ike and Abel. They were young men of seemingly vicious dispositions. Their faces were unwashed and unshaven and they reeked with smoke and dirt and sweat. They originated from Georgia and were bachelors and seemed to be good honest haters of most everything.

"Who are these men?" Michael asked Elizabeth, thinking what little dependence could be placed upon them. There were so many it would be necessary to get rid of.

"Men I have hired," she said, and she told him she would rather trust in these men and be deceived than to wound anyone by doubting too much.

"We will be going into the country with a band of strangers."

"Men earned their money when they worked for Major Coughlin," she said, "and with me it'll not be any different."

What little she knew of these men she did not want to believe. Summers of hope, winters of despair, she knew as well as anyone, people were in their straits for one reason or another. They were men without masters and desperately in search of other masters.

"You cannot deny them their liquor," Michael said.

"I am afraid if I do not the bottle will be handled too freely."

He reminded himself he'd agreed to the venture. He would keep his word. His concerns were navigation, arms and ammunition, the security of the stock, their camping ground, posting of the night watches, and killing the buffalo if they should get that far. His job right now was to go in advance and spy out the land. Preparation was prevention. Caution was protection. He'd rely on old habits and practices proven with time.

"They are men like everyone else," she said, "with a desire for something to have. They are committed to making money."

"I hope that's enough."

"Isn't it always?"

"What does the penman have to say?"

"We have talked," Elizabeth said. "He has quite a story to tell. He would simply like the chance to prove himself and I said he could. It's necessary for them to keep together, for the boy to look after the old gentleman, who is very shaky on his feet."

"And what of the boy?"

"He costs us nothing and his grandfather wants him to become a man."

"If he can't keep up, it becomes an issue," Michael said.

"Not for you," she said, and with that he was dismissed.

The days were running sunny and very warm. Determined to husband the stock, the men took them on short and easy drives so that the teams would become habituated to the work. They would travel twelve to fifteen miles a day and when the roads were fine possibly twenty miles.

When the departure day arrived each stood by waiting for the command to begin. The men yawned and grumbled a little, and stretched themselves violently, and yawned again as they waited.

By the setting sun Michael was in the saddle and Elizabeth astride Granby with her broad-brimmed hat, man's shirt, an old cavalry jacket, leather chaps, and heavy congress boots. A holstered revolver hung close at hand, the ivory-handled butt of the big weapon ready to the grasp. In her breast pocket was a pair of French gray spectacles.

"Are you ready?" he said. The moon would soon rise above the trees and the light would be soft and white, bathing the country they would travel.

Her cheeks flushed at the question and she turned, her eyes on the road to town. There was a glow in her hair. She began to breathe, some emotion rising up inside her, and then the Reverend Doctor Purefoy rode in. Under his coat he wore a black vest and his churchman's cravat and collar. Elizabeth had asked him to accompany them as her personal and spiritual adviser and by chance he wished to see the country, and if possible, spread the light of the Gospel in that far wilderness and for that purpose a crate of Bibles was stowed in the wagons.

"Ready," she said.

The night was hot and sultry and without a trace of wind.

Michael rode out and shortly thereafter the teams started their loads and the wagons were moving. The oxen bellowed and the men cried gee and haw and came the clang of cowbells, the jarring and croaking of the wagons, the whiplashes cracking in the air as the great elongated body began to move.

They'd travel across the plain in a southwesterly direction and then due south, seeking the southern herd below the Kansas line. Somewhere between the north fork of the Canadian and Red Rivers of Texas, and from about the 100th meridian to the eastern border of New Mexico, the last herd of buffalo moved.

CHAPTER 9

After holding the same course for three days, the train of wagons parked on a small creek near a thicket of cottonwoods and red willows. The banks were low on each side and the stream not too deep and shaded. The land beyond was a broad interminable sheet of blazing white. Soon the air was sweet with wood smoke and dripping fat from skewers of meat. Aubuchon had prepared a grouse soup thickened with flour and flavored with bacon. He took his own lunch alone and walked in the afternoon along the creek, where he found bullfrogs fifteen inches from nose to toes and several soft-shell turtles and these he'd turn into a fricassee.

Michael had ridden thirty-five miles out and back and again, changing horses evening, morning, and before noon. He took a tin cup of coffee from beside the campfire. He walked away to the water's edge where he drank off the coffee in his cup and dipped it full of water.

He unfolded David's sketch maps illustrating their journey, a scale of twelve miles to the inch, the physical features of the land penciled in. He found the complementary pages in David's journal written two months ago and began to read.

June 8. — The route today has been a rolling prairie, in many places covered, with the dwarf oak bushes. Saw many deer but had no desire to hunt them. Encamped upon a creek of clear and wholesome water. I am homesick. A bad spirit has again taken possession of me. As always, I am a victim of my own imagination. It comes over me a black tide. My spirit is being undone and I try not to forget virtue and beauty, I but think I must end my sorrowful life . . .

I am a gloomy character these days and so painful to be around. I am unsettled in my mind and there are days I feel to be as crazy as a bedbug. I do not know how much longer I can endure the moodiness, dejection, and despair.

I try to think how good it is to be alive. I can now see more clearly than ever in my life before that I have been striving and working without any end in view.

The Lord gave me a cup so bitter. If the farm were not so deeply in debt, the land and the buildings so heavily mortgaged . . . The wolf is at the door and I have sunk into a horrible mistrust of myself.

His heart beating wildly, Michael began tearing out the sad pages as he read them and letting them float away on the current to a place where they would never be read again.

Some days I feel to be lifted above the mere accident of life, and other days, blue days, life is chaos and too much to survive. My sleep is broken and troubled and full of fearful dreams. The terrors come to me so naturally. Old wounds have come back to ache again and the past, the scars of conflict, seem unbearable. An unnamed fear haunts me. How can the days seem so brief and yet interminable at the same time, immense, monotonous? How can I ever again lead good men? I hold no dream of return. They say he who believes will have everlasting life. Maybe that is enough. I have written to Michael. I will pray to God tonight that he will come.

Sabi came to lie beside him and in her

sleep she dreamed of birds and whimpered softly. He pulled low the brim of his hat, still seeing his name on the page in his brother's hand. He tried to think of other things. Today he had come across two antelope skulls, their antlers locked together, and later he'd watched an antelope kill a rattlesnake. When they left the train in Lawrence, Kansas, they had good hunting all the way and he saw meteors in the evening, principally from the northwest. One day they encountered a man hanging from the beams that supported a bridge. It was on this day he first glimpsed the black runner and the big sorrel and would see them again and again as he made his journey west. All along the way, the land was being broken and towns were being built. In one town a pawnbroker was murdered. They found him dead in his bed as well as his wife and baby, all three with skulls crushed. It was a bustling, money-getting world, America. There was so much ambition, so many bold and reckless spirits flocking to the frontier: freed slaves, crippled navies, broken soldiers, outlaws, poor immigrants. The times were truly volatile.

After lunch, Elizabeth rode along the creek a half hour and a half hour back. She rode in and out of shade, the heat waves rising beneath her. She saw glimmering mirages, sheets of delusive water, a cloud of dust, antelope, and wild horses. For some the deceptive and inhospitable landscape might be unsettling, but for her it was liberating. Riding Granby felt therapeutic, an aid to the healing she desperately sought.

When she returned, the men were in the short grass along the water's edge or lying in the shade of the trees and bushes scattered over the alluvial flats. She found Michael holding a piece of paper and reading from a book he held in his hands. He folded the paper over and then folded again, slipped it inside his shirtfront, and fastened the button.

She'd pulled on a wrap to cover the linen shift she wore. A towel was draped over her shoulder. She turned her face to the sun, closed her eyes, and then opened them. She waited and then he noticed her.

"What have you been doing today?" she said.

"I am out for a walk," he said, removing the wire-framed green glasses he wore. The skin around his eyes was white and the rest of his face was burned by the sun and wind and dusted with sand and grit. "You should never leave camp alone, even for a stroll."

"Please do not underestimate me," she said.

She'd watched him closely these first days on the road and was learning how strange and capable he was. He had a capacity for silence and was rarely surprised by what he came upon. When tired, he coiled down in sleep and Sabi snuggled egglike into his body, and at any time he was liable to get up, day or night, and have coffee and smoke. Whereas David had been capable of disappearing inside himself for days at a time, Michael always seemed to be alert, present, and expectant, and unlike his brother, he seemed to require just enough for himself, the horse, and the dogs.

"You might wash your face, young man," she said, her mouth a smile, and then asked that he escort her while she bathed.

He dropped his rifle into the hollow of his arm and followed her into the cottonwoods where she shrugged off the wrap, and barefoot, she stepped into the glittering thread of current. The shift floated along behind her as she left the shore and walked into the stream.

At the edge of his vision she was merely a giving of movement. He waited for her and when she came from the creek she carried the sodden pages from David's journal, where she found them caught in the waterside sedge, washed of ink and thought them such a curiosity, paper in the water, so far from anywhere.

Indifferent to the paper she held, he made a shooing gesture with his hand, a flying insect. He lit a cigarette and smoked in silence and then said, as if lost in thought, "We are being followed."

"How can that be?" she said. She carried her own glasses on the trail and had formed the habit of scanning everything that moved just as he did.

"We will have a stranger here before long," he said.

"How do you know that?"

"I have been watching him."

A few hours later a boy came in barefoot and bareheaded. He wore a cowhide jacket and his trouser legs were ragged at his ankles. He was tall, long-armed, and lathy. He had a rash on both cheeks and scales on his head. He carried his toothbrush in a buttonhole, a corncob pipe in another, and about his neck a clasp knife on a leather thong.

"What route do you take from here?" the boy said.

"Are you going home or leaving home?" Michael said.

"Just traveling."

"Somewhere particular?"

He recognized the boy who sold him the envelope of scissored stars. Michael calculated his age as not yet fourteen.

"Why do you follow us?" Michael said.

"I am all alone."

"You must go back to your people."

"I do not have any."

"Whose boy are you?" Elizabeth said.

"My father and mother are dead. Hey, you wouldn't let a fellow starve would you?"

"What is your name?" Elizabeth said.

"Charlie."

"What is the second part?"

"Poteete."

"Do you shave yet?" Michael said.

"No," the boy said, and smiled.

For however rough he'd lived, Charlie seemed still boy-hearted with a goodness in his soul. He began to fidget. Apparently he carried birds in his pockets, and possum babies, and these he began to shift around and some he set free. The birds, they lit from his fingers like tiny flames and the possum babies he stroked and petted and found a deeper pocket.

"Who is your father?" Michael said when Charlie turned back his attention.

"He is a beeliner," Charlie said. A last bird

emerged from his cuff, and surprised, he tossed it in the air where it took flight.

"And your mother?" Elizabeth said, expecting another bird at any moment.

"I have never seen her."

"Why not?"

"She is dead."

"What set you on the road?" Michael said.

"My father put an apple on my head and was to shoot it off."

"What kind of work can you do?" Michael said.

"When I do something I do it properly," the boy said, working a finger into his nose.

"Such as what?"

"I can see in the dark."

"What else can you do?"

"I can do this," he said, and dropping to the ground he put both heels behind his neck and walked about on his hands.

"What else can you do?"

"Most anything. Find me a bee cave or a bee tree and I'll show you what this ol' boy can do."

"Come and eat," Elizabeth said. "I believe there is a little leftover."

With a pair of hooks, Aubuchon lifted a pot of meat, beans, and potatoes from the fire pit. From the mess box he brought bread and a cherry pie, and the boy dug in.

Soon his face was shiny with grease and crumbs of bread. He'd look up, the face of a starveling, his eyes blinking like an owl, and dig in again as if afraid he'd never see food again.

"Do you like that?" Elizabeth said to Charlie.

"Oh, ma'am, it is very good," Charlie said, taking bites from the stew and the cherry pie.

"Have you not eaten in some time or do you have a hollow leg?"

"A hollow leg?"

"He lost his leg, you know," Elizabeth said, pointing to Aubuchon.

"But he has two legs."

"Yes, he must have found it then," she said, and then she sent him to the creek to bathe.

When washed he was a fair-haired and delicate boy with sloping shoulders and a contracted chest. He was bony but he stood erect and his eyes were bright. By the bruises he wore on his torso, he'd recently received a terrible beating. He asked for tobacco to fill his pipe and Michael tossed him his pouch.

Michael told him to wait where he was. When he returned with Elizabeth she made the boy turn around. The bruises were black and blue, yellow and purple. They were on his shoulders, his ribs, and his back. She made him take down his trousers and they were on his buttocks and the backs of his legs.

However dangerous their journey, she'd not send him back. There would be use for a boy such as him. He could take his turn performing the night guard. He'd watch the oxen as they grazed upon the pasturage. He'd fetch and be sent on errands. In time he would improve and with the right kind of influences even prosper.

"Can you milk cows?" Elizabeth said.

"If I want to."

That evening after Michael rode off to scout the trail ahead, a man came into camp looking for the boy. He was moody and blear-eyed, his skin the color of oakum. He conveyed the sense of a dark, vindictive spirit, of cherished hatred. He too was barefoot, with the bottoms of his pants rolled up several inches. He was lame in one leg, his foot deformed by injury.

"Who is he?" the reverend doctor asked.

"He's the worst man of his name," the boy said from the shadows.

"Why does he walk that way?"

"He was cutting down a bee tree to get the honey. His foot got caught and he crushed it."

"What has that birdbrain been saying to you?" the boy's father wanted to know. His voice was loud and nettlesome.

"He was telling me about your foot," the reverend doctor said.

"Did he tell you I started a fire and with my own knife seared the bleeders? That I lay in the forest for three days and then I walked home?"

"Apparently your boy would throw in with us."

"He's an id-jit," the boy's father said, and he cuffed him about the ear, knocking him to the ground.

"Shame on you," Elizabeth cried.

"That boy is God's own fool."

"You will not hit that boy," Elizabeth said.

"He is my son and it is my right to do as I please."

"He is always teaching me manners," Charlie said. He righted himself to stand with his mouth open and his hands clasped before him.

"The boy wants to do everything, but he doesn't want to do anything long," the man said.

"You were a boy at one time," Elizabeth said.

"Where are you headed for?"

"The buffalo pastures."

"I wouldn't go there unless I wanted my throat cut," the man said.

"You always said 'tis the land of milk and honey, a place where a man might make a new start," the boy said to his father.

"If he is so simple a boy and a good for nothing, what do you want him for?" the reverend doctor said.

"You have a bad heart if you think I'd sell my son," the man said, looking off.

The reverend doctor took out a leather pouch and shook the coins inside.

"Maybe we can be friends," the man said, turning to him. "Maybe we could do bid'ness."

"Is he a hard keeper?"

"No. I wouldn't say that."

The reverend doctor handed the man a twenty-dollar gold piece. "Take it or leave it," he said.

"Your hand is against me," the boy's father said. "I won't have it."

"Stop your sniveling," Elizabeth said.

"Your bones will rest there," the father said, wiping his mouth with the back of his hand. "All of you."

"You will eat something before you go?" Elizabeth said.

"He is not hungry," the reverend doctor said.

"It's a poor conclusion," the man said to his son after taking the heavy coin and then, "Good luck to you," and he turned his limping gait up the road and hobbled on without looking back.

Chapter 10

Elizabeth closed her eyes against the sunlight. For a time she'd fallen asleep in the saddle from sheer exhaustion. When she startled awake the reverend doctor was riding beside her.

"I must have fallen asleep," she said.

"I was prepared to catch you," the reverend doctor said.

"Your constant friendship is a great boon to me," she said. "You are very understanding."

"The heart is not so complicated."

"No," she said. "I do not suppose it is, though it seems it should be."

"Vanity of vanities," he said. "Man is mere breath and his days like a passing shadow."

"Yes," she said, then laughed aloud, her mind strengthened for how simple it could be.

They stopped to rest in the heat of the day. There was a fire started under the wash pot and each man was to bring his own armful of wood to keep it going. Charlie stirred with a barrel stave as each deposited his clothes on his way to the creek. There were washboards, coffee, and a basket of gingersnaps from Aubuchon's traveling kitchen. A small looking glass was hung from a branch for shaving.

They'd been out six days and had run through the liquor. The penman was the first to show symptoms of withdrawal. He was shaky and complained of headaches. He vomited and sweated profusely. He'd blackened his hair with boot polish and in the heat it streaked his face. Like so many, he dreamed and compromised and this was the pattern of his failed life. Now he was brittle and crumbled to dust, his mouth dry and his saliva thick as mucous.

When Michael rode in he sought out the penman to check on his condition and found him staring blear-eyed at a newspaper he'd found in the packing. On his breath was the chemical smell of his gut desperate for liquor.

"I am a helpless reader," the penman declared in greeting, a smile working his mouth.

"What is that you're reading?" Michael asked.

"The *Cincinnati Daily Commercial.*"

The penman let the newspaper slip. He mopped his brow with a threadbare handkerchief. He told Michael he was badly swindled by a man in Cincinnati who took subscriptions to begin a school in his name and absconded with the money. It required every bit of his small savings to pay off the debt and avoid prison. The shame of it was unendurable.

"You and your grandson will not make it," Michael said.

The penman, rheumatism in his hands, tapped his forehead when he spoke.

"We have nowhere else to go." Tap. Tap.

"You must think me indifferent," Michael said, "but I really don't mean to be."

"Willy's father died in the war, and after his father was killed, his mother, my daughter, poured boiling water on herself and shot herself. She was declared insane and sent to the lunatic asylum at Columbus. When she came out she threw herself into a threshing machine."

"I am sorry," Michael said.

"You have lost too," the penman said. There was an intricate network of wrinkles around his eyes. He was shaking and sweat was running down his chin and neck. Waving a trembling hand before his eyes, he shooed away something only he could see.

"We all have," Michael said.

"You understand, Whitechurch will try to kill you," the penman whispered.

"I know."

"It's what I heard when copying his documents. He would have me make certain fabrications. I went for my dinner and did not return. I thought it best to leave town."

"You are not safe from them either."

"No."

"Mrs. Coughlin knows all this?"

"I told her everything when I made my petition to join," the penman said.

"If you cannot make it, that is your fate," Michael said, chafing at the burden of responsibility. It wasn't due to Elizabeth they were here. It was because of his crossing the threshold of Whitechurch's office. That crossing — what else he'd set in motion he could only wonder.

"Young man, sympathy for others is something inside all of us."

"I know you believe that," Michael said.

Michael joined Elizabeth and the reverend doctor eating beneath an awning they'd hung. They'd spread a cloth and unfolded canvas chairs. There was a table with legs that folded. Beside them the creek shimmered in the light, and beyond was the land in the heat waves and an occasional cloud of red dust. There was wine to drink and the reverend doctor brought a bottle of whiskey to the table.

"What did you two talk about?" Elizabeth asked Michael.

"He doesn't talk much," Michael said.

"What's wrong with him?" the reverend doctor said. "Is he ill?"

"He is very friendly and I am sure he is honest," Elizabeth said.

"I would say they are all drunks and they need their liquor," Michael said.

"They've handled their bottles too freely and now it's gone," the reverend doctor said. "More is the last thing they need. I say it's the sun. I myself had a slight sunstroke today. Poisoning from the sun can be very dangerous. I said to young Gough the other day, You are drunk, sir, and he said to me, No, sir, it is the sun."

"Actually, it is something they do need," Elizabeth said, and explained that many of the soldiers in hospital were addicted to liquor. Many went into battle full as a goose and were wounded and suddenly without the bottle they succumbed to the torment of delirium tremens and often died. In response she and the other nurses began to secretly provide a drink or two and slowly weaned them of their dependency.

"I suppose it's no use," the reverend doctor said. "You start by opposing intoxicating liquor and you have to settle for no habitual drunkenness."

"We must separate the sin from the sinner," Elizabeth said.

"These men are paid to work and when they are drunk they cannot work. They are therefore stealing from you."

"You speak the truth," Elizabeth said. "But such men as these are haunted by a thousand devils."

"We can't fool away time with a drunken man," the reverend doctor said.

"What's one to do?" she said with a sigh.

"Let them drink," Michael said.

"So much for the progress of temperance," the reverend doctor said.

"I see it must be done," Elizabeth said.

Michael leaned back in his chair and watched a small whirling dust devil as he smoked. Elizabeth took out her pocket watch and looked at it, the press of time always upon her. Someone was blowing a hooo-hoooing noise across the mouth of an empty bottle and someone else started yelling.

"They are worse than children," Elizabeth said, snapping her watch. Every second ticked away the three months promised.

"If we are lucky, they will laugh themselves to death," the reverend doctor said, and he laughed when Elizabeth smiled.

"Watch your mouth, you yappy bastard," Ike Gough yelled. "When you have hurt your back the last thing you want to hear about is someone else hurt their back."

Then a great cry went up and men were high-stepping and they were hollering, "You son of a bitch . . . Damn you to hell . . ."

Revolvers were drawn and shots fired. Michael came forward in his chair. He told Elizabeth to stay where she was.

When he came on the scene there was a gunnysack and a tangle of rattlesnakes slithering from its interior. Men were moving as fast as they could as snakes writhed at their feet. One was coiled at the shoes of the penman's grandson, the boy paralyzed with his fear. Michael caught the snake's neck in his fist and carried it off the ground. The snake slashed its tail about and twined its body round his arm.

With his knife, Michael cut off the head and still it twisted and rolled and its mouth opened and closed. Another he snatched by the tail and whipped on the air, breaking its neck. The rest were shot or hacked to death or escaped.

It was Abel Gough who had carried the sack into their circle and opened it. The brothers thought it very funny and they snorted with laughter and their eyes brimmed with joy.

"Don't cry. Be a man," Ike Gough said to the penman's grandson. The Gough brothers stood shoulder to shoulder, their faces dull and their emotions drained. The glare in their eyes was loaded.

Elizabeth came up with the reverend doctor's bottle of whiskey. She announced she would give up her prohibition. They could have their liquor and she urged a drink upon each, but she would not tolerate any more fighting.

"Take it slow," she said to the penman as she poured a drink. "Is that better?"

"Happy as a butcher's dog," the penman said for the serenity he felt.

She filled their glasses, and then again, and when the bottle was almost empty she asked Aubuchon that he fill a pitcher from the brandy keg.

"It is not a black-and-white world," she said, turning to Michael.

"In some ways that's true," Michael said, holding out his glass for the last of the reverend doctor's whiskey.

The penman swore after this day he would

ride the water wagon for the rest of his life. But once you start drinking something wakes up inside you and you cannot make it go back asleep. That night on the trail the penman complained of feeling bothery and awfully muddle-headed. His body seized and his teeth clenched and he was taken with the delirium tremens. He was twitchy and anxious and he cried out with each vision of the mental hallucinations that held him captive. They tied him up, loaded him into a wagon, and kept on across the plain.

CHAPTER 11

Michael adjusted his direction by compass and the going was favorable. His brother's maps and journal were trustworthy guides and he referenced them often. Each day they kept on in darkness and in the first days traveled a made road and the going was slow and easy, the route plainly mapped. Still, he lived in constant watchfulness. He rode out and back and made his instructions. He changed horses and rode out again. He returned in the earliest morning and when he left he took with him one of the lead horses. When he returned again he brought deer or turkey. Sometimes Meadows and Cochran would drive to meet him and return with a side of beef or a hog bought off a farmer.

They were not the only ones on the road. His brother's journal warned him of *mischievous, cutthroat infidels, who well deserved to be shot, hung, and imprisoned for life. They say that gamblers and all sorts of "toughs" follow a new road. I met today with a wagon train of consumptives having left the east for the drier climate of the west. There are signs of Indians everywhere. We have been dodging them all day long.*

There were big freight trains hauling grain to the forts, the outposts, and the mail stations, and in the sacks of oats they smuggled whiskey. They sold freely the government stores of grain and the whiskey, and Michael kept their party supplied with both.

That afternoon he ate a meal to last through the night. By morning he wanted to make fifteen miles and so he rode until the sun fell. The night came on and was intense and the air was close. He rode through the darkness, the dusty road, the abandoned farms, the ghost villages of failed enterprise, and in the early morning when the deer came to water, he shot one, and when the others flared and sheered, he took steady aim and shot one more. He gralocked both deer and slung them over the packhorse already festooned with the turkeys he'd shot.

The pale gray of the eastern sky began to grow red.

He consulted his brother's map and journal. *Most of the farms and villages, being built near water, lay hidden in the folds of the ground.* There were directions to one such farm and the names of four boys. Their mother named them each John for the disciple Jesus loved most and they went by their middle names. The oldest was John Matthew, sixteen; and then John Mark, fifteen; John Luke, fourteen; and John John, twelve.

A low line of hills rose from the plain to the east, gradually increasing in height. He opened his pocket compass and it showed him the direction he was determined to go. The first faint glimmering of dawn lit the sky in the east. He bent to the creek and some distance off the road there was smoke in the air. Having been in the saddle since nightfall, he was weary and rode slowly, Khyber sleepy, as they picked their way along the sandy trail. He followed the smoke until he came to a rusty stovepipe thrust through the turf. In the field brown stalks rattled in the wind. Evident all around was the blighting presence of the locust. The early morning air was fresh and the ground cool. He descended a draw and came to a lone window hung with calico and a door sunk deep in the bank.

Across the draw was a little log stable where draft horses and mules stood quietly.

The stable looked more habitable than the house might be. There were seven cows, chickens and a hog pen, the frame of a half-built windmill. The corncribs were full and waiting for some freighter to empty them. Fat Emden geese toddled about. A rooster of beautiful plumage gave his voice to the morning. He stepped loftily and crowed again, his tail feathers carried high and graceful.

When he looked once more a woman stood in the door with a revolver in her hand. It was clear she'd never spared herself. She was tall and raw-boned. Her hair was gray and her face weather worn and wrinkled as if scarred.

"What is wanted?" she said.

"Coffee?" he said, pulling on a rope that let the deer slump to the ground.

"Is that red dog yours?"

"He is not so much mine as I am his."

"Dogs can study out many things better than men can. Dogs and horses know the people who care for them."

"I would agree with you," Michael said.

"Come," she said.

He entered through the doorway in the draw side, the deep crack in the earth where they lived. The room was plastered and whitewashed, the plaster laid directly upon the earth walls. In a corner were the spades and shovels they'd used to build their house.

Four strapping boys in cotton overalls with suspenders sat at the table.

They were fair skinned and freckled from the sun and their heads were shaved bare. Their father sat on a bench cut into the earth behind the stove, idly chewing on a tuft of straw-colored beard he held between his teeth. His mind and his thoughts were so clearly somewhere else. On a shelf over his head were a Bible, a copy of Virgil, and a Greek grammar. There were the collected books of Washington Irving.

"My husband and my four noble sons," the woman said.

There were plenty of biscuits and a large kettle of beans smoking hot that she swung from over the fire. She ladled him a bowl with a fat chunk of salt pork. There was coffee and for the boys there were cakes covered with sugar and cinnamon.

"You've had a bad accident here?" Michael said.

The boys dipped their heads as their mother told how her husband was digging a well for a neighbor and injured himself and never fully recovered. But it seemed more than that. His heartiness was gone. There was a trouble in his mind, a weakness, an eccentricity. She did not know.

"He's never been of a lazy sort," she said, her eyes as if fixed on a mystery.

"They say that danger follows a new road."

"They say true. We have been here since eighteen sixty-five and we have seen it." She told him how last fall several of their cattle drowned in a miry place, another one strangled herself, and a week ago the Indians butchered four of their neighbors while they were digging potatoes. They were hacked to pieces by their own hoes and then the hog pen was opened up and the hogs let onto them to eat their bodies.

"But I am not one to bury my face in my hands," she said.

"My brother was to hire your boys," Michael said.

Her mouth softened, but her eyes were still brilliant. Her face pinked.

"The boys are very good?" he said.

"They work with right goodwill," she said.

"Do they have shoes," he asked, and she nodded yes, they did. "The place we are going will be a dangerous place."

"Ma, we must take our chances," Matthew, the oldest, said.

"I don't give a damn how dangerous it is," Mark, the next oldest, said.

She swatted at him across the table. "You wash your dirty mouth," she said. "Get the man a feed of corn for his horse."

When they stood from the table they filled the room. They were stout, well-grown boys for their age with clear blue eyes and open, intelligent faces. The four of them walked off in silence and Michael was alone in the house with their mother and her husband who'd let go of his beard and was fretting with a sliver he found in his thumb.

"I am surprised he's not come sooner," the woman said.

"He has died."

"He was a good man," she said. "Most people are bad but not him."

A sound floated through to him, a sweetness. One of the boys at his work was singing beautifully, "Oh my luve's like a red red rose."

"Where are you taking my boys?"

"The Wolf Creek country south of the Canadian is full of buffalo."

"Not safe, they say."

"There is no denying the risk."

"We are all poor folks here and don't hardly make enough to keep up. They wish to have a better future," she said.

Her hands on her cup were whitened and creased from the wet and cold. For so long she'd feared the coming of this day.

"You will be all right here?"

She set down her cup and unbent her fingers, her hands to the wood of the table and wandering over its surface.

"I will," she said, folding her fingers into her palms.

When the boys returned he asked them again if they were still thinking of going.

"How long do you think we may be gone?" Matthew said.

"Through the winter," Michael said. He knew they had no choice and he felt a pang in his heart for their mother. He was taking them away from her.

She moved toward the open door, sunk in a moment of despair. She remained in the light huddled in the opening. The boys looked down at their feet. One of them searched after something in his pocket. The rooster was standing at their mother's feet, looking inside. His plumage of green, orange, and purple showed in the sunlight like burnished metal.

"Tell the man what you have decided," the woman said, shooing away the rooster.

"We are as we were," Matthew said.

"We are going off to buffalo," Mark said.

"You are to do whatever this man tells you," she instructed her sons. "They think they're smart," she said, a flash in her loving eyes. "You've got to give them a little hell every once in a while," and then she said, "I warn you right now, they will eat you out of house and home."

She went to each boy and placed her hands on his shoulders. "Act as men," she said to them, and then she turned to Michael. "I want them home for Easter."

"You'll make her Easter," Michael said to John, the youngest, and the boy smiled.

"I'm kind of tired of talking," the woman said. "Your father's blessing goes with you."

Michael paid their mother half their wages in advance. There'd be enough for her to leave and winter among townsmen, enough to pay a doctor to treat her husband.

He told them to follow the creek west to the crossing and wait on the wagon train and when it arrived they were to tell Mrs. Coughlin that Michael Coughlin had hired them for the season. He told them to hang the turkeys and dress out the deer for their mother before they left.

That morning as the boys reached the path opening by which they were to go away, they turned and took a long look back, their mother waving, a hand held over her heart.

Midday the wagon train reached the bank

of another river, where they crossed. They deflected from the road and followed the creek and Michael could see them coming with Darby bringing them in. The four boys tramped along in their cotton overalls with their shoes knotted together and slung over their necks, bouncing against their chests. Matthew carried a late-model Winchester over his shoulder.

Aubuchon directed the boys in digging a trench and laying the fire. He would cook and they would eat and rest and remain through the heat of the day before traveling into the darkness. They found their shady spots and spread their bedding. They pulled their hats to cover their faces and fall asleep.

In the days to come, Michael would begin to distinguish each in ways beyond their birth order. The youngest brother was a mischief-maker and the next youngest was a great whistler and imitator of bird language, conducting lengthy conversations with crows, jays, meadowlarks, mockingbirds. The second oldest was the singer, a tenor who arrested the attention of even the hardest among them. The oldest was the foremost. He was heavy-molded with a bashful smile, but otherwise his face impenetrable. For his family he maintained a stubborn fidelity, was tender and brave.

■ ■ ■ ■

"Where is Charlie?" Michael said to Aubuchon.

"I am here," Charlie said, scrambling from under a wagon.

"Bring a axe and a pail," he said, and the two set off down the stream not far until they came to a hollow tree where high up was a hive and with bees all about.

"Time to prove your worth," Michael said.

Charlie was as if touched by electricity. He stroked the tree's massive sides and then rapped with his knuckles. He was looking for something and when he found it he took hold and peeled away a sheet of bark. With the axe he chopped away at the base until he'd broken through to a hollow that ran the length of the trunk. He made knots of dried grass and piled them in front of the hole and struck a match.

It wasn't long before smoke began to curl from the top like a chimney.

After Charlie smoked the bees a good long while, he flung a rope to the tallest branch and a second rope to which he tied the bucket. Hand over hand he pulled himself up the rope and then moved higher from branch to branch. Perching himself at the hive opening, he pulled up the bucket and began filling it with great chunks of honeycomb he fished from the bee hole.

Michael fed more green twigs into the fire, watching from the ground, the boy's figure lost in the smoke that curled from cracks and holes and joined in the air, and then Charlie came back to earth with a pailful, twenty pounds or better. Michael told the boy that in Africa there were little honey birds, light gray in color, that led a person following it to a wild bees' nest, and once the hive was open and the honey extracted, the honey bird fed on the remaining wax and larvae.

"It ain't easy to keep up with a bird," Charlie said.

"It looks back every once in a while to wait for you. When it arrives at the hollow tree it points with its beak. After you take that one it leads you to two or three more."

"I knew they had those snakes," Charlie said, still thinking about the men the other night. "They said they were gonna eat them."

"I do not believe I could eat a snake," Michael said.

"I have eaten a lot worse. Will you go back to Africa?"

"I hadn't really thought about it."

"If you do, will you take me with you?"
"I will think about it."
"I have thoughts too," Charlie said.
"Penny for them," Michael said.
"Penny for what?"
"Your thoughts."
"Do you think all cats are gray at night?"
"Why do you ask me that?"
"Ike Gough said all cats are gray in the dark."
"What were they talking about?"
"The grass widow."
"Who is the grass widow?'
"I don't know," Charlie said, holding out his hand. "I will take my penny now."

That afternoon they watched as the river behind them swelled to a foaming yellow flood and threatened to breach its banks from a heavy rain above. And then the great heavily loaded wagons were again creaking along over the heavy sands.

Chapter 12

The day began with a peculiar stillness and a pervasive quiet. The weather was sultry, without wind and a white sun. As the hours passed the sun became powerful. It hadn't rained in days and everything was parched to a crisp. The rivers were low and the water so alkali that the last few days they'd boiled what they drank or used for coffee or cooking. They flavored it with sugar and lemon extract and it was still sharp.

When Michael rode in at noon Cochran and Meadows had yet to return with the game he'd shot. Aubuchon made up for it with a bacon vegetable stew and dumplings.

"Where do you think they are?" Elizabeth said.

"Somewhere in the wind," Michael said.

"We can't wait," Elizabeth said.

"Perhaps they are broke down," the reverend doctor said.

"I do not believe it," Michael said.

"Then they have abandoned the hunt," Elizabeth said. "It is their right."

"But not to steal your property," Michael said.

"What do you propose?" Elizabeth said.

"I will go after them. It is my own fault for tempting a thief."

He transferred his saddle to Khyber, remounted, and went out. He recrossed the creek to the north and rode to the top of a hill. Below was the plain they'd traveled and everything was open and with the glasses he could see for miles and there was no sign of Cochran and Meadows. Behind him was a splashing and when he looked it was the reverend doctor riding hard to catch up with him.

He moved north and then west, the reverend doctor lagging behind, and in an hour he'd cut their trail. They were traveling west parallel to the mainline of overland travel in the direction of the faraway silver mines.

Threading his way through the brushy trail, Michael came upon them. The front right wheel of the wagon had come off and was broken on the ground. Seeing the hopelessness of further flight, they'd kindled a small fire and roasted some of the venison they were transporting. So sudden and intense the encounter, there was a balanced moment when they could have shot each other, but it passed. They sat in the grass with their rifles in their laps. Cochran's shirt was open and there was a bright scarlet mark about his neck and breast where he'd taken a tumble when the wheel came off. Meadows calmly lit his pipe.

"As you can see," he said, "we are broke down."

"You are lost as well," Michael said as the red dog caught up and sat beside Khyber.

"Aye," Cochran said. "And thirsty."

"You've not been thoughtless, have you?" Michael said. The temptation of sudden wealth in the silver mines was strong enough to make any man forget his obligations.

Much to their relief, the reverend doctor came riding up, his horse heated and lathered.

"You men are not running off, are you?" he said.

"That's a load of shite," Cochran said.

"Ah, lad!" Meadows said to Michael, "we'd never run on you, if that's your thinking, and that's a promise."

Michael tossed his canteen down to Meadows. The man drank a little and smacked his lips.

"That's food and drink to me," Meadows said, passing the canteen to Cochran who gave it a sniff and smelled the liquor. He looked up at Michael with a smile, gestured a thank-you, and then he took a swallow.

They passed the canteen back and forth until it was half-empty and then handed it back up to Michael. The reverend doctor had dismounted and was inspecting the damage. He took off his coat and rolled up his shirtsleeves.

"We mustn't dally any longer," the reverend doctor said. "We need to get this wagon back to camp for repair. We will move the rear wheel to the front. Then we will cut a long pole and extend it from the front of the wagon at an angle to beneath the rear axle and let it drag on the ground while it carries the rear end."

Cochran and Meadows laughed at how simple the plan.

"Brilliant," Cochran said, and Meadows agreed.

"Give us a hand," the reverend doctor said, and the men set to work.

After they returned to camp to make the repair, there was still too much sun in the sky for the wagon train to travel. Michael set out, and when he reached the next horizon, he paused. He wiped his forehead and lifted the glasses to his eyes. For as far as he could see nothing was green, not grass nor brush nor tree. Across the land in front of him from east to west and as far as he could see south, the country was burned over, black and desolate.

Khyber stepped into the burn and poked along. Michael spotted antelope that'd been caught in the flames. Some were dead and others so badly injured they could not crawl to cover. As Michael advanced he saw great clouds of smoke rolling up from the plain, rising by degrees, thickening and spreading over the whole face of the country. Out there the plains were wrapped in a great conflagration, the long grass so dry and feeding the flames. The fire shot up bushes and trees, rising on great columns, darkening the atmosphere.

They traveled all night, Cochran and Meadows moving from one shadowy antelope to the next, anxious to prove themselves, taking what meat they could harvest. They picked their way forward for some miles until morning when Michael found good grass and the next river, at least three hundred yards wide. It was a broad and shallow double curve, its current troubled and rapid and the bottom filled with quick sands and mud holes. The river was overclouded with moving vapor, the mingling of its cooler air and the smoke of conflagration.

Each bend enclosed a bottom where cottonwoods grew up from a watered meadow. Michael directed they should cut sticks and sharpen one end while he shucked off his boots and stockings. He entered the water at the fording place to try the bottom and find the safest ground. He shifted upstream, and halfway across, finding what he was looking for, he began planting his sticks to the opposite bank. By the time they made their crossing, the sun was high and it was time to lay by and wait for the sun to begin its descent.

When he rode back into camp that afternoon he told Elizabeth it looked as if the flames had scorched the earth beyond the river to its very limits. He spread the map out on the ground and placed the compass upon it. He turned both to make the north of the map coincide with the direction of the needle. He directed her eye with his gloved hand.

"The grass is burned ahead and there's fire hopscotching all over the country. Here. Here. And here. Beyond the burn there is good grass." He then suggested they make camp where they were and rest and wait until the threat of fire disappeared.

"Can we keep going if we choose to?" she said.

"We can."

She consulted her watch as if its ordered way would provide an answer.

"There will be grass," he said, and explained there was a wide swath of land to the next river as yet unburned.

"You give me no help," she said.

"What is unburned can burn," he said. "The decision is yours."

"Then we could burn right here."

"Here we can get into the river."

"What would you do?" She was coming to rely on Michael in all things, although she'd learned that she had to ferret it out of him.

"I don't know," he said, and it was the truth. Decisions such as this were based on chains of incidents, history, hunches. Presented with the same facts one day you would do one thing, and the next day another. On this day he leaned toward caution. On another day he'd be bold. Sometimes he was right and sometimes he was wrong, but mostly he was right.

"My will is not your will," he said. "Flip the coin if you must."

"You'll not second-guess?"

"No."

"Then nothing can be gained by dillydallying," she said.

Late that afternoon the boys were instructed to fetch in the oxen. Charlie hung on to the tail of one, letting it pull him from the water to the crest of the slope. Darby rode back in to say the conditions had not changed.

So they journeyed in late daylight into grass and soon could see evidence of the fires in progress. The smoke was at a great distance, and in places there must have been trees because they could see distant flames grow spectacularly tall as they consumed the canopies. The sky was flushed at sundown by the red smoke and turbidly yellow from the invisible burning prairie.

As the twilight grew into darkness the wheels rolled onto blackened ground and all around them were deep and somber shadows. The air did not cool but was close and warm and smelled burned. The rolling wheels and the feet of the oxen churned up the sooty ash and those in the rear came forward until finally they drove abreast and were as if the teeth in a great rake leaving a rising black billow of murky vapor behind them to float and settle again.

They were parched and their irritated eyes stung with their own tears. They pulled their hat brims as low as they could and their neckerchiefs over their noses and where they breathed the material wetted and caked black. As the night wore on the skies glowed with the reflection of the distant fires and it was as if they were driving beside hell itself. They moved onto the good grass. To the west a bright line of fire could be seen as if a thousand torches were sweeping across the plains. Out there, the air was full of burning ash and flying cinders, clouds of black pumping smoke.

Then the wind changed.

A heavy smoke began to shut out the starlight. Coming from the west were animals, driven before the flames the way they were driven in war by an advancing army. There were deer and antelope, wolves and coyotes, their tails tucked between their legs. Birds flocked the air.

"What's best to be done now?" Elizabeth asked.

"Hold on our course. Go quickly. Get to the river."

"What about turning back?"

"The fire is already behind us."

"Good Lord," the reverend doctor said, and they turned to see a pillar of fire shoot into the sky. Upward and upward it rose, as if a geyser and its treacherous flames consuming whatever invisible tree gave it life.

Bright flashes shot up here and there. The flames had found the good grass and the men knew to drive. Soon there would be firebrands swept up by the fire gale and streaking down from its highest bloom. The black clouds were upon them in a mighty pall spreading over the earth from west to east. Then came a rift in the black smoke clouds. It was the bright light of the fire and this made for a new horror, as the flames were seeking out what they would destroy. The men wetted their neckerchiefs and hid their heads to prevent being smothered. They choked on the particles of soot they breathed. They began to move quickly as it would soon be impossible to survive without shelter as the flames rapidly swept on.

The wind did not abate and nearer and louder it came, blasting the land, lifting turf and sand and stones and sending them airborne and the wind hurling them along in its fury as ever more fire made fire and made more fire in ever-increasing fury.

"Keep the fire on your right," Michael yelled to Elizabeth. "Drive on the river as fast as you can."

He wheeled Khyber around and rode in the direction of the oncoming flames.

"Michael," she yelled, "Michael," but he was already enveloped in the smoke of the firestorm.

Michael pulled up and dismounted. He went down on a knee and deep in the grass he struck match after match to set a backfire. His little fire gained and was soon a small roar and growing. The flames grew with the wind coming from the west and they picked up speed and began to dash east across their intended path.

He paused but a moment before guiding Khyber into the rear of the little blaze. He followed the fire he started as if chasing it along. It was picking up speed and beginning to fan out from the single point of combustion. Behind him the greater tide of flame was rapidly closing in. He watched the coming of the fury. At his feet, however black with ash, there was still so much left to burn.

Elizabeth stopped suddenly as a wall of roaring flame swept across their front with Michael following close behind. They waited until it passed and then went forward again and onto the newly burned earth. With a mighty roar the flames reached the burned-over land and then stopped while to their rear the towering flames continued east and crossed behind them. There was again the sound of yokes rattling, gears creaking, and springs clashing as the wagons jounced over blackened furrows and hummocks. Axles, wheels, hooves, dangling buckets, their own shoes they could hear again.

Grand and irregular thunder began to boom over the plain much to their relief and could be heard above the roaring of the fire wind. Now and again spurs of light would flash. There was more thunder in the darkness and then the whole air in their immediate vicinity began to vibrate and tremble. The thunder was continuous and there came close and dangerous lightning, three pulses between thunder and flash. Michael counted again the number of seconds. Forked lightning stitched the sky, two seconds, and there came more thunder in quick, sharp percussions.

There was another crash of lightning and a little rain and the men turned up their faces. It began to rain a downpour as if a waterspout bursting over their heads. The gleams of quivering lightning lit up the wagons and horses and their burned landscape for a long second, then a deafening roll of thunder followed by another burst. They were grateful and they cheered. They let the water wash and cool their faces.

The swift slants of sharp rain came in torrents and the road began to grow heavy and in some places the water was collecting. The ravines channeling water to the main were flooded, the water rising over the embankments and cutting them away, and before long the level ground on which they traveled was covered with water.

Some bolts pierced the earth straight and lancelike and some forked and others were shafts that zigzagged. The darkness between flashes shortened and it was as if they were forever illuminated to show the plunging horses and riders, the plodding oxen, and men in daylight. There was a flash and a tree at the roadside was torn to pieces in a blinding explosion. The oxen bellowed and went to their knees as they felt the stun of it.

He tried to reconstruct the land so changed from his earlier reconnaissance. The river was so dreadfully swollen. He touched at Khyber and she leaped ahead that they would be the first to step off the edge. He chose a place of entering the river above the destination so the current would assist in carrying animals and wagons across on the oblique. If the animals should stop in the river the wheels would sink rapidly in quicksand.

They reached the river proper and Khyber plunged and staggered. The water deepened to her belly, but her feet found bottom and she struggled on. They made the other side and he turned and before he could stop them Elizabeth and the reverend doctor were making their own crossing. He directed them to a high bluff and reentered the river as the first team, the Miller brothers, stepped off. They shouted and pushed and twisted the oxen's tails. He got to them as near as he could, caught a rope around a horn, dragged them into line, and the gaunt team followed to the distant shore, the lead yokes finding their footing, climbing the bank, and pulling the others through.

"Drive on!" he yelled. "Drive on!" as he went back into the water, the flashes of light stabbing the night.

Next came the Gough brothers and then Cochran and Meadows with Daragh, kicking, whipping, and shouting, their teams, plowing through the swift water, and they were followed hard on by the penman and his grandson. Finally came Aubuchon with Charlie and the boys and Darby riding behind with the spare horses, chasing the cows. They reached the shore and began to climb out when their wagon dropped a foot with a jolt and Charlie fell out the back and into the river floating on a crate. The crate rolled and broke open. The water was too fast and swimming was impossible as his clothes filled with floating sand. Michael went down one bank and Darby the other. They rode as fast as they could to get ahead of Charlie. Elizabeth and the reverend doctor were already on the move.

The reverend doctor had the first chance at him. He turned his horse and they bravely plunged in, but Charlie'd already shot past and the reverend doctor and his horse were too bogged down to get another try. Elizabeth saw him next and cut left, and Granby took her into the water where it was swift but not so deep. As Charlie came near she could think of nothing else to do except lean over and make a grab for him. If it took her from the saddle, so be it. It was his only hope. As the boy came swirling through, it was evident he'd not be floating much longer as his clothes were so weighed down. She left Granby and went in after him, the water ripping at her thighs. Charlie knocked into her and they both went under. She fought to stand and lifted him to breathe. She knew it'd be the last moment for the both of them as she felt the bottom washing away beneath her feet.

This is how it ends, she thought, and she found the strength to fight for another moment, and then Michael was in front of her, blunting the flow of water, and Darby was behind, dropping a rope around Elizabeth holding Charlie.

At last the men erected wagon sheets and wet and shivering, they crawled under and into blankets, where they huddled. Scattered bolts of lightning boomed and crashed. They'd driven the wagon with the red pennant as far off as they could. Everybody and everything was soaked through. And yet with kerosene and broken crates they were able to start a small sputtering fire for Aubuchon to boil coffee. He opened boxes of crackers and carved a big cheese and each man filled his open palms.

Story Miller climbed in the wagon to forage for more victuals, pickles, sardines, and canned peaches. He called to Daragh to step up and fetch down the boxes. Daragh climbed to the fore box and sat with a leg over the side. As he was waiting for Story a golden bolt of lightning struck him on his head, and after boring a clean round hole through his hat and skull, the electric fluid passed out through his side above the hip and ran down the iron rung of the wagon into the earth.

Ripped from their throats were groans and shrill piercing cries as splinters of wood flew everywhere. They cowered and went down and quivered on the wet earth and all about them was the smell of sulfur.

Michael was the first to stand. The iron rung was melted and fused with the nails in Daragh's boot. He found a tarpaulin to use as a winding sheet. He and Aubuchon arrayed Daragh's body on the cloth. They wrapped him and tied him closed.

After this first death a silence fell over the camp and each was left to his own thoughts as the time began to lengthen between flashes of lightning and the clap of thunder. Who knew what his end would be? Accident, fate, destiny, the luck of the draw: to each was his own explanation why it was Daragh's end and not someone else.

The four brothers did not speak a word of the world they'd entered. They sat together at their own little fire, gazing into the flames. Matthew held his little brother John in his lap. Beside their fire the wet sticks of wood they gathered steamed dry.

The Gough brothers also stayed to themselves as did the two Englishmen. The Englishmen sat on a blanket stripped to the waist. On their bodies they wore the blue tattoos that mapped their life in Her Majesty's service. The one favored tigers and the other the cobra. Their minds were on gold and silver bullion. Their working biceps flexed the hips of hula girls.

"You've got very wet," the reverend doctor said to Elizabeth.

"Yes, I am washed clean," she said, the light of a little alcohol lamp flickering on her face, her teeth chattering from time to time.

"You were very brave," the reverend doctor said, and made a heartening smile.

In the flashes of light the river gleamed in every direction as far as they could see. The land was ruined for travel.

"I have been struck by lightning several times," Charlie said.

"You know perfectly well you are telling a lie," the reverend doctor said.

Charlie said he wasn't lying and performed a pantomime of being struck by lightning to prove it.

"When I was struck by lightning," he said, "a tree grew in my chest."

"Would God approve of your stories?" the reverend doctor asked.

"I do not believe in God."

"Young man, do you think God cares what you believe?"

"Please," Elizabeth said, and it was enough to remind them a man had been killed, a man who had a family and she'd known since the war. Mark began to sing, "There is a green hill faraway," and Elizabeth was taken home in her mind and she wondered if the boy could possibly know how sad and beautiful he sounded.

All night the storm renewed and raged with unabated strength and each time the lightning lit the land they could see the water was climbing around their little island on the bluff. Hour after hour they lay beneath their tarps under their blankets unable to sleep, and listened to the wind and rain. Story Miller started up from sleep and said his wife's name as if it was a question. He looked about, and when he found his brother Temple nearby, he lay back down.

In the morning they learned they'd indeed crossed the river and were camped on the bank with barely enough height to raise them above the flooded land. Rags of smoke and vapor drifted over the water and the air was dense and stifling to breathe.

Aubuchon put on the coffeepot and made a kettle of oyster soup. During the night the wolfer and his woman had slogged in wet and hungry.

"I have never seen such a misery," the wolfer said.

"The elements seem to be against us," the penman said.

"There is no purpose in nature," the wolfer said. "It just is."

"It's the order of living things," the penman said.

"There's progress," the reverend doctor said, "even if it does not seem so."

"The notion of progress has yet to be proven," the wolfer said.

Elizabeth listened to the men as they talked. Inside her there was something gray. She thought to sift out the meaning of recent events. There were signs to be read and there was accident and there was good luck and bad luck. It was as if she'd passed from one world into another and all she wanted was to rest and move on again even deeper into the country.

"Well, that's something done," she said, and she stood and she told them tomorrow would be another day and each day would bring them closer. She directed them and they lassoed driftwood and opened a dozen more tins of canned fruit and salmon and all day long kept the coffeepot hot on the fire while the water began its recession.

The next day the sun appeared like a molten ball, intensely red. The water was shallowing fast and soon gone, and left behind was a mud flat as far as the eye could see. There was enough new land revealed to bury Daragh and for two more days they waited on their little island as the land baked and cracked, and on the fourth day when they awoke the land was parched and cratered. Michael and the boys were bringing in the oxen and the dangerous river they crossed had disappeared.

Chapter 13

The days went on as if an eternal passage through hell. Relentless and unremitting night turned into day and day into night. Daragh was missed and then he wasn't missed. Fire, flood, injury, accident, death — each was an episode to be experienced and endured and forgotten as they plodded south by southwest with the increasing sense there would be no arrival and with no arrival there could be no return.

As the sun climbed, its rays refracted and reverberated from the heated ground. A great part of the road lay through a very sandy country with little water. The sun was wearying, but the oxen were fit. The landscape was alive with mirage. What Elizabeth thought to be water was a mineral efflorescence in the dry sands. In the vapory distance, straggling antelope loomed huge on the shore of a sparkling lake, then a miraculous city, its skyline rivaling New

York's or Chicago's, gleamed out of some tantalizing future lit from within. She knew what this was and yet she could not resist riding in its direction. Perhaps her willingness was the girl inside her, the dreams of an imagination, hope, and want. If only she could arrive it would be there. She looked again and Michael appeared to be crossing the prairie in midair and then he passed from her vision as if over the lip of the earth.

They trailed south down the line of the 100th meridian, keeping an average of ten miles east on the sandy and dusty freight road to Camp Supply and the valley of the buffalo. According to David's maps, they were south of Snake Creek and north of Buffalo Creek.

For several days Michael sensed doom. Out there something terrible was happening. Then it was over and the aftermath was waiting ahead.

He cut the tracks of another wagon train and followed up behind. He'd been following their trail most of yesterday, and through the cold night, the wheels of their wagons rolled ever southward. He determined there were three wagons, smaller and lightly loaded. For some reason they'd left the advantage of the military road and they were cutting their own trail. He climbed to the top of a little sand hill, looking out with the field glasses. On his right was the common trail and on his left was their trail and it stretched southeast into seeming nothingness for mile after weary mile. It made no sense. It was as if they'd left the shore road and set forth onto the trackless sea.

That day he'd come upon the half-calcined bones of two men burned to death. They were surveyors and in the sand of a creek bank he found their tools, a reflecting telescope, transit, theodolite, Gunter's chain. He watched his back trail as he moved down the offside, taking the same detour they did. There was a dread he could not shake as the horse strides brought him closer to where they might be. Not here, but out there was sadness and sorrow, death from violence.

He came upon a burial the wolves had scratched out of the ground and there was nothing left but a strew of rags and cracked and broken bones, an old man's bones, shrunken and brittle. He took from their case the field glasses. He adjusted them and looked for some time to the south and southwest. He studied every fold in the earth. He saw nothing and proceeded along.

The rolling plain was cut up by irregular and closely located sand hills. He waited there for a long time but saw nothing come in sight and rode on again. Already their track was vanishing and then, suddenly, it disappeared. His compass in hand he took his bearings and matched them with the map he carried in his head. He'd ride another length and then he'd break off his search, his curiosity best unsatisfied. The red dog was off somewhere and not yet returned. He slowed his pace as he saw a spectral flock of black vultures hovering on the wing. With the field glasses he studied the edges of the land. He picked up the remnants of their train.

He came across a yoke key and then standards and other trappings belonging to a wagon train scattered along their trailside. There were plowshares, hen coops, boxes, millstone, a split-open crate of pocket Bibles. Strung for half a mile were fragments of broken cups and musical instruments, torn leaves of books, remnants of dresses, silks and velvets, a small satin slipper, a wedding gown, china, books, furniture, a spinning wheel, bonnets, crockery, a cradle, tools.

He was loath to get off the horse, but he did. He knelt in front of Khyber to sort the scattered books and found a volume of Dickens he'd not read before. Khyber nosed him. He quietly reached up and ran his hand down her neck, caressing the tight muscle over her shoulder. The book he stuffed in his saddlebag and quickly re-mounted. Khyber danced her impatience beneath him.

The red dog finally came in, his nose lifted into the wind the way he did when he smelled blood.

"What's the matter?" he said, and the dog trotted ahead.

They picked their way along, the only sound the occasional stroke of Khyber's hoof. He was grateful it was Khyber he was riding, a horse with the courage to face a lion. At any moment they were poised to run hard and away from this horrible place.

He reached a small stream where the water's edge was littered with broken bottles, meat tins, rags, and paper. There was a case of patent medicine that'd been broken into and the contents drunk. Some Indian was probably blinded or poisoned to death. He could smell the rank and unmistakable stench of decaying bodies. He lit a cigarette and held it in his teeth.

He suddenly had a dim vision of a scene where all hell had broken loose. He let his hand rest on one of the revolvers draped over the saddle horn.

Khyber signaled by throwing up her head and snorting. He rode a few strides nearer and floating in the water was a man. His body lay in several inches of water and was not yet swollen and bloated. His corpse was full of arrows, which made him resemble a porcupine. His eyes were pecked from his head and his eyeholes were ringed with black halos.

They crossed the small stream and in a burst Khyber ascended the banking to an open grassy spot just beyond where buzzards floated lazily in circles.

"The slaughter pen," he said. He let the reins hang loose, knowing the horse understood his work. They were in a sag between two higher points of land. Tick mattresses had been slashed and the stuffing still carried in the air like pollen. The men and women had been stripped and scalped. There was a dog and it had also been scalped. An ox stood by, its sides quilled with arrows.

Vultures fed everywhere.

A cavalry saber was left protruding from the body of a woman with child.

Who can imagine the shrieks and lamentations of the women, the final moments of their fear and torment?

There was the dead and mutilated body

of more than one child, their heads scalped and clotted and dried in the sun, the black stains of their dried blood, their little shoes.

They'd not stopped until the bodies of the men and women and children were hacked and burned and severed and covered with blood and not stopped until the bodies were opened to the air and the sun and their blood had turned purple and black.

In his mind he recomposed the families. There was the white-haired grandfather, the mother, two grown-up girls, a boy, and three little children. There was a father and wife and their children. There was the man's brother and his family. There was the young bride, the shot hole under her chin telling plainly enough her fear of capture, and her husband stoned to death. There were the rest of them.

He made a wide circuit, cutting a pony trail headed west-southwest. He came to a travois track going in the same direction. He discovered the tracks of shod horses among numerous tracks of ponies, horses taken in raids. They were on the move. There were women and children, horses, dogs, and men. There were coins, buttons, and buckles. There was the blood of the wounded on them. The trail was not old and there were fifty or more.

CHAPTER 14

When Michael appeared again late in the afternoon, riding through the pale deceptive light, Elizabeth was much relieved. They were camped at a crossing, the tarps unfurled to provide them as much shade as possible.

"What is it?" Elizabeth said, the reverend doctor at her shoulder.

He told her what he'd discovered to the southeast. He told her it was Comanche traveling west and suggested they wait a day until they cleared the country ahead.

"We must attend to them," the reverend doctor said.

"I would not go back there," Michael said.

"Then I will go myself," the reverend doctor said.

"I will go," Michael said. He knew there was no argument to be made that would convince the reverend doctor how pointless his intentions.

Michael ordered another horse to be brought and his saddle transferred. He took Darby aside and told him what he knew and that the men should keep their rifles handy.

The reverend doctor came up on his gray gelding, a shovel across the pommel.

"I am coming with you."

"Suit yourself," Michael said, spurring the fresh horse forward.

As he made his return to the site Michael again approached cautiously. He continued to study the folds and curves of the ground. In the path beside the crate of Bibles were sitting two immense gray wolves as if waiting for him.

"Do you think they brought those Bibles for the heathens or for themselves?" Michael said.

"They are missionary Bibles," the reverend doctor said, "published by the American Bible Society."

The wolves had no fear and seemed mildly curious of them. They panted with the heat, their tongues lolling from their open mouths.

"Do you want one as a souvenir?"

"No thank you," the reverend doctor said, drawing his rifle, but Michael stayed him, no noise.

Michael cracked his whip and spurred the

horse forward. He crossed the stream and climbed the sandy hill. He imagined them in this place, their sinking wheels almost to the axles, unloading their wagons as fast as they could, trying to escape the inevitable.

At the top of the hill, in the sag of land, the wolves had joined the vultures and were at them, their bloody heads drawn down between their shoulders, their long tongues licking at patches of bloodstained earth.

A wolf was gnawing at a half-stripped head it held in its paws. The wolf looked up at them, squeezing its eyes. It stood and stared at the red dog as if mildly interested. The red dog kept coming until the two were side by side, head to tail, sniffing each other. Suddenly the wolf rose up and its teeth were in the back of the red dog's neck. The red dog went down and rose back up and tore himself free. The wolf swirled and the red dog's powerful jaws closed on the wolf's hind leg. The wolf flung back its head and snapped at the air behind. The red dog twisted and the wolf screamed as its leg bone cracked. The red dog let go and on three legs the wolf limped away. Michael cracked his whip again and the birds flapped their great wings and flew away with hoarse and guttural croaks. The other wolves slunk off with their tails between their legs, but they didn't go far from this place of feeding.

The reverend doctor crested the hill and looked down the offside in horror. He covered his mouth and however hard he tried he could not stop himself from retching. He leaned over to one side and emptied his gut down one of his legs. He then composed himself and he apologized.

Michael went down the hill to the upright saber. He leaned over from the saddle, withdrew the saber from the body and wiped it clean. Not far away he spotted the scabbard flung into the grass and this he attached to his saddle. He found a polished mirror catching the sun's light and next to it a wooden box with hinges on one side and locks on the other. He unlatched the door to see the even backs of books. It was a traveler's library of uniform size and binding.

He ran his hand along the smooth spines of the books. Robinson Crusoe. *Swiss Family Robinson.* It was a library of literature, travel, history, and biography titles, Sir Walter Scott, Richard Henry Dana, Washington Irving, Charles Darwin, Charlotte Brontë, William Makepeace Thackeray. He removed the books and slid them into his saddlebag.

"Would you like to say a few words," he

said to the horse, then to the red dog.

He lit a cigarette and stared into the shimmering heat. He drew heavily on the cigarette. When the reverend doctor came up he passed the cigarette to him. The reverend doctor drew in the smoke and choked and coughed, but it seemed to help and he let out a deep sigh.

"My God," the reverend doctor sighed.

"It's an old-fashioned world," Michael said.

He turned the glasses south and then west. They were out there somewhere. After a while he lowered the glasses and replaced them in their case.

"Do you think she will marry again?" the reverend doctor said.

"Who?" Michael said.

"Elizabeth."

"I don't know," Michael said. "You ought to ask her."

"But I cannot ask her," he said, shaking his head. "It could be misunderstood. What about you? May I ask what your intentions are?"

"That is not the way I regard her," Michael said.

"We are not so different, you and I."

"Yes, we are."

"You have no intentions?"

"That's how different the difference."

"I was mistaken then. I apologize."

Michael took down his canteen. He took a drink, sloshed it around, and took another. He passed it up to the reverend doctor, warning him the water inside was fortified. The reverend doctor took a drink and another and he was much restored.

"Have you seen all you wish to see?" Michael said. "If you feel for her the way you claim, you will convince her to turn around."

"Can this be all of them?" the reverend doctor said.

"Do not ask that question," Michael said.

"Let us bow our heads in prayer," the reverend doctor said, taking off his hat, holding his hat as he spoke words in the manner of someone talking to himself.

"No. I think instead get ready to leave," Michael said, interrupting him, and they started from that dreadful place.

That night around the campfire the men told stories of death, torture, and capture; stories of men tied to stakes and strips of flesh cut away, red hot pokers thrust into the wounds. They wondered whether it was fear, or loss of blood or shock, or pain, or anguish that brought an end to the horror. They all agreed when things were at their bleakest, one last bullet should always be saved.

Their voices carried and Elizabeth and Michael could hear their discussion.

"They are talking about their obligation to kill me before they kill themselves," she said.

"It's not unthinkable," Michael said, his hands clasped behind his back.

"Maybe for you," she said.

She then apologized for being sharp with him. However cautious and quiet and even secretive he was, she understood with him she was not alone in the world. She waved a hand in the air, so many days gone by and so much had happened and her life at Meadowlark another mirage in her distant past.

"Do you always see everything and understand everything?" she said.

"What I know I know."

But how do you know, she was desperate to say. She studied him in the darkness. She knew the question was unanswerable.

"It is good counsel," she said, "that we wait a day or two, but I am growing impatient. Our stores are dwindling, we have lost a good man, and we have not made a dime in return."

Michael asked after the reverend doctor

and Elizabeth said he'd sequestered himself upon their return.

"There was a look in his eye," she said.

"Not a good one," Michael said.

"He said hell itself had let loose."

"You see what people can do to each other."

"I'd not let them get her," one of the Gough brothers said loudly.

Michael stood and stepped in their direction. The red dog sprang to his side as if from nowhere.

"By God, you will hold your tongue," he said, and the men went silent. He then told them to move their asses and to double the watch and then he returned to his canvas chair beside Elizabeth.

"If they come on us," he told her, "there will be no mercy."

He wanted to say more, but there was nothing more to say. He wondered if she was learning the importance of hate when living in the world of men. He made himself a drink of limewater and found his pipe and tobacco.

"Say something," she said, impatient with his mood.

"Is there a certain thing you would like to hear?"

"Tell me the truth," she said.

"I believe the immediate danger has passed."

"Would you keep going?"

"Yes," he said. "Yes, I would, but I do not want you to."

"Your rule of life is to do what you want to do," she said. "This is what I am learning to do."

That night the animals were brought in and secured and he sent out mounted pickets. He found a height of ground that provided a survey of the surrounding country and each man in turn would take his coffee jar, biscuits, cold venison, and rifle and sit watch.

That night the reverend doctor came awake under canvas at 3:00 a.m., an hour before his watch. Nothing was stirring. The air had cleared and there were stars in the sky and the plain was blue and as if a sleeping ocean. He came from a dream scene that left him weak and gloomy. He'd seen a lot of dead people but nothing like that. He reminded himself he was safe and alive, but still the dream haunted him. Restless with an idea, he opened his portfolio and arranged his steel pens, penholder, ink, and wiper. He lit a candle, placed his revolver within reach, and was as if in a quiet room.

His hand was shaking. All his life he'd

been torn between the sacred word and the secular world. There was an emptiness he desperately needed to fill. It was a need to feel something never felt before, to say something never said before.

He had done his first writing when he was a young exhorter and prayer leader and living a lonesome itinerant life. He'd left behind in Massachusetts a comfortable world of academic excellence and a prominent clerical family. His first success was a pamphlet he sold for a penny, a scathing polemic excoriating slavery. Then he authored a bondage narrative written in the name of Nero Jones. The book was promoted by the Massachusetts Anti-Slavery Society as a great step forward. The book sold well and Nero Jones, in care of the publisher, received invitations to lecture in London and address public meetings throughout the Northeast, which he had to decline. After that, he wrote another book, the story of a reformed alcoholic with the nom de plume of Josiah Kirwin who was laid low by liquor and in his desperation turned to God and was embraced by the Cold Water Army. Josiah Kirwin's story took him three weeks and was serialized in twenty-four issues of *Harper's Monthly* and later printed in a single volume.

His mind and thoughts cleared. He shot his cuffs, and his body erect, he bowed his head to the paper and began to write.

At the broken wagon, the red dog sniffed the air and showed his white fangs. His lips drew up and his spine stiffened. He made a sound deep in his throat and warily I dismounted. I went down on one knee and followed the dog's bloodshot eyes. They were cast on a girl's face deep inside the overturned wagon. She held a water bottle and was wrapped in a tick mattress.

She may have been fourteen years of age. Crouched beneath the wagon, she directed her large blue eyes full on my face and continued to gaze in mute surprise and terror.

She was long and slender and her complexion was white as ivory and there were freckles on her cheeks and nose. Her hair was the color of corn silk, and long and braided, and the braids hung to her waist. She wore long gray stockings and another pair she'd dragged up her arms to her shoulders.

"Can you speak?" I said.

Her response was a whimper and it built to a cry.

"Girl," I said, "there is nothing to be afraid of."

I removed a glove and reached out a hand. I asked her name.

"Charlotte," she said. "Charlotte."

"Charlotte, don't be afraid," I said. "Come to me."

She knit her fingers among my own and I helped her crawl from her den. The girl unfolded herself. She looked about and then she began to shake. She collapsed to the ground moaning and weeping. It was the wail of a lost soul, despairing and pleading for mercy.

"Charlotte," she said. "They took my sister Charlotte."

I picked her off the ground and wiped her hot, sandy face and pushed back her hair. I looked kindly at her and touched the back of my wrist to her mouth and then her cheeks and eyes. I told her I would find her sister even if it cost me my life.

Chapter 15

They came upon the first buffalo signs, piles of dung and wallows six feet in diameter, and then their first buffalo. It was a tangle of hair, scraps of hide, and broken bones scattered all around. The wolves had dragged it down and been at it. They'd hollowed out the carcass, torn it to pieces, and crushed the bones for the marrow.

They crossed the Buffalo and Sand Creeks, the men whipping up the oxen and managing to roll their heavy loads across, the axles in water as the wheels bumped and sank and bumped again. Michael guided them downstream and into camp a goodly distance from the freight road where they might lay up for a few days. They made rest beneath cottonwoods with huge trunks and spreading arms near a sandbar with a clean white beach. The men unyoked the oxen and set them to graze.

The next morning Michael took Darby

with him. They entered the Wolf Creek valley between the two Canadian Rivers and bent west toward the 100th meridian. According to David's journal, the old road ran to the crossing of Wolf Creek through an immense field of wild sunflowers. They grew to such a tremendous height they could not see over their drooping heads even on horseback. Up the course of this creek lay the route to the Comanche and Kiowa and the buffalo pastures.

Wolf Creek cuts a broad, shallow canyon across the vast high plains, David had written. *The rocks, tertiary sands, gravels, and marls . . . Spring-fed streams enter from north and south and pour their waters into its sandy channel. The creek flows for a considerable distance. Custer and the Seventh were here in '68.*

As they left the sunflowers, the rolling swells of the prairie melted away before them into the vast level plain of a new world.

"This is where you turn back," Michael said to Darby. "Keep your eyes peeled. Rest up and bring them on. I will meet you tomorrow afternoon at the bottom of the sunflowers and guide you in. Can you do that?"

"I can do it."

"Make sure you get back without dying."

A mile after breaking through the field of sunflowers Michael encountered more wallows and crushed grass and buffalo dung fresh and moist. There were countless herds of deer, wild horses, and buffalo. There was elk, antelope, turkey, jackrabbit, quail, grouse, and chickens. There were honeybees and songbirds and the sky shadowed with raptors. There were bee caves and bee trees flowing with honey. The lush grass ran to the horizon and seamlessly filled the laterals running into the Wolf and he thought this is how the world was in the beginning.

Not far, he found a black gelding with a bloody saddle and blood-drenched shoulders and mane, though healthy and alert. The blood was so much and days old. He was a good horse, sound and gentle, and Michael named him Starbuck for the pretty white star on his forehead and led him on.

Soon he could see thousands of buffalo roaming the plains and he filled with a strange and powerful feeling, the passage of receding time. There were so many of them he felt diminished, infinitesimally small, insignificant. He lost his breath. It made him wonder on the courage of the first man. Man the shadow. Man the child. Man standing erect. Man just beginning and the wars of civilizations yet to take place.

He traveled south by southwest and soon he'd reached the invisible border of open and hostile country. There were three wild horses and he watched them through the glasses. They were a mare with her daughter and granddaughter. The daughter was nursing from the mare and the granddaughter from her mother.

How rich and fecund the country, how it smelled of earth and manure, decay and return, hot, steamy, and reeky, the thousands upon thousands of years of grazing and manuring and birthing and dying on these generative plains. The land, the water, the very air generating life, sustaining life, and receiving its return to the earth as it used to in the old days.

The plain's trail led him deeper into the country. All about were sharp hoofprints in the pounded soil. The cut banks of dried laterals were beaten down and packed hard. Tufts of brown fluffy hair were snagged in the hawthorns and rough bark of the cottonwoods. He continued on, making his way to a darker line until he could see below the silver trace of water entering a wide and spreading world to the east. The banks ran high above the cutting water and the green plain ran to the edge without much sign to mark its course and there the land fell away as if a false horizon to the steady current below. The creek was wide, shallow, and swift, a beautiful clear-running creek, David's place of live water, fuel, fodder, and buffalo.

He followed the water a short distance east to find a small valley situated in a cup among low hills. Here it was, the course so accurately drawn by his brother that he hit the mark without deflecting. It was an unnatural place, a parklike meadow bounded on three sides by the curving stream. It was unnatural in the way it lay stranded. It would need to be looked for or stumbled upon by accident. Blue-and-white cranes fished in the shallows. There, fire would not be seen and its smoke would float east and close to the water before rising.

David had written, *Some labor will be required to make a serviceable wagon road. There is a ford to cross where the water is shallow, and the bed hard gravel where can lay a corduroy road. Once on the bluff, a wagon can follow the points of the compass wherever a buffalo trail may lead . . . farther west an easy ford to the south. A spring of ample water threads from the bank side. An ideal hunters' camp: plenty of fresh water, good grass, and wood in abundance. Turkeys roost by the thousands; deer, antelope, in great herds.*

He imagined David, a few months ago, pen scratching on paper, his joy of discovery. This place would be the solution to his insolvency. This place would save him and Elizabeth from bankruptcy. Khyber stepped forward and, sure-footed, she picked her way down the long, bushy slope. The water barely came above her hooves. From here the land was the fragment of a natural amphitheater. The creek bed opened into a wider bottomland, where it shined beneath the trees through which it wove. Mulberries, plums, choke cherries, gooseberries, currants, and other fruits were still in abundance. Upstream and downstream, deep trails were worn into the bluffs where the vast buffalo herds had crossed and recrossed for generations. The trails were wide and so deep a man on horseback was little above the surrounding soil. There were groves of trees where lived great flocks of turkeys and shallow eddies where the deer and the antelope came to water. There were reeds and tall wiry grass. There were deeper pools with fish.

Michael cast a rope around a fallen limb and dragged it to the fire he would make. It was hot that late afternoon and on the warm air was the boom of bees. The air was still and beyond the brink of the cutbank, was the silence of desolation. A rattlesnake, as thick as his arm and more than four feet long, lay coiled on a rock. It was looking at him with its massive pointed head and glittering eyes. He looked again and the snake was gone.

His appetite was sharp. His last meal was in the saddle: corn bread, bacon, sardines, a boiled egg. He ascended to the plains, the gelding in tow.

He heard them before he saw them. It was September and still the rutting season. He rose to his full length in the stirrups, shading his eyes from the sun's last glare as he stared ahead. He dismounted and drove an iron pin in the ground and picketed the gelding. He remounted Khyber and rode out.

They were a small herd feeding slowly in the direction of the creek. Big timber wolves hung on their rear and flanks, ready to cut out a stray calf or those weakened by age. There was a good breeze blowing and he could smell them. He rode as near as they would allow and was surprised how close he came before they took notice and gave off their bellowlike grunts.

They gazed at him for one moment and then another and then tossed their heads, spiked their tails, turned, and fled. A bull bounded at once from a crouch to an erect position. He moved off with a rolling gait reaching for full speed and swiftness and not to be caught by the fastest horse. A second, younger bull lowered his sharp horns. He made a burst of speed in a rush toward Khyber and would have run her through if he'd not stumbled and fallen to his knees.

Khyber wheeled and faced about. The bull collected and charged again. Khyber stepped aside and offered her flank and he lost his forward speed when she turned and turned again. The bull snorted and puffed and gored the ground and started off once more following the circle Khyber made and soon he was too exhausted to carry on. In his heat and fury he panted and lolled out his tongue. He turned his enormous shaggy head and looked at the horse and rider out the corner of his deep-set eye.

Michael drew the saber from its steel scabbard. He touched Khyber and they took after a cow. Khyber gained steady pace. Her neck lengthened and weaved the air as headlong she rushed on in pursuit. As they gained upon the cow, she slowed her pace from a canter to a trot, her tail flying out behind her, and she slewed a little to one side.

Khyber went in close and then left and in that moment Michael reached down with the saber and slashed the tendons in her back legs as Khyber veered off. The saber stroke brought the cow's hind end to the ground with a deep-mouthed groan. A young bull calf bawled and trotted in intent on nursing milk from its fallen mother. He let the bull calf find the teats and drink and then he shot him.

He drew his steel and pulled out the tongues. He sliced them free, near five pounds each, and tied them at the back of his saddle. He then took the livers for dinner and a loin for breakfast.

He retrieved the gelding and went back to cutting: the hump roasts came off the shoulders 4 pounds each, butt roasts 11 pounds each, loins 12 pounds each, tenderloins 20 pounds each, and still he kept cutting until he calculated the load at 250 pounds and calculated another 600 pounds of meat and tallow left on the ground in the dark red carcasses. He sprinkled a pinch of gall upon a slice of liver and ate it.

When the bloody work was finally done, the carcasses lay gleaming in the twilight air. He shaded his eyes with his hand.

Wolves seated on the hill were waiting for him to leave. They were stationed all about in packs of five and six. They'd come upon the blood and more were arriving.

Something came to him, something on the wind. He stood from the work and looked about. He looked to the red dog. The red dog heard it too, or was the red dog responding to him?

He washed his hands with canteen water, mounted Khyber, and led the gelding over the bluff and into harbor. He hung the meat in the trees and washed his hands again, and his face, in the cold water of the creek. He drank some and as David wrote, *It is neither bitter nor gyppy.* From beyond the creek came a chorus of howls as if in challenge to his arrival.

In another hour the turkeys came in. A half mile east was a large roost where they gathered. They came in by the thousands and there was the loud crack of a thick limb they'd overloaded with their weight and they tumbled to the ground. He wondered what they ate and what it made them taste like. He followed the turkey sounds to their roost and when he returned he carried six over his shoulders and dragged another four behind him. He stretched a rope between trees and threw the birds, tied two together, across the rope where they could mellow.

He mounted Khyber and they crossed the creek and ascended the bluff. In the darkness the wolves were crunching the bones. To be heard were the snapping of jaws and the rending of flesh. A blazing sunset was burning away the edges of the bright blue sky. It burned across the wide circle of the horizon and stained the sky overhead and pinked the darkness coming from the east, the earth firm, smooth, and level, lurid yellow and red. He thought of Africa and remembered the years he had spent there. He was so often thinking of things that were far away and he knew how dangerous this was. When he hunted, whole villages followed him into the bush, a hundred or more, the elephants so monstrous they rolled out the guts, entered the rib cavity and butchered them from the inside out.

He thought he observed something of a tawny color moving in the brush along the creek bluff, a good distance to the east. He could not make out what it was and before he could uncase his field glasses the animal or whatever it was had disappeared. The red dog walked in and sat beside him. The darkness was coming rapidly. He held up the glasses and the lenses collected what little light there was. Misty people seemed to appear out of nowhere. He watched as the dark figures rose from the grassy turf to stand and walk in on the wolves. They carried spears thrust before them and then they were running on the wolves, blades of shining metal, long knives flashing.

The clouds moved again and the scene was eclipsed as suddenly as it had appeared. He leaned forward and his body quivered with life. What could it be out there in the shrouded darkness, these horseless ancient hunters, materialized from the gloom? Everything looked mysteriously beautiful in the starlight. He wondered if he saw what he had seen. He remembered how hungry and tired and sun struck he was.

It was hot that evening and on the warm air was the rush and laving of the waters, the vague sounds from the wilderness, the dreary howl of the wolves, the whine of the coyotes, the grunting and bellowing of the buffalo. The red dog moved out to the deepest shadows about the campfire while he ate and finished his tea. He lit a cigarette and the owls came out. From the darkness there came screams and cries and a heartrending shriek. He prepared a place of concealment away from the fire circle and lay down for the night. The red dog came back in and they lay close together.

Michael looked up at the infinite expanse of night sky. He pressed his hands against his eyes and opened them again. He felt no fear, just melancholia. The moon was close for a while and there was good light and he could have read his book if he wanted to. Unbidden, her memory came to him and he reached a hand forward as if to touch the image in his mind. She smiled when she looked at him and her lips reddened and her face colored as she sat up and turned her bare feet onto the tiled floor. She stretched, lifted her hair, and let it fall.

"Luisa," he whispered.

The light blued the chattering creek and silvered the land and after a while he fell asleep. He'd not slept long when a dream took him to Africa and soon he was being hunted by lions. He woke and smiled. The lions hadn't gotten him yet. Then he returned to sleep and she came to him in his sleeping mind. In his sleep he laughed and held out his hand. She came closer and he took her into his arms.

"Don't let me go," she said. "Hold on to me, now you're here." She took his face in her hands and she kissed him.

CHAPTER 16

When he awoke, the wind blew lightly from the south. He took his coffee by the stream. He looked to the sun. The wagon train was on the move by now and he imagined where they'd be. He then had another thought. He retrieved the saber from beside his bed and returned to the stream. He hefted the saber in its scabbard. He let the ricasso to the light, the fuller, the cutting edge. He turned east and held the steel until its bright luster gleamed in the sun. The shallow hallmark read AMES MFG. CO. CHICOPEE MASS. He slotted the blade and without another thought he pitched it into the deepest water, swallowed forever.

He saddled Khyber. He'd ride onto the dead, flat plain and north to the sunflowers to guide them in. He ascended the bluff and lit a pipeful of black honeydew tobacco. The valley was black with the big animals for as far as the eye could see. He said her name and Khyber stepped off. He made a wide circuit of the surrounding land before heading to the rendezvous. When he reached the end of the road he dismounted. He loosened the cinch on Khyber's saddle, took out his reading book, and lay down. He would wait here for the wagons to arrive.

Soon they came down through the wild oats and the drooping sunflowers. The men lashed the air as the oxen brought on their great creaking canvas-covered loads, straining against the weight of their yokes, the wheels turning on their hickory axels.

Darby had started them at midnight; they were weary and the oxen moaned as if they knew there would be release and rest at the end.

Elizabeth dismounted first, looking both weary and intent.

"I have found them," he said to her.

"How far?" she said, her tired eyes suddenly brilliant and sparkling. There were moments she'd grasped what greatness she'd set in motion, but she hadn't thought it would be like this. She felt fearful, awake and alive.

"Twenty miles, and long, flat ones."

"How many are down there?"

"I cannot tell you. You wouldn't believe me."

"There's no turning back now," she said.
"Yes, there is. There always is."
"Cochran and Meadows," she said, "they have deserted, but two new men, Findley and O'Malley, wandered in and I have signed them on."
"The faithless men," he said. "Some loss is always to be expected," he added, angry with himself for trusting them from the first. It always held: the true man is true, and the false is false. As far as he was concerned they were just so much rubbish and gone forever. One way or another, they'd repent the mistake they made.
"They stole a wagon and a very good team," she said.
"They are days gone," he said. "That's the finish of it. If they make it, they'll have a story to tell."
As they proceeded there were hundreds and hundreds of buffalo on either side of the trail chewing their cuds and they had to be chased away to protect the oxen.
Michael brought them to the bluff that overlooked the creek.
"We have arrived," Elizabeth said.
"The kingdom come," Temple Miller said.
"Jerusalem," the penman said, and he performed a little jig step in the joy of arrival.

Charlie bent low and ran ahead as if charging a stiff wind. He tucked his shoulder and tumbled over the bluff and rolled to the creek. He splashed across and ran on determined to be the first after Michael.

"Gentlemen," Michael said, "break out your picks and shovels."

At his direction they set to work to clear the brush and cut down the bluff. They were eager to make the descent, cross the creek, and enter the park below. The first wagons were lightly laden and as a precaution they secured the back wheels by means of the drag chains lest they run up on the back legs of the oxen that pulled them. Story Miller braked against the oxen and one of the wheel oxen stumbled and went down on its knees and was dragged to the creek bottom, where it got back on its feet. The turning rims of the wheels milled the water as they completed their crossing.

The descent to the creek was still too steep and the crossing below was rough and jolted the wagon. Though the wagon crossed safely, improvements were needed if they were to make the descent and the crossing three and four times a day. They started farther back with their spades and cut deeper. They lessened the slope and successfully attempted a large wagon and the rest followed.

From the creek bottom they proceeded a quarter mile down the stream and into the park. They knocked the pins from the oxbows and slid them from the yokes, and the oxen were set free in the lush grass of the peninsula, where they capered and pranced with sudden energy. From their long days on the road all the men and Elizabeth were dirty, worn down, and shabby. Their clothes were stained and penetrated with dust and grime, but there was no inclination to rest. The men immediately set to work building the camp. Every one of them was anxious to get onto the buffalo and begin earning their money.

Aubuchon was at the earth with a shovel, the blade flashing the dirt aside. The trench he dug deepened and lengthened until it was four feet long, a foot deep and eight inches wide. As he worked a canvas pavilion was being erected around him. Dead limbs were dragged to its edge, where they were bucked to length. The dry dung of the buffalo was gathered and heaped in a pile. Aubuchon knotted dry grass and twigs, soaked them in kerosene, and set his fire in the bottom. The black smoke cleared and it burned brightly, and the iron grates were laid over the flames. Soon the coffeepot hung from the crane and was sputtering hot. There were kettles of beans and side pork, the turkeys and joints of buffalo Michael had hung in the trees. There were cake pans of corn bread dusty with ash. Aubuchon laid the thick buffalo steaks to roast on the reddening iron grill, where they sizzled and popped. When one side was ready he flopped them over and began cutting off pieces while the other side cooked.

The men came to the fireside with sore backs and feeble with tiredness. Their throats and nostrils stung with the smoke as they leaned in to spear pieces of roasted meat. They drank their coffee and ate the beans scalding hot. They crumbled biscuits into their bowls, soaked up the liquid, and spooned the soggy mess into their mouths. The tired sag left their shoulders. Charlie compressed the corn cake in his hand and ate a fistful in a single bite.

Restored, Abel Gough stood erect, gave his neck a twist, and crowed like a rooster. They all laughed and went back to work. They yoked a pair of oxen and hooked them to a running gear and began building a woodpile.

Michael took Charlie aside and told him of a bee tree he'd found that they would return to when they had a little time. Then he rode to the bluff and onto the plain where ravens were flipping over the buffalo chips, looking for grubs. There was no sign of their camp below. There was no smell of smoke, and what smoke there was, it followed the creek east into the willow and cottonwood forest. There was no sound. There was nothing that could be seen. David had chosen well.

By the time he returned Story and Temple Miller were twitching logs to the crossing and the boys were laying them side by side in the creek. They hooked on to an empty wagon and took it across. The oxen pawed and thudded dully against the logs laid in the bed, the water streaming between. The wheels bumped across, the sideboards rattling in their sockets and they made the bluff and turned and came back down and it all went smoothly with little effort.

In the days to come they'd build a press of sapling posts with a lever and chain to flatten the folded hides for the freighters to cart away. They'd build a smokehouse of forked poles placed in the ground and covered with green hides, twenty feet long, and at the end a fire to smoke the inside. They'd erect scaffolds and other contrivances for sugaring, pickling, jerking, and drying meat.

Toward evening the men went down the water trail, then stripped to their undergarments and waded out into the channel, where they squatted and soaked. The darkness thinned away as the moon and stars came out in a perfect sky of southern blue. They worked the brown soap into lather and splashed away the suds. When they were done they stood in the last light. John brought them coffee and a basket of hot biscuits, a round of butter and blackberry jam. Charlie followed behind carrying a sack of peanuts, a bottle, and a thimble measure, and for each of the men there was a gill of whiskey.

Elizabeth's new home was two wall tents pitched together. The back apartment was a sleeping chamber and the front a parlor, office, and sitting room. A canvas curtain divided them, and carpets covered a canvas floor. She had brought her washbowl and pitcher, her husband's field desk and stand, his folding chair and folding table with a drawer. There was a little bed lamp with a capacity of oil for fifteen minutes of reading. There was a stove in each apartment and their pipes passed through pieces of tin fastened in the slanted roofs of the tents. Her bedstead was made of iron. She'd brought also her bathtub made of tin.

The dim light from the new moon made the tent walls glow inside. She lighted a kerosene lantern that hung from a chain above David's campaign desk, now her own. Inside the drawer was a chocolate she slipped into her pocket. She had so much work to do. Darby would soon leave for Fort Worth to conduct her business and to guide in the freighters. She'd have Michael for two more months and then she'd be on her own. She steeled herself. There was so much she needed to learn from him: how to read the land, sky, and water, the sun and the stars, men and animals. She needed to find the power inside herself to do this. She would be at the mercy of no one; she would be self-reliant, self-supporting, and live an autonomous life. She had no choice but to be strong.

Chapter 17

Elizabeth rose early to the smell of bread carried from the bake oven. The sunlight through the canvas was soft and warm, but soon it would be warmer and the prickly heat of the day would make itself felt. She looked forward to the day and dressed hurriedly in a flannel shirt and corduroy riding trousers tucked into riding boots, a hat with a red ribbon.

Aubuchon was at the honey pail. A circular mass of waxy honeycomb was perched on top and oozing golden liquid through a square of muslin.

"The land of milk and honey," Elizabeth said with all delight as she lifted the cloth that covered the pail. There had to be fifteen pounds of honey inside. She dipped her finger into the honey and then into her mouth.

"Where is Michael?" she asked.

"He was in the saddle long before the sun

rose. He rode west in search of the buffalo."

"We have lost the buffalo?"

"He said they are on the wind."

It angered her how badly she took the news. She would be more patient. She would wait to hear what Michael had to say.

"And what is for breakfast, old friend?"

"For breakfast there are eggs and veal from the calf and the liver of its mother."

The horses grazed the dew that was on the grass in the peninsula. The sun grew stronger, burning off the little fog that was close to the water. The men came awake and they were still tired, unpleasant, and dissipated. They wandered to the cook tent and drained the coffeepot again and again. How tired they felt as they lay back in the stillness. Like the oxen in the pasture, they were exhausted with heat and work and felt feverish.

In the afternoon when Michael returned, he had no news of the buffalo and yet did not seem concerned. He directed Charlie and John to each fetch a bar of lead from the burlap bags in the powder wagon to the fireside and he carefully placed them in a kettle he'd set over the flames. He erected a table and spread a canvas over its top. There was an array of tools required for long-range shells. While the lead melted he named each tool and explained to the boys its purpose: wad cutter, bullet seater, shell reducer, and loading tube of nickel-plated brass, bullet mold, a little hand brush. Elizabeth came by to watch over the process. The reverend doctor also joined them, carrying a pencil and paper and taking notes.

The lead melted slowly and then all at once. Michael spread the handles of the hinged bullet mold and with a greased rag cleaned the cavities inside and clamped it shut. He placed it beside the kettle, letting the smoke run through the little funnels leading into each cavity. When the kettle began to bubble he ladled molten lead into the tiny funnels filling each cavity beneath.

"Be careful," he warned them. "It can burn you viciously."

The mold full, Michael thrust it into a bucket of water, where it hissed and the water foamed. He then spread the handles and the bullets spilled onto the canvas surface. Some needed a scrape or two with the file and some he threw back in the kettle. Each one he kept he rubbed its base with beeswax.

They followed him to the powder wagon for a box of caps, brass shells, and a can of powder.

"The shells will be good for fifty times,"

he told them, “and after that they’ll be no good anymore.”

From the box he thrust a cap into the shell and tamped it in place. He took the loading tube, explaining to them that the amount of powder must be precise so the bullet would not pass through the animal but concentrate its full power on entering the body, doing its work, and coming to rest against the far side of the interior where the skinners would reclaim the spent lead and they’d mold it all over again.

“The shells fifty times,” he said, “but the lead forever.”

He poured the powder an inch from the mouth of the shell. Over this he put a thin wad of drafting paper and then the bullet. With the bullet seater he pressed the bullet gently to the powder and the cartridge was complete. He told them they were his cartridge factory and he’d need 150 every day. Elizabeth and the reverend doctor were the most enthusiastic about loading shells. They worked alongside the boys, casting the lead and pouring in the powder.

Michael left to feel out the country and locate the herd while the camp continued to build all around them. The men dug out the water trickling from the bank and formed a catch basin, where they built a curb of stone and inserted a barrel. Where the water cascaded from the barrel they set a long wooden sluice to catch the overflow and carry water into camp.

Three days had gone by and the men were restless and some were angry and blameful. They'd come all this way and had yet to make any money. It'd been their habit to address Michael and not Elizabeth, as if he were the one employing them. She'd accepted this and not chafed, but now she was the one subjected to their asides and innuendos.

When Elizabeth returned from her rounds she found the reverend doctor occupied with his notes. He was cutting a pencil and she did not want to disturb him, but he waved her near and she sat with him where they could see Michael and the boys beside the creek.

"Why is it, dear friend," she asked the reverend doctor after recounting the shift in her experience with the men.

"Why not take it as proof that they knew all along this is your adventure?" he said.

"Because I am a woman?" she said.

"A remarkable woman," he said.

"You are easy company," she said, patting the back of his hand. She reflected on their protracted journey to the buffalo fields. Not once had the reverend doctor been less than even-tempered. However harsh the experience, he'd always had a kind word and maintained a spirit optimistic.

At daybreak, before the clearing away of the morning mist, it tasted like Africa, the red dust of Africa blown to America. Wherever the buffalo were, they'd be moving to water right now.

The water was a trifle brown, but David believed there would be catfish and a species of bass. Michael would see what he could catch and later he'd take Sabi and reconnoiter the countryside and shoot some birds.

Charlie and John joined him by the water. He removed from its cloth sleeve the elegant jointed rod and shining new reel that were David's, as well as a leather wallet of artificial flies. He drew the silk through the nickel loops and selected a fly from the wallet. The casting began and soon he was placing the fly exactly where he wanted it. The morning was cool as he stood by the creek with the boys listening to the scrape, the murmur and plash of the water. Occasionally a snake or turtle would slide from a log into the creek.

He let the fly float twenty or so yards

downstream, where it stopped and the momentary illusion was of the fly making its way back to him against the current when suddenly it was struck. He set the hook, the rod bent double, and the reel began to run, the line cutting the water. He let line and took line and slowly he brought the fish into the shallows. Kicking off his moccasins, he waded into the creek up to his knees. It was a bass, jet black and sparkling in the light, three pounds or better. He gave the hook a quick flip and the fish came free and fell back into the water, where it floated before coming to life, twisting and finning away.

John was the first to see the water was changing dirty and was to say so, but then Michael saw it too. The buffalo were crossing the creek upstream and breaking onto the western plain.

He asked the boys if they were ready. He rushed to put on his boots and gather the rifles and cartridge belts and mount Khyber.

"Tell the skinners," Michael yelled, and he was off, with Elizabeth on Granby galloping behind.

Chapter 18

Upon crossing a low ridge, they beheld the whole country and it was black with buffalo and trailing wolves. Elizabeth could not help herself and gasped. She shaded her eyes from the bright sunlight and then she looked at them through the glasses. Never before had she seen so much wandering life and nothing broke the intense stillness of that first moment.

It was so many it would have been impossible to count. They were rising from the creek and wandering at their leisure from grass to grass, the cloud shadows blotting out thousands and revealing thousands more when the clouds drifted on. Michael had never seen the like of it. Not in America when he was a boy, not in Africa, not in India, not anywhere a congregation of so many warm-blooded creatures.

They moved up from the water, and their

thirsts slaked, they moved again onto their grazing.

"My God, what a sight," she said. "It seems more than the ocean. I did not know my eye could reach so far."

They picketed the horses and made their approach against the wind. The last fifty yards they moved on hands and knees and then Michael laid himself flat along the earth, and inch by inch crept to the outer edge of a hill overlooking a shallow little basin. Here, he found them again, a small herd, a hundred or more in a secluded fold of the land. The herd was slowly feeding north.

He found the rising ground he wanted. He turned the glasses on them. By now they were a hundred yards from the creek and half of them were lying down. They were a mixed herd, bulls and cows, old and young. He held his breath as a wind snaked through the grass. The wind was theirs. He dug a small hole for his hip joint to rest in and lined it with a horse blanket, then planted the sharp end of his steel shooting stick in the earth. He stuffed cotton in his ears and passed the wadding to Elizabeth so she might also.

Without taking his eyes off the animal before him, he asked that she also cover her ears with her hands. He waited until the buffalo he wanted turned his body for what would be the last time. He took aim, close behind the foreleg and a foot above the brisket. The mark shone brightly inside the scope.

"Open your mouth and breathe a little," he said, letting his own mouth to open.

He took steady aim and fired. The bullet left the ringing steel. Just as in Africa, he was firing at the shoulder with a very heavy rifle. But instead of distances twenty or fifty yards, he lay on a ridge and fired at distances between one hundred and three hundred yards.

The .50 shot high velocity, low trajectory, and long range with penetration and precision. By the time the ball stopped it'd shredded the buffalo's lungs. The big bull he shot, tormented and mystified, blew and pawed at the ground, throwing clumps of red earth high in the air. The others raised their heads to sip the breeze and went back to their feed. Forming on the bull's lips and nostrils was a mass of bloody foam.

Elizabeth watched through the glasses. The bull shook his ponderous head. He seemed to settle himself a moment before rocking sideways and then slipping to his knees. He held that position and then keeled over, slowly at first and then with a rush to the ground. A cow walked over and sniffed at the dead bull. Michael raised the stock of the second rifle to his shoulder. He took one quick sight, fired again, and struck the cow deep in her massive lungs.

"You should go now," Michael said.

"Don't mind me," she said, and on her knees she moved closer.

He held out the cotton and indicated she should press more into her ears.

"Just a few more," she said. "I will go soon."

After what seemed the longest time Charlie and John heard the first percussion of the big .50-caliber shocking the air. It was the sound of thunder over thunder. John pulled a string from his pocket, and after the boys counted ten such shots on their fingers, he tied a knot in the string. At five knots in the string Charlie would run down the slope to rouse the men to fetch the oxen, to yoke them and hook them to the wagons, to gather their knives and make sure the water barrels were full.

Michael shot and he shot again, exchanging rifles every minute or so to let the barrels cool down. Thirty buffalo he killed in thirty minutes. It was not killing by hand, or even killing, but was like the harvesting of corn or wheat or the ripe vegetables in the garden. He showed Elizabeth how to cool the barrel by pouring canteen water down the muzzle and then levering open the breach block and letting the water run out. He showed her how to swab out the barrel with a greased rag in the eyelet of the wiping stick and then he commenced shooting again. He killed them until his head ached with the boom and his shoulder with the recoil and his body with the heat of the day.

He stopped to look back at Khyber and Granby who stood quietly swishing the flies from their sides. When he finished there were 110 dead and dying, and the skinners would soon be specks in the distance coming onto the field followed by Aubuchon and the butcher boys. By nightfall they would be skinned and pegged. Tongues, saddles, loins, hearts, and harslets would be taken for smoking, brining, drying, pickling, and sausage, for grill or cauldron. Machine-like their grim work had begun and at day's end they would return in darkness and in the firelight would be as if the workmen of the devil.

For five days the boys climbed the bluff with their string. For five days Michael shot the buffalo and on the fifth day he secured a buffalo shot for shot. He fired 178 times and there were 178 dead. Hundreds of hides were already stretched, poisoned, and pegged to the ground.

On the sixth day, from the low knoll he looked down at his kingdom of death. It was a windswept and solitary place. The ravens, the wolves, the coyotes, the skinners, the butchers — they waited as if they were paralyzed and had yet to recover from the sound of the rifles. The rest of the herd, grazing and ruminating, drifted west, the cloud shadows slowly going before.

He wiped at the corner of his mouth with his thumb. His beard was dirty and his face caked with dust and black with powder. He'd begun his part in the great vanishing and he knew it. It was as if he was taking apart the world around him one life at a time.

The seventh day he was on the buffalo again. He shot all that day, and when it was over, his nose was bleeding and he could not move for the cramps in his arms and legs. After the day's killing came the lighting of a cigarette, sitting quietly, trying to find himself again. On the wind was the ferrous smell of blood. He held the cigarette in his teeth as he lit it. The red dog came in and sat nearby. One hundred eighty times he pulled the trigger and 168 buffalo fell down and died. His ears dinned with the damage of the ceaseless rifle fire and he could not hear his own voice. He thought about a bucket of hot water and Epsom salt to soak his feet, maybe a bath, clean socks.

Through the glass he watched Aubuchon as he directed the skinners in the taking of the hides and the boys in the taking of saddles and loins, tongues, humps. He watched as each one of them recovered lead for Charlie and John to melt and cast again.

"The Lord says don't look back on your past because I have given you a new future," he said to the red dog. "What do you think about that?"

He breathed deeply as the cigarette stub smoldered between his lips. He thumbed away the shell on a hard-boiled egg, and then another, and a third he offered to the red dog, which would not eat it in front of him.

By then Michael had begun to dream of the buffalo. At first there were no buffalo and all was wrapped in darkness and then a roaring wind, strange and hollow, and a rock split and the buffalo poured from the mouth of this cave. They came bellowing, tramping, splashing, and snorting onto the vast rolling pastureland. There were thousands and thousands and thousands and thousands.

Chapter 19

One by one in the morning darkness Matthew woke his three brothers. Young as he was, from an early age he'd been his own master, and the three looked to him with respect, love, and affection.

"The night is for sleeping," Luke whined.

"Get offa me," John cried.

"Who has my pants?" Mark said, and then, "Where are my shoes?"

"You have big feet," Luke said, tossing him one of his shoes.

"Quit your dawdling," Matthew said and then, "What is it, John?"

"I feel lonesome," the youngest boy said.

"We are old travelers now," Matthew said, gathering his littlest brother into his lap. John was quiet and pensive and favored by the other three, as if his goodness and purity were inborn.

"Will you write to Mother soon?" John said. The boy held his collar and his white thumb in his mouth.

"Yes. Maybe tonight. Before the freighters get here."

"Don't forget to send her a lock of my hair."

"We have a good cause," Matthew said, solemn thoughts coming to his mind as he considered their enterprise.

"I guess I'll see the thing through," John said.

"Good for you," Matthew said as the boy began searching for his shoes.

By the gray light they knew it would be daybreak in another hour. The air was sharp and warming.

When they went to breakfast Aubuchon was at his kneading trough by a little fireside, preparing bread for the oven. He wore an apron, a red flannel shirt, and tow-cloth trousers and was dusted white with wheat flour. Their coffee was already spluttering on the iron grate.

"Hatching mischief?" he said, and gave Matthew a wink.

They ate, hurriedly peeling their eggs and stuffing their mouths with buttered bread and ragged pieces of boudin nearly black with sun and smoke.

"As-tu écrit à ta chère maman?" Aubuchon said, placing his hands on Matthew's shoul-

ders, and then, "Have you written your dear mother?"

"I will, sir."

"Then be off with you," Aubuchon said. He shook each of their hands and they thanked him and they went off to spend their morning stretching, pegging, and poisoning hides.

Another day's killing done, the work of flaying and butchering had begun. On the hot wind was the stench of decaying animal matter and the smell of new blood. Each man wore on his belt a flat leather scabbard with a ripping knife, butcher's steel, and broad-pointed skinning knife. The Gough brothers, the Miller brothers, Findley, and O'Malley — their wrists and forearms were as coils unsprung.

On this day Elizabeth went out with the skinners while Aubuchon and the boys would collect the meat and the green hides and make as many trips as possible to bring them in.

After the Gough brothers finished taking a hide she glanced at her watch to set the start time in her mind for the next one. She noted that when they moved they carried a butcher's steel in one hand and knife in the other, swiping the steel as they walked, to sharpen it. They worked quickly while the carcass was still warm, the easier to take the hide. Ike grasped a foreleg and heaved it over, levering the buffalo onto its back. With his ripping knife Abel made a slit from under the jaw the length of the belly to the root of the tail. Ike pulled hard when Abel made his cut and the belly hide made a ripping sound as it opened to the ghostly whiteness beneath. While Ike made a slit around each ankle and cut down from the front hooves over the knee to the brisket, Abel made the same slits and cut down the hind legs to the tail.

With each pause their steels came out and they vigorously swiped their blades two, three times to sharpen them. They cut the hide away from the rib cage, rocking the animal back forth until they were ready to roll it over and drag the hide from beneath. Then they folded in the legs and rolled it up head to tail into a bundle three feet wide. Ike tied a knot in their string and they moved on to their next one, their blades going snick, snick, snick on the steels.

The animal they left behind was much smaller.

Elizabeth glanced at her watch, fifteen minutes. She timed them again and again and they consistently took hides in fifteen to twenty minutes. She did the arithmetic. In a twelve-hour day, that would be thirty-five to fifty hides. Say at forty hides, that would be five dollars a day apiece for the brothers and for her, less their pay, there would be a hundred and ten dollars a day just from these two skinners. Could it possibly be? She took a notebook from her pocket and did the multiplying on paper. It was.

Aubuchon and the butcher boys came in and began to open up the carcasses. The meat was cut into long, narrow strips and hung in festoons upon racks, where they dried in the sun. Chunks and shreds were taken, and the intestines collected, and these would become sausage. Some took the hump ribs, while others took hearts and livers — Aubuchon called them the *petits morceaux* — and wrapped them in canvas. Bones were to be chopped to pieces with axes for the marrow to enrich Aubuchon's soups, to butter their bread, to add to the sausages. Aubuchon told the boys when you eat the animal you eat its life. You eat whatever it ate. You eat its blood and muscle. You eat its breath. You eat the grass and the earth. You eat the water.

She moved up the wind to time the Miller brothers and then Findley and O'Malley.

They were not as fast as the Gough brothers, but they were not that far behind. Maybe a bonus for bringing in the most hides would cause them to improve.

The penman and his grandson worked side by side and unfortunately they were as if weak and lost. The grandson's glasses kept slipping down his nose with his sweat and each time he set them right he managed to daub more grease and blood on his face until finally he took off his spectacles and folded them into a pocket sewed inside his shirt.

She would have to take them off piecework and offer to pay them a wage. They could butcher and make sausage, tend the smokehouse, cook food for the men in the field, ferry hides and meat into camp.

As the day went on, dark masses of clouds arose on the horizon. The men cursed the animal as they ripped it. They cursed the animal as they skinned it. Hats were pushed far on the backs of heads. Faces shined with grease and blood. In turns they stood and stretched their backs. They wiped their faces with their forearms. They uncurled their stiffened fingers and then grasped their knives again.

When Michael returned from the next valley he turned the glasses and watched the skinners and butchers on the plain. There was an oppressive feeling in the atmosphere, the threat of weather. They saw it too. Thunder rumbled in the distance.

They were warned, but they would not relent and they labored on as if factory men. He watched them until a little before sundown and then bent his way homeward, returning to the camp on Wolf Creek. From the bluff he could see the glint of the water; the white peaks of the Sibley tents; the cowshed, smokehouse, brining pits, and cookhouse; the chickens scoured in the yard; and hundreds and hundreds of hides pegged into the banking along the creek and sprinkled with arsenic water. Hundreds were in the presses and hundreds more were already bundled.

He settled himself back into the saddle and slowed the mare to a walk off the bluff. It was now a camp of buffalo hunters and the flesh smell of the abattoir was in the air.

Aubuchon was back at his cook fire. John was raking the coals. He'd found another large soft-shell turtle, of a hundred pounds or better, basking on the bank of the creek. He'd roast it in the shell and tonight there would be soup.

Michael went down to the creek with a bucket and a bar of soap, Khyber following behind. He drew water and washed his hands and arms and the grime on his face. Before stooping to drink, he looked around. He scanned the high bank. Then he took Khyber into the water and washed her and scraped her dry and curried her and brushed her.

At his tent he dragged his cot from the confines of his tent and into the cool evening and lay down. His was the long habit of wakefulness at night, but tonight he was all played out and would sleep. If anyone should come during the night, Khyber would know and give him warning.

He slipped into his moccasins. Charlie came racing by with new belts of ammunition.

"Where are you going so fast?" he called to the boy.

"Aubuchon," he said.

"Who gave you that black eye?"

"I fell down."

"Was it one of the Gough boys?"

"I told you I fell down."

"Repeating a lie does not make it true."

"Leave it alone," the boy said, and took up his run again.

He lay down and Sabi climbed in beside him, but he could not sleep. He felt in the air the beginnings of something to come.

He read awhile and then fell asleep, his head pillowed on the book. When Aubuchon called for dinner he opened his eyes to see Elizabeth looking down at him. There was twilight on the bluff, but it was almost dark beneath it and the skinners were not back yet.

"Would you join us for dinner?" she asked.

On the table was a white tablecloth and brass candlesticks. There was a small fire and there was every delicacy: tongues, brains, marrowbones, kidneys, venison, as well as turtle soup. Fifteen days since they'd begun the harvest and 1,650 buffalo were slaughtered for their hides and meat.

"God was good to us today," the reverend doctor said, holding aloft a glass of wine.

"First rate, indeed," Elizabeth said.

She was still doing calculations in her mind, subtly moving her fingers the way some people do when they listen to music. The numbers were very good, near five thousand dollars less four hundred for the skinners, and they hadn't been on the buffalo but two weeks and that tally did not include the butchering at three cents a pound, tongues at six dollars a dozen. A hundred pounds sold to the eastern markets was worth three dollars and would come to thousands. If only she had more men, economic autonomy would be hers. She felt inside herself the powerfully surging life of the times.

"How goes the writing?" Elizabeth said.

"You are writing?" Michael said.

The reverend doctor explained he was writing two books, one useful to the settler and the investor when the country opened up and a second one he called a new divinity.

After soup and other delicacies, they ate heartily of the fat steaks and marrow bones. Then the men scraped the bowls of their pipes and filled them with tobacco. Elizabeth asked that Michael make her a cigarette. They lit their pipes, and Elizabeth her cigarette, and they sat back against the night waiting for the skinners, warm, drowsy, and tranquil.

The blue smoke curled lazily, flattened, and floated east. Michael opened and closed his mouth to get his hearing back. Elizabeth looked up at the stars revealed in the waning twilight. The moon was low to the horizon and in the air overhead was the wheep sound of bat wings breaking the night silence.

Charlie came running and then Aubuchon and John. Charlie was breathless, pointing down the creek into the darkness. Michael said something, but Elizabeth could not hear what it was.

"There's something moving," he repeated. He stood so quickly he knocked over his chair.

"Who are those fellows?" Elizabeth asked of the shadowy figures.

"Don't stand there," Michael called out, his hand on the grips of his revolver. "Come into the light where I can see you."

They came as if from the dusky twilight. They were half-starved, half-naked wretches. There were four of them. One man wore cast-off military from the last war. Another wore a coarse blanket tied with string at the neck and holes cut through for his arms. They carried stout wooden shafts with spear points fashioned from kitchen knives and scythe blades.

"You come in now where I can see you," Michael shouted. "Step into the light."

They were led by a tall, slender man not yet in the middle of age. His face indicated a refined and sensitive nature. His forehead was high and narrow. His mouth was large and against his black skin his teeth were white and straight. When he spoke his voice was quiet and impressive. He alone wore a pair of heavy cowhide shoes.

"Who are you?" Elizabeth said.

"I am Pastor Starling," he said, "and these men are Elijah, Gideon, and Henry Ward Beecher, members of my congregation."

Elizabeth stepped forward. She took Pastor Starling's hand into her own and said she was happy to meet him. She turned to Aubuchon and asked him to fill the boiler again and make another pot of coffee, and if there was pie, could they have some of that also?

Pastor Starling had brought his people four hundred miles from the piney woods of Arkansas, bound for Kansas to have a better future. They'd come through the Indian Territory. They came through an impenetrable belt of forest, matted and tangled with undergrowth, shinneries of scrub oak, blackjack, post oak, sumac, bracken, and fern.

In the days after the war, being black and free was a crime. Pastor Starling told them how he was preaching on a Sunday when men wearing masks interrupted his service. The masked men tied him to a tree and severely whipped him before his gathered congregation. They salted and brined his wounds and he was charged with sedition and incitement to riot. To pay the cost of incarceration, he was transported deep into the pine forest to work the isolated turpentine farms with other men, women, and children. Each man was responsible for boxing ten thousand trees spread over a hundred acres. They worked twelve-hour days and their sentences seemed never to expire.

One day they awoke to find that the overseer had been killed in his sleep. Dense smoke poured from the fire heating the furnace, but the stiller and his wife were nowhere to be found. Neither were the men who guarded them. In the warden's house was a safe with the door swung open and paper strewn across the floor, and in the huge open cauldron they found the stiller and his wife floating on top.

Escaping was punishable by death, but so too were thievery and murder. So they filled their socks with all the pepper they could find to keep off the bloodhounds and the patrollers. They used saltpeter and turpentine. They dragged the skins of whatever animal they shot or trapped to cover their scent and they all traveled west, every man, woman, and child. As their oxen withered and failed they were butchered for food until they were down to one with a dislocated hip. It was here they'd come to a halt.

The lid on the boiler rattled with the heat and Aubuchon began pouring cups of coffee. The wolfer came in from the shadows, his rifle in the crook of his arm.

"Where are the rest of your people?" Elizabeth said.

"Our people are back a ways," Pastor Starling said, with a nod to the east.

"How many more are there?" Michael said.

"Some of our men and your men lay side by side with their bayonets through one another," Elijah said to Michael.

The wolfer stepped forward and explained to Elizabeth that Starling's people had been scavenging meat. Some were made sick by the strychnine set out for the wolves and some of them died.

"Hunger will break through a stone wall," Henry Ward Beecher said. The man was bent and wiry and looked nearly a hundred years old.

"Will you work?" Elizabeth said.

"We would," Pastor Starling said. If it ever crossed his mind that his people were there first and by the hunter's code owned the hunting rights, he did not say.

"I only want men whose hearts are in the work. I hire all my labor at a good rate."

After a moment's pause, Pastor Starling inquired how much she was offering and she wondered how many times in his life he'd had the opportunity to ask. She told him the same as the other men, plus all the meat they could eat as well as rations of corn, coffee, flour, and sugar, which she would provide.

"For your kitchen," she said, "there will be hot biscuit and corn cake."

"We will hold up to your opinion," Henry Ward Beecher said.

"White men sit pretty heavy, they do," Elijah said.

"White men are lazy," Henry Ward Beecher said with a mischievous smile, and they all laughed at this.

"I think it good wages," Elijah said, though he'd never received a wage in his life.

"It's a very good wage," the reverend doctor said, announcing his name and stepping in to shake hands with Pastor Starling and the others. "I can vouch for it, as well as the honesty of this woman."

"You are?" Pastor Starling said.

"Methodist."

"Yes, I am too," Pastor Starling said. He stepped forward and said to the reverend doctor something private that made him laugh.

Pastor Starling stepped back and turned to Elizabeth.

"The last days we have shared a pot of mush and it is now gone. Might we receive in advance a bushel of corn to parch?"

"Of course you can," she said. "There is a hand mill bolted to the side of the provision wagon in case you want to grind any of it. There's meat and beans just baked. Do you have sufficient blankets?"

"We do," Pastor Starling said.

Elizabeth turned to Aubuchon and said, "Please dig up the bean pot from its bake hole and prepare it for transport. Send with them sausage and a roast and draw five blankets for their use."

The men and boys came off the bluff, their long day in the field over. The wagons were filled with the last of the hides they'd stretch and peg in the morning. They were tired and hungry and needed to tend to the animals. They carried their bloody knotted strings and wanted their tallies recorded in Mrs. Coughlin's ledger book so they could add today to their total and dream how they'd spend it.

Their voices could be heard over the creak of the wheels and the tramp of the oxen.

"We cut a big hog in the ass today," Ike Gough was saying.

"Another day, another dollar," Story Miller said.

Michael told Charlie to run and tell them to wait before they came down the path. Pastor Starling took out a large silver hunting watch.

"And what time would you expect us?" Pastor Starling said.

"Do you work on the Sabbath? I believe it is the Sabbath tomorrow," Elizabeth said.

Pastor Starling turned to the other men and they conferred for a moment before he turned back to Elizabeth.

"We do if there is work," Pastor Starling said.

"The men usually gather to go out late morning. Does that suit you?"

"Yes, it suits us just fine."

"I will loan you a wagon and a team and as many sets of knives as you can make use of. You will bring me your count every day."

"I will."

"Fair enough," she said, and this was followed by another round of handshakes. As they were to depart, Pastor Starling turned to Elizabeth one last time.

"When the time comes, you will pay us what we are owed?" he said.

"There will be profit for you and for myself."

"You have your own camp?" Michael said.

"We wish to remain separate."

"Then I will trust you to keep to yourselves."

The men could be held back no longer. They were coming down the path. They were tired and blood-sotted. The thighs of their trousers shined with grease in the pattern of wiping hands and knives. Michael went up the path to meet them.

"That's a good lot of niggers," Ike Gough said when Michael stopped them.

"What's the confabulation?" Story Miller asked, jutting out his chin.

"New men hired," Michael said, and the news shocked them.

"We worked our guts out today and for what?" Temple Miller said.

"Your own hook," Michael said, and he kept them there until Elizabeth finished her business with Pastor Starling and his people.

"There ain't enough hides to go around," Story Miller said.

"I believe the Negroes will do as much work as it is possible for any white man to do, Mr. Gough. It is your choice whether to stay or leave. Either way, I will be going forward with these new men," Elizabeth said.

"We will work with them, but we will not eat with them," Findley said.

"They prefer to keep their own camp,"

Elizabeth said.

"How are we to sleep with those savages at our backs?" O'Malley asked, turning to Findley.

"You can make a nigger work," Ike said, "but you cannot make him think."

Michael stepped forward. These men were not strangers to him. He'd known them in so many places and long since taken their measure.

"We are every day on borrowed time," he said. "If we last, there will be enough for everybody."

At dinner and into the late hour the Gough brothers continued to harp on the deal struck with the Negroes and how any deal with Negroes was wrong and they should be run off the land. They'll not work anyway. They'll soon enough get the Negro sickness, such as headache; pain in their eyes, arms, and legs; their knees hurting; backs, necks, feet, hands, bowels.

Later that evening Michael went out to make his rounds and to set the night watch. He told the men their talk was making the horses uneasy and maybe it was time they shut their g.d. mouths and go to bed. When he returned Elizabeth was sitting with the reverend doctor in front of her tent, and she called to him.

"Are they still griping?" she said.

"They'll be having the sulks for a while," Michael said, but he knew it was a grave situation.

"Guess what he said to me," the reverend doctor said.

"I have no idea," Michael said.

"Starling said he was Methodist, but unless he dunks them in the river they do not believe it takes."

"Have I done wrong?" Elizabeth said.

"Making a decision does not make something so," Michael said.

"It will be a great experiment," the reverend doctor said.

Michael went up the path toward the hired men. Within the glow of light given by the small fire the angry discussion was still going forward. Their words were drunk with fatigue and angry with betrayal and they were as if one long unceasing voice.

"Who will boss them?"

"We know how lazy those boys can be when there is no one to boss them up."

"I never saw such a ill-looking lot of niggers."

"They won't work so hard."

"Well, I'll tell you what I think on it; I'd like it if we could just get rid of 'em. They ought to get some country and put them

where they could be by their own selves."
No one slept much that night.

CHAPTER 20

Michael looked up and held a hand to the sky. Summer was over and the fall was coming. Beneath the blistering sun, he watched them through the glasses, the men and women working in the midst of 135 dead buffalo lying on the ground as if struck down by a single hand. Pastor Starling took off his shirt and his glistening back skin was seamed and ridged with scars from his neck into his waistband. His back was streaked and speckled, dusky white, pink, and pale, as if the color had been whipped out of it. Most of them worked with bare arms and bare feet, half-clothed and wearing handkerchiefs wrapped on their heads. Some of them smoked, what he did not know, and they kept a little fire going to cook their food and light their pipes.

Pastor Starling's people did not work in twos but in gangs of three and four, and the money they earned was money for them all, as they were going to Kansas. To each gang a boy was attached whose business it was to sharpen knives, fetch water, and guide the team as it moved about the field.

There were women who came with the men and they carried babies slung to their breasts with great triangles of cloth they knotted behind their necks. The babies they lay in a dump cart beneath the shade of a blanket while they worked with the men, and when the babies fussed, a woman would go and nurse them. When her milk was dry, it would be the turn of another woman to nurse the babies. Later in the day they re-tied the triangles of cloth and carried the babies on their backs as they worked beside the men.

Ike Gough unholstered his revolver and fired a bullet into the ear hole of a buffalo not yet dead. He pointed his knife at Starling's back, tipped his head, and drew the blade as if across his throat, and the brothers shared a laugh and went back to work.

Large black buzzards sailed slowly, high above the plain. Flocks of larks, quails, and robins settled and dispersed, as did doves, swiftly flying in small companies. Wolves and coyotes could be seen waiting for the darkness when they'd be poisoned by the wolfer.

The women followed the skinners and the butchers from carcass to carcass with long, thin knives. They collected the tripe and the sweetbreads — the pancreas and thymus — and these would go into the iron kettle back at their camp with a flitch of bacon and dried vegetables: corn, squash, and onions. At noon one of the women kindled a small fire and began roasting the hearts and livers for the men to eat. They ate the milk gut raw and drank the chyme until it ran down their chests.

The old man named Elijah wore a brimless hat. At the hips he was wrapped round with a piece of old blanket tied with a rope. His ears were cut and he wore the brand of an *M* for Maroon on his cheek. He shuffled from one place to the next, powered by his hips and thighs. His Achilles tendons had been cut because he'd been a runaway. He asked the Millers if they'd take some food.

"You have a good appetite, old man," Story Miller said, accepting from him a skewer of meat. Story extended his hand in thank you. The old man looked at it before taking it into his own. His hands were as hard and rough as hickory bark and his skin was as black as tar.

"You sure can eat your allowance," Story said.

"Yes, sir, when I can get it," Elijah said, wiping at his gray whiskers.

"There's a genuine cotton nigger for you," Ike Gough said to Abel. "Look at his toes."

Story Miller thought to stand up to the Gough brothers but knew they were men blood hot. They'd give no quarter. They'd kill you if they perceived a threat and in turn you would have to kill them both or suffer the revenge of the other. Story wanted to say, Mrs. Coughlin told us to behave like gentlemen, but he didn't.

Ike Gough rose up and hovered malevolently over Elijah. He then laughed at the old man and went back to his brother.

"You were a horse rider," Elijah said to Story. "I was a horse rider too."

"Where was that?"

"First Mississippi Infantry, African Descent. I was bayoneted in the right breast."

"I was with the Second Massachusetts. Major David Coughlin."

"We were comrades in arms."

When Michael rode in they all stopped to watch him and the loping horse and the red dog and, for Pastor Starling's people, especially the dog.

Michael made the rounds to collect the spent lead they'd recovered. They dropped them into the sack he'd hung behind the saddle along with the two Sharps, the Winchester, and several canteens for cooling the barrels. He saved Pastor Starling for last. He spoke to him quietly, so only the pastor could hear.

"Sit with me a while," he said. "Let them see you smile."

He stepped off with the horse in the direction of the red dog and Pastor Starling followed behind. Michael dismounted and coiled down to the ground sitting on a leg tucked beneath him. He fished a cigarette from his pocket and struck a match, shielding the ember as Pastor Starling sat down beside him, propped on his hands and his legs stretched in front.

"You didn't kill anybody?" Michael said, looking away to the east. He felt safe, as he could see for miles across the blasted land and whoever might be traveling.

"Are you looking for murderers?"

"I am looking for a story I can believe," Michael said.

A tense moment passed between them. A pistol discharged and another buffalo was finished.

"I confidently hope you believe me," Pastor Starling said. His face was perfectly motionless, but his eyes conveyed the strongest emotions.

Michael shrugged and gave a slight turn of his head. A muscle twitched in his cheek. He rubbed out his cigarette in a patch of dirt.

"The things I said, it makes no matter what people say or think, they are what happened," Pastor Starling said.

"We all have our secrets," Michael said, a flicker in his eye.

"Other men you see them and it makes you despise the weakness in yourself. The weaker the animal, the more you despise it."

"I see a sadness in them," Michael said, meaning the buffalo.

"That is your own sadness you see."

"There is sometimes too much in human nature to withstand," Michael said, and then he said, "Thank you for talking to me. I apologize for bringing it up."

Michael stood as if he had been shot up from the ground. He mounted Khyber and looked down at Starling. "If they catch you, it will go hard on you." Khyber shook her head causing the bit ring to jingle. In his pocket he found a square of chewing tobacco and tossed it down.

"I reckon it will," Pastor Starling said, tearing off a corner of the tobacco with his teeth. He made to toss it back, but Michael gestured no.

"Don't all come out here at once," Michael said. "Take turns so all of you don't get caught if it comes down. You will make your money."

Michael whistled up the red dog and wheeled Khyber. He made a nick nick nick sound and she leaped into a gallop. He let her run a hundred yards and another hundred and until he was small and away from where they were.

By the time they finished the day's skinning and butchering, the night was clear and the moon shined brightly. The boys had ferried load after load of green hides and meat back to camp. That first day Pastor Starling's people were capable of processing only twenty buffalo among them, but as the days went by and they ate the warm hearts and the livers and drank the blood, their strength would improve and in short time they would get the knack of it. Now they were all trudging home to their dinners and blankets and sleep. They'd wake up to tomorrow and it would be the same as today.

"There's a wonderful moon this evening," Elijah said.

"Yes," Story said, struck by the moment he was sharing with the old man. It was indeed a wonderful moon. The two of them looked at the sky for a long time and neither man wanted to break the spell of the moment cast. Neither man felt the strangeness of being together.

Feeling dizzy, Elijah suddenly fell against him and Story tried to catch him, but the old man slipped to the ground.

"Are you poorly?" he said, going down on his heels beside Elijah.

"The work tires me a good deal," Elijah said, and his eyelids drooped. At first he seemed reluctant to stand, but then he wanted to try. "Hold on to me, I want to get up," he said.

Elijah supported himself on Story and climbed to his feet. Glassy-eyed and unsteady, he strained his eyes to make out the land ahead of him, but he could see nothing. Story called out and Elijah's people came and loaded him in the wagon. Elijah raised a hand and Story waved.

The two men would never see each other again.

When Pastor Starling brought the count, Elizabeth asked that he stay for tea.

"The number is good. It will get better," she said. "How do you find the work?"

"Like we are living ten days in the week," he said.

"I wish to know more about you," she said.

"You are asking me to remember."

"I did not mean to pry," she said.

"Some of them folks in the turpentine woods didn't even know there was a war," Pastor Starling said.

Once he started telling, he started remembering and he never knew what he would remember. Some people remembered better than others and he was of that kind. When he looked back there were no vanished years. He remembered them completely, acutely, and once again he was living moments of the past.

"We saw soldiers," he said, "but that was all and a while later we started receiving three dollars a month and didn't know why and then we found ourselves in the jailhouse and then the turpentine farm.

"At the outbreak of the war I was fifteen years old. My master had a brother in Texas and I was refugeed there with my mother and my two sisters for safekeeping. One day I went with my master's brother to drive a herd of mules to Louisiana. While I was there he traded me for fifty head of cattle. I imagine he told everybody I was dead."

"You never saw your mother or sisters again?"

"No, ma'am. Not ever again," he said, and he did not look away and his eyes did not wet with tears. He knew Elizabeth Coughlin was a caring woman and yet he hated her in this moment. He knew it was unfair and unreasonable to hate this good woman, but he did. He hated the white material of kindness and sympathy and sentimentality. He hated God and the hypocrisy of his mercy.

He sighed deeply and dropped his gaze to his hands folded in his lap. He laughed ruefully. He especially hated telling his story for no more than a cup of tea.

"Is that a history you would want to remember?" he said.

"I am at a loss for words," she said. "Yours is such a heavy truth. I hope one day you find the freedom you are looking for."

He stood to take his leave. He smiled as he thought of the littlest thing: departing from the presence of a white person on his own initiative. He tipped his hat, gave a wink, and walked away.

CHAPTER 21

It was the Miller brothers, Story and Temple, very reliable men who came to Elizabeth on behalf of the others. They were making better numbers every day. They took off their identical gray felt hats and held them in their hands as a mark of respect. Temple Miller cleared his throat and spoke first.

"Good morning, Mrs. Coughlin. How are you today?"

"You find us as we are," she said with a wave of her hand. The reverend doctor lifted his coffee cup, nodded, and took a sip. Elizabeth motioned to a chair. Temple Miller sat down, fretting with the brim of his hat while his brother stood behind him, his hands crossed in front of himself. Temple sighed and looked to a spot on the ground just beyond the toes of his shoes.

"The men won't go out," Temple said.

"My good man. You lose the morning, you

lose the day," the reverend doctor said.

"They say they won't go."

"We had an agreement," Elizabeth said. She sat back to see him more clearly and beyond to the trickle of smoke ascending from the breakfast fire, flattening and drifting away, the other men gathered where they could watch. She found herself already growing angry.

"It's the Negroes," Temple said.

"The men say, 'Niggers are going too high,' " Story said and then looked down at his hands, his wrists, his hat stained red with blood.

"What does that mean?" she said.

"They are all panting for riches," the reverend doctor said to her. "They want more money."

"We came a long ways to get here," Temple Miller said. "To make our money."

"I know that as well as anyone," Elizabeth said. "You've worked hard."

"It isn't right," Story said. "I do not begrudge them, but I say, let them get their own. We fought and died for their freedom and we are entitled to something more."

"We all want to make the most of it while it lasts," Temple said.

"You are good hands. You will do well if you work hard," Elizabeth said.

"We worked our guts out to get us here, and for them it is easy sailing and they are profit for that," Temple said.

"What does it matter how far someone comes to work?" Elizabeth said, drumming her fingers on the tabletop.

But she knew what it meant. They'd traveled together over the broad prairie of Kansas, crossed the dead line, and plunged deep into the country. They'd weathered the miles, the fire, the rivers, the heat, the snakes, the lightning. The knives and gunpowder, the tents, tools and provisions, all that they'd hauled here, when they could have stayed home.

Temple's voice was thin and yet unconflicted. He believed the things he was saying.

Still, Elizabeth could not help herself. She wondered why men were so ignorant. Like David, she would rather trust a man and be deceived and not live with suspicion and cynicism and it was perhaps these two brothers she trusted the most. But every one of them was now to her a liar, disloyal, and a storyteller.

The reverend doctor was addressing her. "It's the desire to get rich without working," he was saying.

"Mrs. Coughlin, the men will not work

for the same pay as the coloreds," Temple said. "They say a white man is worth more."

"You are all agreed in this?"

"Time is money, ma'am, and we only have so long," Story said. "This ain't going to last forever."

She closed her eyes and breathed in the late morning air. She felt inside the fist of anger. Beyond the bluff to the west the big guns fired methodically, the cracking air a muffled thump by the time it crossed the valley, minute after minute.

"Well, it's work or starve," she said. "Starling's people sure enough know the truth of that."

"We ain't coloreds, ma'am," Story said. There was hurt in his voice. "And I do not hate them, but it ain't right. Every hide they take is one less for us."

"Is that your answer, ma'am?" Temple said.

"My answer? My answer is no."

The gun boomed again, a puff of a sound coming from the west. In her mind she could see the animal shudder, see its head lolling back and forth, see the flush of blood, see it collapse to its knees and onto its side. Tell her the sex, age, and weight of the animal and she could tell its worth in hide, meat, and bone.

"Ma'am," Story said.

"What?"

"They say they'll kill the niggers if they go out."

Her mouth moved, she was too shocked to speak. Were there no rules or laws? Wasn't money enough?

"Who says that?"

"It only takes one to say it," Temple said.

"It is a raw deal, ma'am," Story said, and then he bit his bottom lip.

She thought to invoke David's name, to appeal to their years of service, but would not allow herself to do so. In a month's time she could have a new crew, but what of the threatened bloodshed and what of these good-souled men before her forced to do the devil's bidding?

"I will make it right with you," she said. In her mind she made calculations as she spoke. Her right hand, her fingers all the while were tapping the table and her left hand in her lap, her fingers were doing the arithmetic.

"No, no, no," the reverend doctor said, chopping the air with his hands. "That won't do. You men are talking murder."

The Millers' faces were red and they ducked their heads in shame.

"Reverend Doctor Purefoy," she said, "I

would ask you to please leave us alone for the time being."

"It is the principle of the thing," he insisted.

"I will act for myself," she said quietly. She could not hide behind innocence or outrage. She knew dissension would be ruinous.

Pastor Starling and his people were coming into the clearing. There were only three of them today: Pastor Starling, Gideon, and Henry Ward Beecher. She watched as they stopped and lingered on the outskirts. Clearly they understood there was a tension in the camp. They backed away and dropped from sight.

"My dear friend," she said, "please, the less you say, the better."

"I only wish to help."

"I know that."

The reverend doctor stood and shook down his trouser legs. He opened his mouth as if to speak again, but then he left.

Elizabeth waited. She'd not speak again until one of them did.

"Ma'am?" Temple said.

"Please," she said, as if returning from an inner distraction, "what are your terms?"

"They want more money per hide and they will not work with the colored women and the pickaninnies in the field," Story said.

"Why?" she said.

"Why what?" Temple said.

"Why no women and children?"

"Mrs. Coughlin, it jes' ain't right," Story said, "to have women and children out there with men."

"You're embarrassed," she said. "When you have to make water. Or void your excrement. There is no privacy."

"It ain't right," Story said, his face going from red to scarlet.

"I understand," she said. "I would be uncomfortable too."

She paused to look at her watch. She would offer the women employment in camp assisting with the butchering. She asked the Millers if they'd like tea or coffee, but they declined.

"Do you have a figure in mind? It would be helpful."

When they said they hadn't got that far she waited again. She commented on how fine the weather was running and offered them tea or coffee again, which they declined a second time.

"Can you accept terms on everyone's behalf, or must I present them to the other men myself?"

"We were told to see what we could get," Story said.

"I see."

She took a sip of her tea and then offered them three cents more a hide. She told them that was a 12 percent increase and could mean another ten dollars a week.

"I am sorry, but that is all I can do," she said of the new terms.

"We can do that," Temple said, his relief apparent.

"There is another matter of great concern," she said. "We agreed to terms before leaving Meadowlark and by imposing new demands you have broken your word. How do I know it will not happen again?"

"We promise," Story said.

"I will trust you and forgive you, but you must ask me to. That way, we can let bygones be bygones."

After asking her forgiveness, she insisted they have coffee and she spoke to them quietly for a long time until they felt forgiven.

When Michael returned that afternoon he was summoned to her tent, where he found her at the desk. There were stacks of invoices filling the chairs and she seemed not yet finished. She explained to him what happened that morning.

"What did you do?" he asked.

"It does not concern you to know it."

"Fair enough," he said, standing and reaching for his hat.

"I made concessions."

"That's very courageous of you."

"Are you sincere?" she said.

"Men like them, there is not much you can threaten them with."

"Then I will leave the matter with you."

"What am I to do?"

She held up a sheet of paper in each hand. She scrutinized them, as if reconciling the columns of figures and annotations. The ink was not yet dry. She set them down and picked up two more.

"Maybe there are lessons yet to come," she said, still studying the papers.

"Such as?"

"You will have to kill more buffalo," she said. "To satisfy everyone."

He stood there for several seconds, motionless, watching her closely. There was something new and different about her, a growing strength, an optimism, and if there are moments when a life changes, this seemed to be one of them.

"I have learned so much," she said, and a smile appeared on her face.

Feeling dismissed, Michael went to his

tent for his shotgun. When Sabi saw the fowling piece, she dashed about, her joy unrestrained. He slung the gun, pocketed shells, and draped the setter across his shoulders. They rode north into the sunflowers and waited for the night flight of the migrating doves. He sat against a fallen log and the setter lay quietly beside him. She was panting, her tongue lolling from her mouth and she seemed to be grinning. All manner of birds began coming in. There were wild ducks as well and geese feeding among the sedges, skimming to invisible water and lifting off and continuing their journey south.

He laced his fingers at the back of his neck and stretched out his legs. He was exhausted after his day in the field. He thought about Elizabeth's imperative, her temperance and forbearance, her restraint in the face of provocation. He began to anticipate the morrow. When the dove came in they were following the creek and its laterals and there were vast numbers of them, and with every shot, six or eight or ten fell to the ground.

The next day he killed 117 buffalo and the next day 98 and then 126, 130, and he told the boys they needed to load 200 a day.

Chapter 22

About the first of the month Darby piloted the freighters from Fort Worth into camp. The freighters brought hay and grain, sugar, molasses, shoes, powder, and dry goods. They brought firing pins, poison, tobacco, canvas, salt, and liquor. There were bundles of magazines, newspapers, and mail.

There were six yoke of oxen to the team and each pulled a big Murphy wagon with wheels seven feet in diameter and a smaller wagon trailing behind. The wagons had racks built onto their beds and could hold five hundred hides. The freighters were mostly Mexican and were well armed and spoke little English if they were inclined to speak at all.

The men broke work that day to load the hides. Pastor Starling's people came from the woods and pitched in. One at a time they brought the wagons off the bluff and filled them with hides, boomed them down, and cinched them tight with a haymaker's hitch. They doubled the yoke to twelve, ran the wagon back onto the plain and brought down another one. There were six such wagons to load and four more they filled with barrels of pickled tongues, smoked buffalo hams sewed in canvas, humps, loins, sausage, jerky.

That day they would ship twenty-eight hundred hides and three tons of meat and could have shipped half as much again if they'd had the wagons. The freighters ate their food and climbed the bluff, where the men helped them yoke their teams and then began the slow march to join up with twenty other teams on the rough trail back to Fort Worth with near ten thousand hides. The hides were bound for auction, where every day or two they moved a hundred thousand hides destined to become the drive belts connected to steam engines that drove the mills, factories, and farms as they wove from line shafts to pulleys and turned at tremendous rates with superior grip and tensile strength. Industry wanted every buffalo hide it could get.

The next morning Darby went out with Michael to the buffalo fields.

It was October and the buffalo wore their full new coats, their pelage at its finest and their hides warranting the highest price. Darby brought Michael a letter from Fort Worth, another one from Mr. Salt. Michael had never met Mr. Salt but knew him to be a rich and successful businessman of Scottish descent. He was a member of the House of Commons and a senior partner of a banking house and a commercial house in London and Bombay. Michael knew that he owned a forty-three-thousand-acre estate, set in the midst of a park with lakes, forest, and a distant view of the sea. Mr. Salt theorized men are not that removed in time from the savage and that's why men of vast fortune go to live in desolate places, surround themselves with animals, and hunt and fish every day.

Their transactions were confined to contracts, bills of lading, invoices, and letters. Michael collected birds and animals to fill Mr. Salt's private menagerie and Mr. Salt paid him handsomely. The letter informed Michael that his associates, the Métis and the Lord, would soon arrive in Galveston Bay on his steam yacht and from there would mount an expedition into the interior, and he hoped Michael would still be their guide. He was interested in buffalo, antelope, deer, wolves, coyotes, rattlesnakes. He wanted two of each, a breeding pair.

He'd collected India and Africa and now he was interested in collecting the Americas. Based on his success with Eskimos, Nubians, Lapps, and Hottentots, he wanted a Comanche family for an ethnographic study. Michael would receive as usual a very generous commission, and if in the meantime he received any counter offers, these he would match.

"Your man, Mr. Salt," Darby said.

"Does everybody know?" Michael said.

"People talk. How many more days before you leave?"

"A while yet."

"Does she know?"

"Not precisely. I just found out my own self."

"We will make do," Darby said. "It's easy hard work."

"I believe that," Michael said, but both men knew the hardship yet to come. They were in a place where violence ran free. There would be winter cold and darkness, accident, fever, snakebite, pestilence, infection. A man could lose his mind.

"We will miss you," Darby said.

"I am glad to be so needed," Michael said.

The day turned hot, dusty, almost hallucinatory. Three miles out and Michael and Darby came suddenly upon a buffalo road traversing the prairie. Four miles to the west and south they found them again. They rode on and soon they were in the midst of a sea of buffalo.

Michael felt a hunter's joy to have found them and then a sorrow at the prospect of killing every one of them that he possibly could.

That day in the field there were two bulls squared off with each other, their anger mounting. They bellowed and tossed their heads and neither would give ground.

"That'll stir your blood," Darby said, his eye at the telescopic scope.

They pawed the earth with their hoofs throwing the sod high in the sky. When they crashed into each they heard them as far away as they were, and shivers went through the men for how violent the collision. Once more and finally it was decided. Not today would they kill each other. They turned from each other and as they slowly walked away Michael shot one and Darby shot the other.

The skinners were crossing the creek, humping onto the bluff, and beginning their drifting in the direction of the rifle fire. They had spent time with the oxen, worked with the oxen, lived with the oxen, and had become more like the oxen than the oxen like them. They strode forward with their heads thrust downward. Beside them the great beasts toed in toward each other and toed away, shrugging themselves forward against their oxbows and empty wagons.

"Harrup!" one of the men called, exploding the air with the whip's tightly braided leather. The greased axles turned smoothly, the chains taut and letting as they took and gave. The men and the oxen followed the miles the sound of the big rifles. As they neared, one after another took out their knives and steel and they made with their grimy hands the sound that went with them: snick, snick, snick . . . snick, snick, snick, the white men going first and the black men following.

Chapter 23

As night darkened Michael sat with the men, his legs crossed beneath him, gazing into the smoldering embers. There were beans and skewers of meat spitting and popping on the hot grill. He looked into the fire and warned himself against it. The light candled the eyes and he would have to turn away if he was to see in the darkness.

The red dog stood with a forepaw on Michael's knee and leaned forward until his chin rested on Michael's shoulder. He made a sound in his throat as if whispering a secret. When the red dog lay back down, Sabi, fluidlike, found her place in Michael's lap.

The men were tired, glassy-eyed, red-faced, and quietly drinking.

"Looks as if a storm is coming," someone said.

Lightning cracked on the bluff, and the whole camp was illuminated in its white light. The red dog gave a threatening growl and was awake in an instant.

Suddenly both dogs bristled, having scented something in the night.

"What is it," Michael whispered.

Sabi danced from his lap, making low sounds in her throat. Then the red dog sprang up, a mass of bristles and growled softly.

Amid the ragged mist of the crossing was the outline of a horse and rider followed by another. The setter barked and swirled and came to him shivering in her whole body while the red dog, surly and aggressive, advanced on the riders.

"How the hell?" Ike Gough yelled, and suddenly the night was alive with the men laboring to their feet, snatching up the revolvers and rifles at hand, bullets being chambered, triggers cocked back. There came lightning and the thunder was as if artillery fire and rumbled on every side.

The rider wore a white shirt, breechcloth and buckskin leggings, the seams fringed with long locks of hair. His moccasins were embroidered with beads and the dyed quills of the porcupine. In his belt in a leather sheath he carried a butcher's knife, the handle ornamented with round-headed brass trunk tacks. Over his shoulders he wore a fine robe of jaguar skins, and his black hair was plaited into a long braid ornamented with eagle feathers and silver buckles and pieced out with hair from humans and the tails of horses until it was lengthened enough to reach the ground. His horse was cream-colored, painted with eagles and serpents.

Story Miller came off the bluff with his rifle. He tripped and fell and his rifle discharged into the air. At that moment anything could have happened.

"Don't shoot," the second rider cried, surging past the first rider. "Don't shoot."

"Get off that horse or I'll blow your heart out," Ike Gough cried, his rifle pointed at the second rider's chest.

The second rider dismounted and led the horse forward. It was a woman in the middle of age. She held a long official-looking envelope out in front of her. Michael walked forward and took the envelope.

Temple Miller brought a light from the fire. It was written permission for an Indian called Iron Pony to visit his family on the Canadian River. It stipulated he must follow the Canadian coming and going and he must not be gone from the agency more than thirty days. The document had expired two years ago.

"You see," she said, pointing to the document. "You see."

Michael stepped back to scrutinize Iron Pony, the man on horseback.

The blonde scalps of three women hung from the headstall. In his belt along with the sheath knife, he carried a long ice pick. Two pairs of dead hands were tied behind his saddle. All about him was the smell of death.

Michael pulled John aside and quietly told him to fetch the wolfer and then asked Darby to warn Starling's people. "Take rifles and cartridges," he said, "and stay with them."

Iron Pony handed down his lance, a straight piece of steel, two feet and a half long, tapering to a sharpened point and fixed into a slender handle of bois d'arc four feet and a half long. As he tried to dismount he collapsed to the ground. He'd been shot from the rear by a large-caliber bullet. On one side his hip, pelvis, and thighbone were shattered. The wound was days old and the source of the fetid odor that attended him. He would die soon. There was nothing to do.

Elizabeth heard the shouts from her desk. She leaned back in her chair to listen more intently. Throwing her robe over her shoulders, she went to the tent door.

"What is it," the reverend doctor said, coming to the door of his tent.

"I have no idea," she said.

She brought out her little brass hurricane lantern and went up the path with the reverend doctor following behind, buttoning his suspenders.

She held the light that she might see Iron Pony's face. She drew in her breath. His right eye was shaded with scar tissue knotting his brow. He wore three brass rings in the upper cartilage of each ear and from each hung separate works of bead, shell, stone, and bone, the longest a foot in length. On each finger he wore a brass or silver ring and on his biceps above his elbows eight and ten hoops of brass. His face was marked with pox scars.

"Help me," Elizabeth said, and they lifted his shirt.

The bullet had gone through his bowels and there was also buckshot in his back. She sent for her medical kit, but aside from stanching the blood and washing and binding up the wounds, there was little else she could do.

The wolfer stepped into the light, took his look, and then stepped back into darkness. He spoke to Iron Pony from the darkness and there seemed a moment of recognition. He then turned his attention to the woman and scrutinized her. The woman was spare and tall and unadorned. She wore an old blue military coat with tarnished buttons. Her hair was thick and black and tied in braids she wore down her back.

"You know him?" Michael said.

"I know him," the wolfer said.

"He is Iron Pony?"

"He is."

The wolfer had known Iron Pony since he was a boy. Before the war Iron Pony ranged from the Sabine to the Rockies. He'd had a great many slaves and many horses from raids into Mexico. During the Civil War he'd fought with Stand Watie at Pea Ridge, Old Fort Wayne, Cabin Creek, and Wagoner, where the surrendered were butchered.

"He was a real old homicidal Indian," the wolfer said.

"You knew him well," Michael said.

"I know him all right," the wolfer said. "I wear my knowledge."

"The woman?" Elizabeth said.

"She has blue eyes," the wolfer said.

Elizabeth turned to Michael and asked that they might speak in private.

"He will not live much longer," Elizabeth said.

"No," Michael said.
"What should we do?"
"With her?"
"Yes, with her."
"Do not persist in asking me that."
"Why?"
"There is no right answer."
Michael told her they needed to mount a more vigorous watch and she gave him leave to do so. He gathered bedding and moved onto the bluff, where he listened and kept watch with the dogs in the deathlike stillness. After a while Charlie arrived with a lidded kettle and a screw-top jar of hot coffee wrapped inside a cloth.
"Mrs. Coughlin sent me," he said. "There's bean stew and dumplings."
"What is the news down in hell?"
"Nothing," Charlie said.
"Shift your ass," Michael said, stretching out his legs and digging in. He forked out beans and links of burned sausage. He ate some himself and fed some into the boy's mouth. By the time Michael finished eating, Charlie had fallen asleep close by his side. He lay on his back, his hands on his chest as if in prayer.
Michael rolled the boy in his blanket and pulled his coat around him. He looked up into a sky full of stars. He took a drink of

coffee from the screw-top jar and looked to where the moon fell across the sleeping boy like a robe of silver. His thumb was in his nursing mouth.

In his breast pocket Michael carried a rosary, a silver cross, and two Indian Mutiny Medals with Lucknow clasps. He'd plucked them from Iron Pony's belt where they dangled on strings of rawhide.

"I hope they were very hard to kill," he whispered to the darkness.

He took a pipe out of his pocket and filled the bowl and tamped with his thumb. The pipe stem gripped in his teeth, he was to strike a match but instead knocked the tobacco into his palm, wadded it up, and stuffed it in his mouth.

As the night bore on, Iron Pony's life ebbed away. Elizabeth told the men they should sleep, but they were frightened. O'Malley expounded on the miraculous appearance of Iron Pony and the woman. He claimed the banshees were afield this night and they better beware.

Iron Pony's head lolled and tipped at the angle of death. His cloudy eye fell from its socket onto the ground. At his feet the woman began to weep quietly. Elizabeth touched a gentle hand to her back. Her own loss was so recent. A hand was laid on her arm. She turned uneasily. It was the reverend doctor and she was relieved for his presence.

"We cannot let her go back," the reverend doctor said.

"What do you mean?"

The reverend doctor called for a rope. With all suddenness the woman rose up. She hissed and spit at him, a flash of vicious hatred in her eyes. She screamed and clawed at the air trying to reach his face. Several of the men held her down while the rope was brought and her arms tied at her sides. A twisted neckerchief was tied across her mouth.

"My God," Elizabeth cried. Whatever respect she thought she'd gained from him she learned was an illusion.

"I respect you," the reverend doctor said, "but in this I know best."

"Where is your mind?" Elizabeth said. She would not be bullied. With steeliness in her voice she turned to the penman. "Mr. Penniman, you and your grandson will take charge of this woman. Walk her to my tent and stay with her until I arrive."

"You would take this responsibility?" the reverend doctor said.

"No man will touch that woman," Elizabeth said.

"I am afraid you are making a great mistake," the reverend doctor said.

"Nevertheless," she said, "it is my mistake to make."

The men snickered to themselves seeing their presumed betters at cross-purpose. They waited a bit longer and then they stripped Iron Pony of his clothes and all possessions and divided his belongings into lots and would draw from a deck of cards for rights. On behalf of his brothers, Matthew negotiated for the horses and their furnishings, and for this they agreed to drop out of the drawing.

"What about the other two?" Story said of the penman and his grandson.

"They ain't here, are they?" Ike said.

"No."

"Well, there's six of us, we voted and that's their loss."

Left to the men were collectible items: the robe of jaguar skins, rings, earrings, heavy silver armlet, eagle plumes, a disk of beaten gold embossed with a turtle, bear-claw necklace, knives, ice pick, rifle, bow and quiver with a clutch of arrows, clothes, glass eye, scalps, the dead hands, and his ornamented braid measuring eleven feet long.

"What about the woman?" Findley said. "She's worth something. I know of a trader that deals in returning white women at profit."

"What's one worth?" Ike said.

"Some will pay any price to get their people back. You ransom them and then you resell them to their people," Findley said. "He does a brisk trade."

"How much do you think she's worth?"

"Depends on who wants her back."

"There ain't much left to want. She looks like she's been worked to death."

Ike riffled the deck. He was impatient to get started. "If I was you," Ike said, "I'd take it up with Lady Coughlin," and to this they all laughed.

Alone with Elizabeth inside the tent, the woman seemed lost in profound abstraction and was undistracted by anything that surrounded her — the chairs and the table, the desktop, the reading books and account books, bundles of papers tied with red tape, bottles of ink, pewter inkstand, quill pens. From time to time she concentrated her eyes upon Elizabeth without appearing to see her, even as she unknotted the rope.

"I am sorry for your loss," Elizabeth said.

The woman's eyes began to shine. They lost their vagueness. She was returning from wherever she'd secluded herself. Her grief renewed and swept through her with heart-stopping force. She shook and gasped for breath.

"We are both widows," Elizabeth whispered, and beyond that there were no more words to express the sadness of her heart. Try as she might there were no consoling thoughts, no balm for the black despair.

The woman keened and it seemed to gain inside her.

Elizabeth too began to cry. She cried on behalf of this woman and she cried on behalf of herself.

From her clothes the woman took a small knife. She hacked at her braided hair, then slashed at her arms and breasts, drawing thin streams of blood from beneath her skin. She went to the ash bucket and with her blood painted her face and arms, then lay down and curled small. Elizabeth draped a blanket over her and took another to a chair by the door.

It was around midnight when the woman whispered something as if afraid of her own voice, her English slowly returning. She accepted a cup of tea and fingered the tablecloth on the tea table, the muslin curtains that divided the tents. She touched at the calico coverlid until finally letting her hand rest on the cloth and telling her story to

Elizabeth.

She did not know how many years, maybe thirty, she was just a girl when her family was killed and she was carried away. There were five taken, including a baby, and when rescuers closed in she was the only one not killed. They traveled for days until they reached the mountains. It was soon after that Iron Pony took her for a wife and she gave up the idea of return. She'd lost a baby, but she still had two sons with Iron Pony and they were many days to the west in the winter canyon. She remembered a brindled dog and a black-and-white cow. She remembered her bed of blue-and-white-striped ticking.

Before dawn Elizabeth found Charlie asleep in a wagon and sent him to saddle the woman's horse. Charlie told her that Matthew and his brothers now owned the horse.

"Find me a horse that can travel," she said sternly.

She stirred the woman from her sleep and told her it would soon be light. The horse Charlie brought was a large-boned chestnut named Lancaster. She went down on one knee, her other knee a bench. The woman grabbed Lancaster's mane, stepped onto Elizabeth's knee, and vaulted into the saddle. The horse edged away as the woman took the reins and suddenly she was at speed, splashing across the creek and ascending the bluff.

Michael stood and watched as she rode by. He followed her flight until she disappeared in the west as if she'd never been.

As the morning sun flooded the plain, from the creek the gurgle of water, the reverend doctor met Elizabeth coming up the path.

"What have you decided on?" he said.

"She said she was going home and I let her."

The reverend doctor flushed with shock and anger. He raised his open hands to his face. He squinted his eyes and his lips moved as if he were counting.

"Do you know what have you gone and done?" he said, upon composing himself.

"You needn't look at me so," she said. She was exhausted, and try as she might to hold them back, her eyes filled with tears. She was silent for a moment and then spoke again.

"She said she would return to be with her sons," Elizabeth said.

"She was a white woman."

"What difference does that make?"

"I do hope your trust and kindness will be

reciprocated," he said, and then, "They always revenge themselves."

"My Christian friend," she said. "What's done is done."

"My feelings right now I cannot express."

"You have been a dear to me, but what you did last night was a disappointment. It cut me to the heart."

"God, forgive me. I am sorry," he said. He turned gentle and soft-spoken. "I did not realize. My intentions were only the best."

She wanted to say, I do not know if I can ever forgive you. But what was the truth worth if it could not be understood?

Instead she said, "I would still have your counsel. We are both learning." She let him take her hand in his. She looked at the ground. "I am sorry too."

She could think of nothing else worth saying. She understood the warmth of his feelings, but he was a man of faith — rigid and, in this matter, punitive.

The reverend doctor returned to his writing desk. He held a new nib to the candle's flame and another he slipped in his mouth. He would have saved the woman from what she did not know. He would have learned from her and returned her to her family, to her God, to civilization.

He took up his pen and resumed his writing.

When I first saw her, she stared upon me with such a look of hope, of doubt, of fear, and of madness as I shall never forget. There were hollow shadows under her dusky eyes. She was nude except for the shredded remnants of her wedding dress. She was badly frightened and threw up her hands in an appealing way. Her arms crept round my neck and all the humane characteristics I ever possessed came to the front of me, and old campaigner that I am, I confess I shed tears.

"Thank God, you came in time," she said.

"You poor lost lamb," I murmured.

"Where are my people?"

"Murdered by the savages," I said.

"Every one of them?"

"Your sister yet lives."

Long, ragged sobs shook from her spasmodic, quivering body and I whispered words of comfort and gently stroked her golden hair.

"Poor girl," I said. "What can I do for you?"

"Something to cover my body," she said.

His penmanship had become uniform,

perfect. He wrote two more lines and then sharpened the nib more finely. From somewhere to the west the metronomic booms of the .50-caliber rifles were breaking the atmosphere. He startled when he heard Charlie cry, "Eighty! . . . Eighty! . . . Eighty to the northeast!"

A whiplash cracked the air and then another and someone bellowed, "Draw you devils . . . Draw!"

Chapter 24

Even though it would soon be December, the men still slept outside in the hammocks they'd strung for the healthfulness of the cold fresh air. The fresh air fumigated and sobered them. They claimed they could hear better, see better, sleep better, wake better.

While they slept a mother skunk led her four kittens into camp. She found an arm hanging down from over the side of a hammock, the hand dangling quite close to the ground and she began to feed on it. After a while she climbed onto the sleeper's chest. She scratched back the blanket and found the soft meat of his cheek.

There was a scream of horror that rent the night. The men were yelling and there was running. Then there were gunshots and then another scream, and Elizabeth's deepest fears rose up inside her. The shooting kept up until someone cried, "I'm shot! I'm shot!" and then Temple Miller was at her tent and Michael, by instinct, was headed for the bluff.

"My God, what is it, man?" Elizabeth said. She could not help herself. She'd become so impatient with recent events.

"It were a skunk."

"I'll be right there," she said.

The skunk had bitten Abel Gough. His fingers were gnawed and he was eaten at the cheek and he couldn't get the animal to release its sharp white teeth. It had clung to his face as it spewed its sulfurous fluid in a wide radius.

"Who saw it?" Elizabeth said, a handkerchief to her nose, the smell so overpowering.

"Were it a phoby cat?" Abel cried. "Were it?"

"Settle down," she said. "We will get it sorted."

Elizabeth washed his fingers and face and told him it was no more dangerous than the bite of any other little animal. Ike insisted on a red-hot iron to the site of the wounds to prevent the rabies.

Michael came in from the darkness. He rolled a cigarette. He held it up to the reverend doctor, who accepted. He rolled another and placed it between his lips. The whiskey bottles were coming out one by one. The men were liquoring up again and soon they'd be reeling about.

"Go on to sleep," Michael said to Elizabeth. "We'll set out a while."

"It isn't good?" the reverend doctor said.

"No, it isn't," Michael said.

"We need to put out more strychnine," she said.

Then Abel was screaming as Ike pressed the glowing iron to his brother's cheek and again when his hand went into the fire.

Not long after, Ike came to them. "We need to find a mad stone," he said.

"You're drunk," Michael said. "You couldn't find your own prick in the dark."

"I need a horse," Ike said.

"I will not have you killing any of these horses."

Ike lost his balance and moved his feet quickly to keep from falling. His stomach lurched up and he swallowed it back down.

"Please help me, Mrs. Coughlin," Ike cried. "He is my brother."

"What is it?" she said.

"The gallstone from the gut of a white deer," Michael said. "You soak it in milk and apply it to the wound where it draws out the poison. After it is saturated with the poison you put it back in the milk and the milk turns green and you apply it to the wound again."

"Does it work?" she said.

"In Africa I knew an elephant hunter in Matabililand who possessed a snake stone that saved the lives of people and horses. His daughter was bitten by a cobra. She turned nearly black before the stone was applied. They placed the stone in a glass of ammonia and the poison looked like a thin white thread coming from the stone. When no more poison came from the stone it was placed again on the wound until all the poison was extracted."

"You saw this?"

"No."

"Faith is letting go," the reverend doctor said. "I will look for this mad stone."

"We can try," Elizabeth said to Michael.

Michael relented and the Millers agreed to go as well. The men rode out in different directions. Michael rode east and the reverend doctor west. The Millers crossed the creek to the south and Ike went north.

Having reached an outer bend of a creek, Michael stopped. Above the eastern verge of the sky was a streak of cold red sky. There were deer emerging onto the curly grass, pausing at every step. They were coming single file. There was no white deer, it being exceedingly rare, so he settled for a buckskin and shot it.

When he rode in he learned that Ike had already found one.

"Even a blind hog finds an acorn once in a while," Ike said, and a knowing look passed between them.

From one of the cows they stripped out a quart of warm milk and began the application of the mad stone to Abel's cheek. Quite drunk already, Abel became jolly and voluble and said he could feel it working.

But the next day Abel, who by nature was morose and surly, was even gloomier and more silent and lagged behind the rest. His brother encouraged him on, but he said he wished to be left alone. He had a headache and a small fever. This made him more irritable and quarrelsome than usual and he went about swearing at everyone.

"That's the grippe," Ike said. "It's been comin' onto you all week."

Abel said it was true. He'd been feeling the grippe days before he was skunk bit. This cheered him up some and for fun he began to growl and grovel and spit. He chased Charlie about and threatened to bite him and laughed and Ike joined in his charade.

Five days later Abel's arm lurched into the clutch of an intolerable tingling, his throat constricted, and his brain felt strangely wet inside his head. He knew that death was inevitable.

"I am afraid Abel's gone bad," Ike said to Michael.

"I am sorry," Michael said. All his life he'd known men like the Gough brothers, born complete, instinctual, fated, potent. They rarely gave or accepted quarter.

"He's suffering bad," Ike said.

"You know what must be done," Michael said.

"No," Ike said. "No."

Toward night, his throat muscles spasming, Abel became raving mad and the symptoms of furious rabies could not be denied. He slavered at the mouth, and unprovoked, he attacked Ike, trying to bite him and claw at his face.

"We have a bad situation here," Michael said to Elizabeth.

"How is he?" Elizabeth said.

"Not good," Michael said. He knew it fell on him to do something. He went into the camp and with the other men he tried to restrain Abel lest he try and bite someone, but Abel broke and rushed into a thicket of willows.

"Let him go," Findley said, but Ike would not give up on his brother and threatened to kill Findley for suggesting they do.

In the morning they cornered him in a little gully. Foam frothed upon his lips and at the corners of his mouth. Veins stood out on his neck and he twisted his head as if to loosen them. His red-sheened eyes flashed wildly in his swollen and mutilated face.

"Stay where you are. I am dangerous," he said, his lifted hand a threat.

"Abel," Ike said. "It's me, your brother."

Abel raised himself to his knees and the sun shone with unbroken radiance upon his face. He spoke in a voice that was hollow and unnatural, the tears breaking over his wasted cheeks. He arranged himself into a sitting posture, sinking his face between his knees. From there he rolled to the ground, gnashing his teeth, and more foam came to his mouth. Still, he retained his senses, and this was difficult for them. He was as if a man transforming into a wolf and midway between the two beings.

"Leave him go to hell," Findley said again.

"Mr. Findley," Ike said, reaching for his revolver, "you have let your tongue run too far."

"I have half a mind to kill you both," Michael said, and the moment passed.

They went into the gully and Abel begged them not to approach, but they did, and wearing their gloves they bound him with a rope and tied him to a tree, but that night when they returned he begged Ike cut to him loose so he could sleep and Ike did.

Abel was gone all that next day, but at nighttime he was back. He sat on the periphery of the firelight. He was skinny and pitiful and watched them with his dark gleaming eyes. They could see the animal inside his face. When they looked again he was gone.

Charlie fetched Michael the next time Abel came back. They captured him again and Michael sent for a chain, but Ike would not let them chain him. He drew his revolver and told them Abel was his brother and he would take care of him. They backed away and in the morning Abel was gone again.

"For the love of God," Elizabeth said, "something has to be done."

"This is paralyzing us," the reverend doctor said, looking to Michael. "We must do something. None of us are safe."

The next day was hot when Michael rode out. The herd was feeding on the edge of a small valley, drifting across the hillside. The wind was coming straight up the hill, carrying his scent away to the east.

Michael gazed out toward the grazing herd and saw Abel Gough in their midst, and bent in a posture of rictus, he was crossing the valley. He got down on all fours and began to crawl forward. He stopped and his head suddenly jolted from side to side. Long strings of drool hung from his mouth. He was as if invisible to the buffalo, which grazed all around him.

Michael threw forward the long, heavy rifle. He placed the barrel in the notch of the sharp-pronged rest fixed firmly in the ground. His cheek against the stock, he trained the telescopic sight on Abel and found him in the crosshairs. Abel rose up on his knees as if in prayer. Michael watched him try to stand, but Abel sank to his haunches as if waiting. The eye he saw was no longer human, or even animal, but was the vised eye of fear and wildness.

I have to do this, Michael thought, and under his skin every nerve and muscle began to twitch. When he looked again, two hundred yards away Abel had turned his body and was staring at him. He thought of David and the words he'd written in this place. Here was another man whose mind had turned strange and alien and for whatever reason was leading him to his destruction. He did not try to make sense out it. He did not think what reasons could be.

There are no reasons in an unreasonable world.

Michael took a deep breath, exhaled quietly, and squeezed the stiff trigger. The distance was immense, and yet the ball passed clean through the man's body. Then the sharp booming sound of the rifle was heard, and the man was fallen and weltering in his poisoned blood.

In days to come he would wonder if he saw what he saw in Abel's face: expectation, understanding, acceptance. The fleet soul breathed with relief and gently floated away. Michael tried to think it was not so, but it was. He saw what he saw.

Abel lay among the buffalo, stone dead, a trickle of blood streaming from his mouth, his body stiffening, a hand unfolded and raised. There was a massive wound in his chest and his eyes were wide open with a look of horror in them. Michael dropped the noose of his lariat onto the raised hand and dragged him from the field before Darby arrived. The wolves would find him and feed on his body and the wolfer would kill them with his strychnine before they became rabid.

That night he told Elizabeth what he'd done. The reverend doctor entered and in disbelief, asked Michael to repeat himself.

"I put him down," Michael said.

"Dear God," the reverend doctor said. "I was just comforting Ike."

The reverend doctor lifted himself from his chair and stalked off into the night. When he returned Ike Gough was with him.

"You killed my brother," Ike said.

"Yes," Michael said. "I did."

"I want justice," Ike said.

"What kind of justice do you want?" Michael said.

"It makes you hateful," Ike said, backing down and then walking away.

"Please, don't let there be any ill blood between you," the reverend doctor called after him. "You will shake hands, sir."

In the days after his brother was killed Ike became scornful and brooding. Privately the other men were grateful, but publicly they commiserated with Ike and they asked of each other what god made Michael the judge and jury of Abel Gough? What would stop him from deciding their lives and deaths.

The next night Elizabeth asked Michael to sit with her until dinner. Michael took off his hat and went inside. His face was still black with powder and his clothes rough and dirty.

Elizabeth was in her dressing gown and her hair was gathered in a ribbon and fell down her back. However much it was her office with inkstand and ledger books, it was a woman's place. Unfolded near the fire was a collapsible bathtub, the water still warm, and he thought how nice it might feel.

She poured him a drink of whiskey.

"The men, they are gossiping," she said.

"It'll pass," he said.

She studied him. She tried to gauge his thinking, but she could not.

"How many more days do I have you?" she said.

"Six or seven," he said.

"Perhaps for the best."

"Perhaps," he said. "Ike will not leave things as they are. He must be sent away."

"He would have charges filed against you so it can be settled."

"Ike?"

"The reverend doctor thought if only it could be adjudicated."

"A judge and jury?"

"I begged him not to," Elizabeth said.

"You don't have to worry about me," Michael said.

"But I do," she said.

He would tell her he'd trust no American to ever decide his fate, but he didn't. When the time came he'd be gone and away in the blink of an eye. He did it before and would do it again.

"The reverend will propose, you know," she said.

"You are not suggesting on my behalf you'd marry him?"

"I know you don't like him," she said.

"It doesn't matter," Michael said. "You'll strike no bargains on my behalf."

He wanted to say more, but her intimation that she should sacrifice herself in marriage to protect him was beyond his understanding. He wondered if sacrifice was her essential and deepest nature. The thought of her marrying the reverend doctor struck him far more deeply than he imagined. He wondered on his own heart and what it wanted, something he'd not done in a very long time.

Chapter 25

The next day Michael was in the buffalo again with 250 cartridges and both rifles. Across the plain, Pastor Starling was approaching Ike Gough. Ike bent his head while he listened to what Starling was saying. Starling was smiling, his hands were out, his palms at angles to the sky. There was something feral in Ike's posture, the way his body held itself curved, the way he stared out from below his forehead. Their faces shined with sweat.

"Back away," Michael said. "Back away," he yelled. "Back away."

They conversed but a moment longer when Ike raised his revolver and shot Pastor Starling in the face. Pastor Starling collapsed to the ground.

Pulling his horse together, Michael gripped with his knees and urged it forward across the plain, the horse gaining speed as it went. When he rode onto the field, the men were gathered around in silence, their mouths open as if to speak but saying nothing.

"What happened here?" Michael shouted, and they all shrank away from him. "Who saw it?"

His questions were met with stony silence. The men, both white and black, looked down and shuffled their feet where they stood.

"What happened here?" he said again. "Who saw it?"

"He threatened me," Ike said, shaking his head. His eyes jerked with panic. "I don't want to get on your bad side."

"That is not true," Henry Ward Beecher said.

"You are no judge of white men," Ike said, stepping in his direction.

"I say what I please."

"Stop your jaw," Michael said, turning on Ike, "or I'll smash your damned mouth."

Michael knelt down beside Pastor Starling. He leaned in close and listened. His ear caught a faint hollow moan, more like a humming sound. There was the sound of shallow air moving inside his chest. There was a hole in his cheek, but his heart still beat and his lungs were making breath. He was alive but made no response in his arms or legs or any part of his body. There was an emptiness in his eyes.

"Do you think he's dead?" Story Miller asked.

"I will ask one last time. Who saw what happened here?" Michael said. He stood and turned to Ike. He could smell the whiskey on his breath.

"They've been taking hides what's not their own," Ike said, his words grudging and malevolent.

"You didn't have to kill the man."

"He ain't dead."

"His brain is turned to mush," Story Miller cried.

"I saw what you did," Michael said, and pointed off to where he'd been.

"He threatened me. Did you hear that?"

Michael spun fiercely and struck Ike a backhanded blow to the side of his face, breaking his lip and knocking him to the ground.

"You shut your mouth or I will cut your guts out and hang you with them."

The men of Pastor Starling's came forward and lifted Pastor Starling into the wagon and settled him down on a bed of green hides. They silently turned away and started off for the clearing where they lived.

"It's time for you to go," Michael said.

"Where am I going to go?" Ike said.

"Wherever you came from."

"I'm stayin' right here," Ike said, his voice weak and thin.

Pastor Starling slid in and out of consciousness. His fingers would stretch, his eyes would clear, and he would respond to those around him and then his eyes would close and he would be out for another few hours. For six hours he did not move from his pallet, tended by the women, and then he was gone to God.

Everyone knew Ike had shot Pastor Starling to revenge himself on Michael. He could not challenge Michael so he'd killed the pastor.

"He ought to be tried and hung," the reverend doctor said.

"We don't hang people," Elizabeth said.

That night Michael thought how the American war was not the end of something but the beginning of learning how to kill more easily, learning that however destructive, however much destruction they did, they were capable of even more. The world would be a warring place. The nations would form and they would take everything they could. The new world would be the old world, only worse. The regimes of wealth, the blood drinkers, the men who glory in their shame — they would determine who had the right to live free. If people would not be used they would be murdered.

The next night Darby came to talk with Elizabeth.

"I have come," he said, "to tell you goodbye. They are going away and I am going away with them."

"To where?" she said. "Where are you going?"

His eyes were distant and his mouth firm and set. She'd known him since he was a boy. It made no sense to her.

"Wherever they will go," he said.

She looked at him, unable to believe that he was sincere, yet she knew his mind was made up.

"Please do not leave," she begged. "I need you here with me."

"They need me more," he said, his eyes wetting.

"The dangers are so many."

"I have made up my mind," Darby said.

"Take them to Meadowlark," she said suddenly, then, "If you could only wait a few days."

"They will not wait in this place. They believe this land is cursed and so do I."

"You will need a wagon and several yoke

of oxen," she said. "Rifles and provisions. Take them. Take whatever you need."

"Thank you," he said.

She studied his face. This place was as if a minister of truth revealing, and those truths were simple and hard and cared little for the manners of human beings. She felt inside the breaking of whatever faith she possessed in mankind. Whatever she'd thought the potential of progressive values and scientific education, human evolution, maybe it was all a kind of foolishness. For all the slave lords the war had killed, a new generation was born in their ashes and born inside the new generation was the enmity of the old.

The reverend doctor came from his quarters, pen in hand.

"What is happening?" he said.

Her spirit seemingly gone, the shadow of a smile formed on her lips. She lifted his pen hand.

"It's nothing," she said. "I must go. I will explain all to you when we gather for dinner this evening."

Michael was with Khyber, leading her about in a tight circle, smoothing her flanks with a brush he held. He stopped when he saw Elizabeth coming.

Why are you crying? he wanted to say, but

he didn't. It wasn't his place to intrude.

"Darby is leaving," she said. "I begged him not to."

"Walk with us for a while if you'd like."

"I'll leave you to your walk," she said.

"Please," he said. "Come along."

She gave in and they crossed the creek and went onto the bluff. He told her he thought her decision was inspired and Meadowlark was the place for Starling's people. They continued to walk west in silence into the last daylight. Soon the skinners would be returning.

"I am afraid Darby will hardly get back on his own," she said.

"There's nothing you can do," Michael said. "He's made up his mind."

"Then you spoke to him?"

"He came to me."

"You'll go out in the morning?" she said.

"Yes," he said. "I will take Matthew and Mark."

Day by day she'd witnessed Michael's recession. Day by day she'd watched him as he hardened and she knew he needed to leave. If only he could hold out a little longer, time enough for Matthew and Mark to learn what he knew.

That night Elizabeth wanted to remember

or forget, but she was not sure which, and it was not a decision she could make for herself, but soon the decision was made and she was remembering and then she was remembering too much.

She recalled the letters she received from the wounded, long since dwindled to a few a year. *I remember the great work you did during the war. You nursed me when I was sick and wounded nigh unto death back to life and health.*

I saw your war, she thought. I saw it every day for three years: cups of coffee, ladles of soup, linen; blood, pus, broken backs; the sick, wounded, and crippled; human bodies shot, ripped, and torn in every conceivable way . . . the great laundry kettles, the mangles driven backward and forward by wheel with rack and pinion, ironing machines and other machines for laundering on largest scale.

And earlier in the war, on the edge of shifting battlefields when shot and shell fell into the hospital, the men and boys in unbearable agony. At night, under the white flag, into the fields with stretchers, listening for the groans of wounded men left behind. In snow and blizzard, in rain and wind, with storm lantern to find the men bleeding and dying and bring them in. Sixteen-year-old babies, weak and wasted, with unwashed bodies wrapped in flannel and fouled by fever and disease, their dead faces and sightless eyes.

Writing bedside farewell letters, collecting the watches and money and any little thing to be sent home: lockets, rings, pins, and brooches they carried into battle; the precious photographs of mother, wife, children, sister, sweetheart; the photographs of hundreds of thousands of orphans, widows, and boyless mothers. Men who fought had left pieces of themselves strewn across the earth and everywhere they went they hopelessly looked for themselves as ghosts are said to do. What awful scenes in my mind. Sleeping or waking they are with me. I hear the cries and the moans of each and every one of them as they went down to the gates of death and passed through to the other side or came back out forever changed.

What victory for me, she wondered. What noble defeat? What memories of comrades in the field singing around the campfire? What whores and liquor? What plunder? What gain? What profit? What glory? What glory?

And yet here she was and in the pursuit of liberating herself she was making decisions that killed men and beasts. It was as if she'd led Daragh to beneath the lightning and Abel to the rabies and Pastor Starling to Ike.

"What more?" she whispered, and thought, *Nothing is left now but to endure.*

Chapter 26

It was their third day on the kill when Matthew and Mark stopped to look where Michael was glassing, south by southeast. Who it was Mark wanted to know and Michael told him they were men he knew and he'd been anticipating, and at the rate they were coming, they'd arrive in three hours' time.

The figures in the little caravan were coming up the valley of the Canadian. They came from the southeast, laboring up through the Red River country, a wickedness of men riding horses and driving oxen and mules hauling steel-barred cages capable of resisting a bear's claws and teeth. The men in the saddles turned their necks right and left, forward and back as their bodies tipped in the opposite direction. The axles were dry and the wheels in the cold transparent air creaked and screeched as they jounced along. The teamsters trudged on at the head of their teams, cracking whips dyed black with oxen's blood.

They were true bloods and half-breeds. They were Americanus, Europeanus, Asiaticus, and Africanus. They were Negroes begotten of white rape: halves, quarters, and eighths, bought, sold, freed, and hated. They were Mexicans still Spanish and Mexicans still Indian with almond-shaped eyes black as obsidian. There were hunting dogs and their Irish dog masters. These were men he'd hunted with on several continents, men who possessed no inner self, men broke free from the great chain of being, men incapable of comprehending their own death and so they lived on. They were men by appearances unhealthy and indestructible.

They were led by his friend the Métis from northernmost Canada, a man whose father was French, descended from a *coureur des bois* and whose mother was Cree, both races war-loving, and with him was another friend, the Lord, driving a two-wheeled, one-horse cart with a fringed top.

The Métis suddenly reined up. He lifted field glasses to his eyes, their reflected light a momentary shock of brilliance across the land. He made his decision and after doing so he was coming directly toward them.

"Friends of yours," Mark said.

"Colleagues," Michael said.

He then made a nicking sound and Khyber wheeled about and they began the long walk back to camp. The brothers, tagging along behind, could not help but glance back, for how unlikely the oncoming caravan.

That afternoon when they rode into camp, Elizabeth saw them before she heard them. In a dust cloud they came on the wagon road, crested the bluff, and descended as a disorderly rabble. She threw aside the novel she was reading and stood, the back of her hand to her mouth. She went quickly up the path to stand by Aubuchon, who was preparing for the return of the hungry men, a mountain of steaks under cloth waiting for the fire. John, Luke, and Charlie joined them from where they'd been down on their knees cutting holes, driving pegs, stretching hides.

Then she heard them, the oxen moaning for water, the shuttering clatter of the steel cages, the howling dogs, the braying of the mules, the knock of bones against wood. They mounted the bluff and came on, stumbling and plunging, some down the road and some off the sides. They poured from its edge, where it was steep, and splashed down into the creek. They fell off their horses and found them and got back on. The dog handlers came next. They were dragged down the wagon road by the seat of their pants and bumped over the corduroy road crossing the creek before they could regain their feet. Then came a black man in top hat smartly driving a two-wheeled cart pulled by a high-stepping pony.

"Stir up the fire," she said, but Aubuchon already was.

The Métis wore a linen coat, a red belt, brown cord trousers, and deer hide gauntlets. He was olive-skinned, well built, and bright-eyed. He had left the northern territories, their lush meadows and evergreen forests; the abundant fish in the rivers and streams; the elk, bear, and buffalo, and like his forefathers, he answered the call to trade and adventure. It was in Africa where Michael had met him and the Lord and all three came to benefit from Mr. Salt as they traveled from one continent to the next.

The Lord was dressed in a scarlet coat and vest with brass buttons, which he wore over buckskin breeches and polished high boots with silver spurs. A silk handkerchief was knotted at his throat and beneath his coat he wore a spotless linen shirt. The Lord's face was ritualistically tattooed and his forehead was gnarled with scarification. His nose had a high prominent bridge and his eyes were large and velvety and black as the night. In Africa the Lord was respected for his intelligence, his political acumen, his ruthless authority. He was a *mganga,* medicine man and sorcerer, whose powers included exorcism, prophecy, and the removal of spells. On his wrist he wore an elephant-hair bangle to keep him safe on his travels and this bracelet he would give to Elizabeth.

In one wagon were the carcasses of a bull, a heifer, and an antelope the hounds had taken down and the men had been eating off since. The meat was green and coated with flies. In another wagon were sacks of snakes, shovels, nets, and snares as well as the bones of Indians they'd looted from their burial mounds for export. Some of the bones did not look so old and Michael saw upon closer inspection that there were knots of leathered flesh and dried blood. No doubt a few of them belonged to men who started up the trail with the Métis and the Lord and perished along the way. It would not be the first time.

The sacks of snakes began to writhe and the deadly sound of them could be heard. No man was immune to the rush of blood and the cold tremor induced by such a sound, but however much the snakes tried, their fangs could not penetrate the enclosing folds. The Lord selected one of the sacks. He unknotted the lash and took out a specimen for all to see. It was of an immense girth, seven feet long, with teeth an eighth of an inch in length. On its tail, it carried fourteen rattles.

He offered it to each of the boys to hold, and cheered on by the men and spellbound, they passed it from one to the next by its throat before letting it drop back into the sack to be cinched and knotted. Long after, each boy would still feel the snake in his hand weighing down his arm, would see the flick of its tongue, its unfolding fangs, the drops of venom.

Aubuchon called to them, and as if the spell removed, the men descended on the big pots with knives and spoons they pulled from their boots, spearing the meat and scooping out the broth, burning their mouths, cursing and swearing, burning them again. They ate until they were bloated and blear-eyed.

The boys brought the buffalo calves they taught to drink by letting them suck their fingers beneath the surface of the milk. The wolfer came in with young wolves and coyotes. Aubuchon took out the brandy and joined the Métis and wolfer, and for a while the three men privately spoke their French, gossiping with pleasure.

Michael lit a pipe and sat down and was soon joined by the Métis and the Lord. The Métis had discarded his linen coat for a blue capote and the Lord had removed his own coat to show a necklace of lion teeth and ivory, heavy brass bracelets, and a gold chain at his vest button attached to a gold watch with Arabic numerals and moon phase calendar made in Geneva, Switzerland.

The Métis untied his hair and let it fall down his back. While they spoke he busied himself with stuffing the skin of an ivory-billed woodpecker he bought in Galveston.

He told Michael he'd been in the north all spring, collecting infant animals to hand-raise and ship when they were hearty, tame, and tractable. They'd started in British Columbia and worked their way south and picked up a very nice pair of wolf cubs and grizzly bear cubs and kits of the carcajou, the wolverine, and they were already ferocious.

He said Mr. Salt wanted a family of Indians, preferably Comanche, and another, a family of American Negroes. He also wanted a white wolf and a white buffalo. He was interested in any albinos they might acquire. Already in the cages, they had coyotes, raccoons, polecats, beaver and otter, but no albinos.

Michael and the Métis stood as Elizabeth and the reverend doctor joined them. Elizabeth looked to where Michael sat by the fire. His countenance was that of a boy, a younger brother. Soon he would leave her to fulfill his contractual obligations with Mr. Salt, the reason he'd come to America in the first place, to hunt and collect. It was how he made his money. It was how he bought the paper on Meadowlark held by Whitechurch, who'd bankrupt her.

She watched him closely. He was as if lost in thought. Suddenly he reached for her hand and took it in his own.

"I will leave Sabi with you?" he said, and then he said, "Where we are going . . . ," but he did not finish his sentence.

"Of course," she said, clasping her other hand over his to say Sabi would be safe with her.

She wondered if she would ever see him again, but she could not bring herself to ask. She wanted to thank him but could not do so.

"What's it like in Africa?" the reverend doctor was asking the Métis.

"There are fish that fly and birds that talk."

"And what's it like up there where you come from?"

"Blizzards, sandstorms, and missionaries," the Métis said, and then he said, "At least you are not a missionary."

However strange and frightening and wicked these men, however violent and savage their lives, it was a joyful encounter. It was as if the rambling circus of the human imagination had come to town. Just as suddenly they were gone, and Michael, with so many thoughts born in his mind, was gone with them.

Chapter 27

The fall had long since merged into winter and it was cold and the one season disappeared into another. With Michael gone, Elizabeth kept steadily to the routine of her work. Each day Matthew and Mark killed buffalo at a furious rate, exceeding all previous tallies. More men came in looking for work. She sized them up and made her decision to hire them or send them on their way after a hot meal.

Then came a day, a bitter frost, and Elizabeth was invaded by worry. It took hold of her as if an illness. She could not sleep that night, waking fitfully, tossing and turning. She was convinced that something was wrong. She thought of all that she'd not said to Michael, all that he'd not said to her, and yet how much he'd become part of her thinking.

There was a new thought she was trying to fashion. She stood and began to pace about. It was so simple and yet the words would not take shape.

She did not want to leave her tent that morning, but it occurred to her how anxious she'd become and how foolish it was to shut herself in. She dressed for the cooler weather. She called Sabi from her warm bed and together they went out.

Aubuchon stood before the fire cutting meat to cook. John was singing to himself a little song as he worked. The horses were feeding. For some reason she expected to see Khyber among them. Aubuchon called to her and asked her where she was going.

"You let me sleep too long," she said.

"I apologize. I thought on your behalf you wished to rest."

"I am going to the top of the bluff," she said, and then, "Where are the men?" and Aubuchon pointed to the southwest.

"He will make it," Aubuchon said, and she smiled grimly.

She walked the wagon road to the top of the bluff and unfolded a camp chair beside John who was knotting the string for his two older brothers. To the west she could hear the boys shooting, the minute-by-minute report of the Sharps. The sky was brittle. The plains were firm and hard. They were the same and boundless. The buffalo kept them pastured short and bare and fertile, and she found this place beside the boy well suited for waiting and thinking as he tied his knots.

"Are you ever homesick, John?" she said to the boy.

"Yes, ma'am."

She listened over the fields strewn distantly with the dead of so many buffalo and wolves and coyotes and birds of prey poisoned by eating their flesh.

"When my husband died, it was as if the life went out of me, and I have been sad with Michael gone. But there comes a new day and after that day there are other days."

"How did your husband die?" John said.

"A horse, John. He was kicked by a horse. It was his own fault. He should have been more careful." Her words were as if self-inflicted. Her breathing caught and her chest ached. She thought she might cry, but she didn't.

"A horse can kill you dead," John said.

"My husband was very sad, John. He'd lost a lot of money."

"What happened to the horse?"

"I put it down. It was a good horse and now I wish I hadn't."

"Do you ever think we will see Michael again?" John said.

"That's what we fear," she said.

From his tent where he was earnestly writing, the reverend doctor watched her go out. He leaned back in his chair to see better, swung his foot, and he was thoughtful and happy.

He stood and looked intently at the sheets of foolscap, the words he'd written in iron gall ink.

Having experienced the delights of whiskey, the Comanche and Kiowa were again on the maraud. The Red Devils shot their arrows to wound and not to kill so they might experience the pleasure and ecstasy their kind found in human torment. For one, a stake was driven through him and his head separated from his body. For another, the tomahawk in his back was deep enough to reveal his spine. Him they scalped, skinned, and roasted alive.

Charlotte surveyed the scene of wet horror from the back of the horse she rode. Her eyes took in the men and women and children, their bodies naked and violated and bound together by their still steaming entrails ripped from their insides while still alive.

"You have no idea of the meaning of the word fear," she said.

"You are safe with me," I said.

"I should not ever like to be taken prisoner again."

"Nor shall you be."

"I am not afraid of death."

"Do not talk like that."

"Promise me something, old campaigner," she said with throat-closing fear.

"Anything," I said.

"Save the last bullet for me."

He clasped his hands behind his back. The writing was four hundred pages and as if automatic and a kind of spiritual dictation. He dipped the nib of his pen in the inkwell, and with a soft clink, he tapped off the excess against the side. *Something calls to me from out of the dark and gloom,* he wrote, the sharp metal point scratching over the paper. *I will go to meet it,* and then he followed Elizabeth as she headed toward her place on the bluff.

The reverend doctor could not help but gaze out at the land that lay before him. He thought about the times he lived in, the latter half of the nineteenth century. He saw the years ahead to be full of promise and permanent greatness and of late his extravagant visions had become gifted revelations. Soon this desolate land of nowhere would all be changed and it was all happening so quickly that he knew he would live to see it happen. The Comanche would be subdued, their naked children and women clothed, their spiritual lives Christianized, civilized, and after the soldiers, surveyors, and cartographers would be men like him of human will, men with spiritual and executive ability, and they would take over the open land and make it ready for law-abiding productive citizens. There would be an end to foreclosures, economic insecurity, and debt. There would be boom times, times of reverence, fulfillment, and human improvement and the end of despair, fear, restiveness, meaninglessness. No darkness but rather light. There would be farms and ranches, fabulous gold and silver lodes in the hill country. The land would be fenced, grazed, planted, harvested. Roads and canals would be built, a lacework of railroads. Rivers would be diverted to irrigate the crops and slake the thirst of the livestock. The plains, liberally fertilized, would become fields of abundance. Rain would follow the plow. The air would fill with the smell of kerosene and oil. He imagined the little children with their dinner pails marching to school. There would be a new masculinity. It would be a land of yeomen farmers and the work they provided for their hired men. Wages would be kept low to prevent working people from wasting their money on alcohol, gambling, and prostitutes.

He then saw her beyond a tussock of grass. She was watching him and he called out to her.

"May I join you," he said.

"Of course," she called out.

"I hope you weren't going to shoot me," the reverend doctor said. "Hello, John," he said to the boy. "How are you this beautiful morning?"

"I am well, sir."

"Very good," he said. "Steady on!"

Elizabeth smiled for how in the bleakest of time the reverend doctor could buoy up her emotions and inspire a kind of cheerfulness in even the hardest man.

John was on his feet holding up the string with ten knots. Elizabeth smiled and nodded as if to say yes, go ahead.

"One hundred," John cried out. "One hundred. Time to move your asses! One hundred to the south!" he cried as he ran off the bluff.

Elizabeth stood aside to watch as the men climbed the bluff with the oxen hauling the big wagons. She felt a thrill run through her from head to foot. She watched them as they traveled west and forded the creek and disappeared south.

"I was thinking, Elizabeth," the reverend doctor said, "if you would just let me look after you. Someone to lean on," he said, and in his voice it was as if she heard his thoughts: someone who will love you and you will love back.

"You are too good and I will try better," she said, "but it's not in my nature."

"It was at one time."

"I am sorry if that was your impression."

"It is what David wanted."

"David?" she said, looking up at him. "You would wound me that way?"

She felt a strange fear, the sinking of her heart. Her eyes were bright and wetting with tears. Would David have wanted such? Would he have said these words to another man?

"As you know," she said, "I read and write and think and I am quite capable of taking care of myself."

"And you have natural moral superiority."

"I assure you I have no moral superiority and want so even less."

"It's not my fate to give up," he said, closing the space between them. "We have a common sympathy and a common purpose."

"Perhaps we should go back to camp," Elizabeth said.

"Don't go," he said. "There is something I want to say to you."

"You've been my good friend," she said.

"Wait. Please," he said, taking her hand.

"I shall probably never marry again," she said, taking back her hand, trying to sound apologetic. There, it was done. She'd revealed herself. She'd brought the matter to a close. Whatever the consequence might be, honesty was the best way to go.

"I have great resources," he said, and he told her everything in a flood of words and promises. He told her of his pen names and ever-mounting royalties, his new manuscript of a white woman's captivity and deliverance. He told her of his recent inheritance of his uncle's house in Boston, a brick mansion fronted by tall elms, the vast dining room, the dim parlor and the oak furniture upholstered in dark green velvet, the brass and clear-cut glass lamps he'd read by as a boy, their oval chimneys and globe shades. He told her in his mind he saw her inhabiting the rooms; walking in the gardens; the two of them sitting at dinner surrounded by authors, professors, theologians, financiers, men of politics. He said he felt a driving and unhindered power inside his body. They were at the center of time and America was history's fulcrum.

The reverend doctor let down his hands and clasped them together. He shook and caught his breath, his face a lighter shade. His vision of her in the straits of a grand house, the walls made of brick. She waited for him to open his eyes before she spoke.

"Please know I like you immensely," she said, "but I have great resources myself." And she did. She'd kept careful records and now her income was no longer insubstantial. She knew how to turn buffalo into money. She knew there would be more to come. She'd already spoken to Matthew and Mark about returning next year and they were willing.

The news was more than he could bear.

"I cannot help but feel betrayed," he said, and hearing himself say the words, he could only think a bad spirit had taken possession of him. All along he'd been sacrificing himself on her behalf and this was the thanks he received. In no way had he anticipated her ingratitude.

"We are all betrayed in the end," she said, her eyes fearless.

"By whom you say?"

"By history, by God."

There was a mournful sound inside him,

dying away. Bewildered, he stared at her as if she'd lost her mind.

"You are not the woman I thought."

"Maybe not," she said. "Maybe before I was nothing and now I am something. I trust you will not pine away and die?"

"Perhaps if we prayed," he said, trying to mask his anguish.

"Not now," she said. God had done all he could for her. "Maybe later."

"I am going to pray to God for you tonight," the reverend doctor said.

Inside he brimmed with anger. That's what it comes to in the end, he thought, and was grateful for what vision and revelation God had recently granted him to blunt the news of Elizabeth's estrangement. Faith was letting go of all dependence and commending oneself into the arms of Jesus. With a freer mind, he'd move to find a faith even more profound.

"Thank you," she said.

"I would have given so much," he said, and finally turned and took his leave, grieving the loss of what he never had.

In the morning the reverend doctor would induce the Miller brothers to accompany him back to Kansas and she learned of his decision only when they came to her.

"It's our families," Temple said. "We have been away a long time."

"Of course, your girls," she said, pausing, and then she said, "What will you do?"

The two men shifted in place. Apparently they'd not decided how to say what more they wanted. The conversation had gone beyond their preparation.

"We were thinking of returning to Meadowlark," Story said.

"Oh," she said, spreading her hands. "This is Meadowlark."

"We were hoping to work on the old Meadowlark," Temple said.

"We are quite ready to stay and work for you," Story said. "If that's your decision."

"How much is he paying you?" she said.

"A thundering lot of money," Story said, and he told her the sum, but it wasn't *a thundering lot of money,* and she thought to tell them the reverend doctor could have reached much more deeply into his purse to secure his journey back to Kansas and they could have driven a much harder bargain and they'd left a substantial amount of money on the table.

"I cannot fault you," she said. "You are go-ahead men. I understand that and I want go-ahead men around me. I will loan you horses and you may draw rations for your travel and you may resume your old jobs upon one condition."

"Yes, ma'am," Temple said. "Anything."

"You are to take Mr. Penniman and his grandson with you, otherwise they will not last." Then she added, "In the meantime, make sure you get your money in writing."

CHAPTER 28

Day by day, his vitality fading, Michael traveled on. To the west he could see the escarpments of the Llano Estacado where the Comanche lived in winter. In this deepest country the red dog's wolfish instincts seemed more pronounced and Khyber was jittery and impatient to be moving as they alternately disappeared beneath the earth and rose again to the sight line. How many nights he'd slept out he could not remember. How many days he awakened to the drenching dews and the chilled air? How many days by noon his body was steaming from the hot sun? Who knows what water he'd drunk? They'd lost three men to water alone: gyppy, salty, alkali. His eyeballs ached and the spangles in his vision had returned. He needed to weather it out. He needed to keep going.

He traveled alongside a creek moving eastward. The creek was here and there, its bed dry for miles except during freshets of rain. When he first found the creek he'd miscalculated and was at its westernmost extreme, a seep, a trickle appearing and disappearing in the earth. The land was broken and furrowed and there were no trees or scrub.

He'd departed the Métis and the Lord at Corpus Christie after the animals were crated, caged, and penned. Specimens were sown in canvas and nailed down in wooden boxes. Skins and heads were sealed in tin cases carefully soldered and by now they were crossing the Atlantic: the wolves, coyotes, buffalo, lions, bobcats, antelope, deer, bear, rattlesnakes, prairie dogs — enough prairie dogs to feed the snakes on the voyage and still have plenty left over. Birds: turkeys, white owl, mockingbird, kingbird, swallow, quail, meadowlark. They trapped eagles in their high aerie beneath which were strewn the bones of deer, antelope, and buffalo.

In boxes were tarantulas, black widow spiders, scorpions, horned frogs, turtles, lizards, centipedes, giant wasps, copperheads, and water moccasins. They were fed a gruel of flour and water. They were fed meat the hounds brought down. They were fed chickens and each other and some could go months without.

The men had been bitten and stung. They were gored, clawed, trampled, lamed, envenomed, and paralyzed. Some died and some recovered. It was their good luck or bad. As far as the Métis and the Lord were concerned, the dead were men who would not need to be paid.

They had found more burial mounds, the dead warriors' skin shrunken, wrinkled, and dry. They collected the corpses, the bows and quivers full of steel-pointed arrows; tomahawks; scalping knives; red clay pipes; and small bags of tobacco, nacre beads, silver rings, and silver bracelets. The deeper they dug, the more they found: parcels of coffee and sugar; revolvers and rifles; saddles, bridles, lariats, and scalps; harquebuses, gorgets, and greaves; and a sword forged in Toledo.

What the Métis and the Lord would do to fulfill Mr. Salt's request for an Indian family and an American Negro family Michael did not know. By then he'd left them and struck his way west by northwest. He told them he'd not be sailing with them, told them he did not know when he'd see them next.

Once more he scanned the distance. Heavy mists hung over the plain.

He was cold, wet, and weary. A chill seemed to have crept into his very bones. He spoke to Khyber. One of her ears pricked and fell back. He spoke again and the other ear fell back. As night came everything became still. Soon would come the howling of the wolf, the cries of the coyote, the wing beat of the night hunters.

He caught himself nodding heavily. Some time ago his back had begun to ache and he wanted to lie down but was afraid he would drop asleep and not wake up. He was now in a place where the creek had gathered enough water to take form and make a trickling of brown current. He crossed a trail where generations of buffalo threshed their way to the water. The red dog stopped and assumed a listening attitude. Water holes at night were not a place to rest.

Since morning he'd had a feeling of illness. He realized that he was experiencing the languor and weariness that presaged the fever. He could taste it in his mouth.

When the malaria finally came, it came hard with a headache that felt like a hammer blow at the base of his skull. He trembled and shuddered and was sick to his stomach. The nausea passed and he sweated and the sweat covering his body was chilling him.

He was faint, light-headed, and tottering in the saddle. He was having trouble breathing and his vertigo became acute.

What a pity, he thought, recovering his senses. He'd run out of quinine days ago. He knew at this particular moment things could quickly go very bad. He plotted out his possible futures. He hoped and believed this wasn't the end. Khyber moved under him. He'd not realized she'd stopped. He dismounted and dragged his blanket, his oilskin coat, and saddlebag after him. Something rustled in the curly grass. The red dog hackled and whatever it was it ran away. He managed to off-saddle and release the bit.

On this return to Wolf Creek the horse had shown her mettle. All other horses would have dropped from fatigue, but she'd not fallen off one iota and this after he'd given her the freedom of her head. She'd already held up fifteen, twenty, miles a day coursing with the hounds, crisscrossing the broken land, and now she was taking him home.

"Khyber," he said to her, the bold heart he trusted so much. His wrists and ankles were as if chilblained. He yawned and thought he fell, but he was still standing. He needed to find a resting place. He blew gently into her nostrils. He waited for her to nose him and she did.

He remembered Charlie and John playing hide-and-go-seek. One of them was behind a big log beside the road. It was Charlie. He was sucking his white thumb and he would not be found. He now seemed strangely present. He was sitting on his coat. His saddlebag was in the grass next to him.

He opened his saddlebag and found his matches. They'd gotten wet and were no more than a paste that rubbed off on his fingers. He rummaged for his whiskey bottle and his brother's journal. He read: *It seems I love you more and more every hour and at night when I sleep I meet you in every dream and when I wake I cannot close my eyes again.*

He closed the leather cover and placed it back in his saddlebag. He hunkered down and drew his saddle blanket over his shoulders, allowing it to droop behind. A cold, biting wind blew across the open land. Cold and chill followed great heat. He knew what was coming. After the chills would come a fever and he felt the fever rising up inside him.

Khyber stretched her neck. She cropped the short grass, looked about, and cropped some more. He took a drink unsteadily, the last of his whiskey. His face felt tight and full of steam. He was breathing through his mouth, almost panting. A slanting rain had begun to fall. A bright arc of electricity lit up the sky. He waited for the thunder, but it did not come. His spine ached and his loins and around his ribs ached also. The ache went into his shoulders.

"We are indeed alone," he said to the red dog. The red dog lifted an eyebrow and then looked away.

Then his temples throbbed and his eyes began to swim. He gathered what strength he could, raised his revolver, and pulled the trigger three times. He lay down on the blanket and curled up in a ball, waiting in distant consciousness. Mercifully the weather cleared and out of habit he looked up to the stars.

"David," he said. He knew David was watching him.

The moon was close and there was good-enough light and it blued the creek and the land, and in time, he did not know when, the world dimmed and he did not know if he was dreaming or his mind was awake and wandering. He lay on the wet ground beneath the horse blanket soaked to the skin. He began to shiver, his teeth, arms and legs jerking in a confusion of fever. Khyber whinnied softly and the red dog came in, turned in circles, and curled down against him.

He was surfacing again. He was breathing hard and beads of moisture had gathered on his upper lip and forehead and soon bathed his face. He rubbed his eyes and he saw her. She was coming to him, walking rapidly against the wind. He felt the warm caress of his wife. She was stroking his hand. His fingers tightened on hers. She was slipping her arm around his waist and she was an angel lifting him up.

Chapter 29

That morning, at her bookkeeping, Elizabeth began to grow uneasy. She buttoned her coat about her and over that her rain slicker. From the saddle hung a holster of stiff leather with the top flap open. She held the reins in her left hand and with the right she slid free the revolver once and twice. She circled the yard at a hand-canter. Her right hand held a whip she carried on her thigh cavalry fashion. The sky was overcast and pitchy darkness still shadowed the eastern shore of the creek water below.

With one hand Charlie held up his string and with the other hand his thumb and forefinger made a zero.

She waited. She looked to the horizon and then to her watch. The horse pawed once and whinnied softly and then stood quite motionless.

"Where are the brothers?" she said.

"They stayed out last night," Charlie said.

"Me and John took 'em food and cartridges."

"Which way?" she said.

"Follow the creek," Charlie said, pointing west and then south.

"Are you warm enough?" she said sternly.

"Sure am," he said, propping the collar of his coat.

She referenced her compass and then spurred the horse and he plunged forward at a headlong gallop in the direction Charlie pointed. She felt the swing and jolt of the saddle beneath her and she let the long-limbed horse race and he built at terrific speed. He stretched out across the open space with such a stride she held tight to keep her seat and urged him on the dead-level plain.

A rain began to fall. Gentle at first, it was soon falling in sheets and she had to close her mouth to keep from breathing in water. It was bitterly cold and then it warmed. She tried to blink away the water in her eyes and pulled low the brim of her hat. She kept riding and after an hour she entered the fields of the last day's killing, the carcasses torn and blown up, and she was riding through and by then it was too late to go back.

She bent south where the grass was high

and the creek was skirted with willows and cottonwood trees. She crossed a lateral creek and moved up the bank. She could hear her heart. She could feel her pulse. Her skin was wet and cold inside her clothes. She urged the horse onward. She could not ride fast enough.

She rode the upslope of another fold and when she reached the top rode over the low crest where a wind up-rose. Beyond was a field of carcasses rotting in the air and infested with flies. Her stomach lurched at the smell and her eyes watered. Innumerable skeletons of buffalo lay in all directions. She lifted her hand over her nose and mouth and struggled not to vomit. She tried to ride the edge, but there was no edge. They were everywhere. There were smaller carcasses to be seen on the surrounding earth. These were wolves and, smaller yet, the coyotes poisoned and slaughtered for their pelts and, smaller yet, raptors, badgers, and birds of carrion: vultures, hawks, and eagles as if struck down from the sky.

She suddenly came upon a pack of gabbling and blood-sotted wolves tearing at the hundred carcasses. The carcasses heaved and their stiff legs rocked in the air as the wolves tore at them from the inside. One by one they emerged from the bellies and turned their eyes to her. She had ridden on them so quickly there was no time to stop or to veer off. She squeezed with her legs and clutched at the horse's mane and he understood to jump. He strutted his forelegs, gathered his hind legs under him, pushed, and rose up into the air. She lifted out of the saddle, letting her weight down into her heels and they were floating for what seemed the longest time.

She did not look down but looked straight ahead. She heard a knock, a hoof on bone, one of the wolves struck in the skull. The horse landed with his trailing foreleg and then lead leg, his hind legs following suit. She took up the bit and rode on. There were streaks of them, ground shadows running alongside her. They were all around and there were as if dozens of them. With a swift flash of ancient memory her heart was water inside her; she knew she was being hunted. In her agony and fear she could not draw enough air into her lungs. She pulled her revolver and fired it to her right as she rode. The explosions threw her wrist about and her hand ached terribly, her wrist and arm, but she held her grip and fired again and again.

There rose upon the air a lone wailing cry. It came from her back trail. It died and rose again. It was mournful and despairing. Another joined in and there were two voices as if in concert. Then a third and this one was closer and the first two found it and the three called back and forth, wild and swelling. All around her was the telling of her passage. She kicked with her spurs. She urged the horse on. He straightened his neck and gave his whole heart to the work. They galloped steadily through the downpour, the big horse stretching itself flat and forward. Her heart beat fast and the blood ran hot in her veins.

When she finally found them it was a strange tableau she encountered. With a strong pull upon the rein, she brought the horse round short. She reined up and swung from the saddle. Matthew and Mark stood off, their rifles ready at their shoulders, deciding what they must do. Khyber stood by with the boys' horses and the red dog stood over Michael, wrapped in his blankets. The red dog, his teeth were bared, his spine was low in his shoulders and an unearthly sound emanated from his throat. He would not let the boys get near. He would kill them if they came any closer.

When they saw Elizabeth ride up their relief was apparent. They let down their rifles and waited for her to tell them what to do. She dismounted and stepped between the boys and the red dog.

"Michael," she said. "Wake up. Please wake up," and it was enough for the red dog to let down his guard and for her to go to him.

CHAPTER 30

"Help me," she said to Aubuchon, and they filled the bath and the hot water with Epsom salts. They unbuttoned his shirt and, rolling him over, got it off him. They dragged off his woolen sleep pants and took off his stockings and lifted him into the tub. She knelt beside him and rubbed his hands and feet. She washed his shins and calves, his ankles and heels. She washed his arms and head; his back and torso; his abdomen, groin, and upper thighs. She washed from his skin the sourness and waste and the acrid smell of his sweat and illness.

As they lifted him out and dried him and dressed him they could hear Mark singing, and then his brothers joined in: ". . . was to certain poor shepherds in fields as they lay."

He tried to talk and his mutterings were insensible and then he began shaking and could not speak for the chatter of his teeth.

"I am right here with you," she said.

"Taking care," he said.

"I will take such good care of you," she told him. "No harm shall come to you."

With the next fit he went under again. It was a very bad one. The buffalo were coming in countless numbers from a country under the ground. They poured from the cavelike opening and swarmed the land and he recognized them as the buffalo he'd killed and they were alive and in his dream he was the one who was dead and lost on the plain. Venomous reptiles coiled among the rocks, panicking the horse he rode, and paralyzed, he was falling to the ground into their midst. He was bitten again and again and each bite was a pinch and a shock of lightning-like electricity. He could see the stream of poison entering the channels of his veins. Their smell was the sulfur of a fiery hell. There were children and the snakes were coiled around their arms and legs and striking with their fangs, and wherever they struck, the children turned black.

In another, he crossed a broad and turbid river, the sand suspended in the water slowly filling his clothes. He was drowning and he was hunted by the beasts of darkness that lived beneath the water. Each time he made the effort to open his eyes and dissolve these dreams he would slip away into another one.

He had seven thousand pounds of ivory to transport in tusk and teeth and had contracted with a slave hunter bound east. They were a coffle of slaves chained at the neck and being smuggled to the coast and behind them were their women and children, also shackled. The slaver led the way in a sedan chair carried by six of his captives, followed by those in chains, down a narrow bush path. The land was wet and there was rank jungle and deep black mud. They set to flight great flocks of ibis, dove, and pheasant. Michael and one of the armed guards hung back behind the rear guard and hunted the curious animals, the reedbuck and wildebeest, that stepped onto the path to see what had just passed.

Suddenly a flock of green pigeons erupted through the loose hanging stems of creepers and into the air and through the treetops and there were so many everybody stopped to look skyward, the iron collars chafing at their necks. When they brought their gaze back to earth, a rhinoceros had emerged from the dripping leafy brush and presented himself beside the path in a profusion of magenta flowers.

Their faces twisted. There was a sickening

moment of fear and inevitability. The world stilled and went silent and then he could hear the bellowing in the grass and everyone understood death had arrived and it was then the rhinoceros charged. When he struck it was the center of the coffle. The man was impaled on the animal's horns and on both sides of him, and one by one, in rapid order, the men's necks were broken as the rhinoceros ran on a hundred yards through the chill grass, dragging the men with him by their necks before it finally stopped and shook free of the man impaled. To one side lay eleven dead men and to the other side lay twelve.

Each day the fever was worse than the day before. Michael's face burned and his throat was parched. He seemed to lurch from violent fever to delirious fever, his breath short and his chest hollow. He lay for many days burning with the malaria and Elizabeth applied wet cloths to his forehead to cool his brow. His eyes were wild and the surface of his body ran with rivulets of sweat so that his clothes and the bedding were soaked. She washed him and fanned him as he tossed and turned in the bed.

She thought his heart must be laboring so heavily and wondered could it sustain the torment of such work. There were times she was afraid to touch him and other times she held him as tightly as she could to arrest the violence in his body. Elizabeth prayed over him, offering God whatever he would have: Please take this . . . and please take this . . . and please, God, make this the last fit of fever he must endure.

When he finally awoke it was with the ache of the long days before. He half-opened his eyes and sorted out where he was. He was alive and he lay listless and apathetic in her bed, covered with blankets. The embers in their chamber threw a dull red light across the rug. It shined on the even backs of books. She was sitting in a canvas chair beside the bed. He could see her shoulder, neck, and abundant black hair piled high on top of her head. She was stroking his hand. He thought to rise up on his elbows, but his legs and body seemed heavy as lead. He was too weak to move. He raised a hand and wiped a little moisture from his lips.

"Good morning," Elizabeth said, turning to him. Her eyes filled with tears. She had been so afraid, but now he was awake and breathing steadily. She touched his cheek and felt his forehead.

Hers was a faraway voice he knew from his life. He stared as if in a dream. He wasn't yet ready to break the stillness of his resting body. All was the quietness of early morning. She blew across her lifted teacup and then she spoke again.

"I am glad to see you," she said.

The dogs rallied to their feet and put their forepaws onto the bed. They made whimpering sounds and stretched to nose him. His shirt was dry and open at the neck, his forearms bare. He reached out his hand to pet them and they licked it.

"I hope you rested well," she said. She wiped his forehead and upper lip. She wiped his chin and neck and she pulled his sleeves over his hands to keep them warm. His mouth was parched, his muscles cramped, and his stomach had shrunk. She asked to see his tongue.

"Matthew and Mark found you on the plain," she said. "The red dog wouldn't let them get near you. I called to you and you stirred and the red dog relented. We thought we might have to shoot the old boy, but we didn't."

He indicated he needed to go and she helped him to the chamber pot. His limbs ached with muscle pains that made him cry. She helped him back to bed, where he soon fell asleep. The tremor of his body passed into hers as she held him and she feared tonight he would again shiver with fever.

He slept through the day and night and in the clear, amber light of the next morning he woke again. On a plate by the bed there were biscuits with jam. There was tea and a glass of brandy and water. There was his dose of quinine, fifty measured grains.

He slipped free a hand and ate a biscuit. He ate a second one and then spoonfuls of jam. When he asked for a cigarette, Elizabeth rolled one and lit it. She held it to his lips until he took it himself and then she sat back in her chair.

"Are you going to eat that last one?" he said.

"You have it," she said.

She was relieved. He had an appetite. He would be all right.

"I thought you were gone," she said, and told him twice his heart stopped and she had to beat on his chest.

"I must look like hell."

She reached out and turned up the lantern wick until it glowed. The oily smell of kerosene smoke drifted over them. She lifted the lantern by its bale and held it close to his face.

"A picture of health," she said, replacing the lantern in the center of the table. She brought a pail of warm water from the stove and began to sponge his face and neck.

"Thank you for saving me," he said, "but it wasn't necessary."

"And why not?"

"A gypsy told me how I would die."

"How?"

"Not this way."

She helped him to a chair close by the fire, where he sat with his elbows on his knees while she changed the bedding and blankets. She then knelt by the stove and held her hands close to the open door. He looked down at her, the curve of her neck.

"How was your foray?"

"Very profitable," he said. "The man named Dimitri lost a finger to a snapping turtle. Every one of them thought it very funny."

"How did it happen?"

She made another cigarette and from the one still burning lit it and handed it to him.

"One of them found the turtle and would eat it. He chopped off the head and when Dimitri picked it up it nipped off his finger."

"Your pain?" she said.

"Tolerable. I was very ill for several days before coming over. It hides in the blood."

"We've got to build you up," she said as she helped him off with his sweat-stiffened shirt and into one that was clean. From the desktop she took the locket he always wore and draped it about his neck. However much she wanted to ask, she did not.

"I will tell you," he said, holding up the locket.

"You needn't tell me anything," she said, and she turned away from him until she thought he was ready to speak.

"It is my wife," he said, and it was then he told her the tragedy of his life.

The Ivory Bazaar was a market for the hunters from the interior, and there at a tavern, Michael had found men whose company he liked. They were English, Dutch, German, French, Spanish, Portuguese, and Irish. They were travelers and they were older and thus far had survived their dangerous lives. They'd traveled to the interior in search of ivory and carried with them a certain unmistakable air of violence and self-reliance. They boxed and gambled. They chewed garlic and smoked cigars to ward off yellow fever, malaria, dengue.

He sought their advice, a factor who might deal with him fairly, an honest man who'd take possession of his goods and trade them in his own name. A man named Heinrich recommended the mercantile agent De Sousa, who carried on a considerable trade in ivory, gold dust, beeswax, and songbirds and several others affirmed his recommendation.

The house of De Sousa had a long sloping roof, wide eaves, and a veranda across the front shaded by the joined canopy of fever trees. At some distance, low acacia thorn had been densely planted to provide a wall of security. Whether the man who greeted him was a slave or a servant he did not know. In that land there was little difference between the two. He asked for De Sousa and waited in the dark of the foyer, the slanted green jalousies admitting bars of tempered light. Eventually the man returned and he was shown through to the garden while he waited.

When he first saw her she wore glasses tinted green, a broad-brimmed straw hat, a pongee shirt pink in color, loose trousers of brown linen, and dust-colored canvas shoes. On her hands she wore gloves made of lace. She was sitting in a canvas deck chair reading a book in the shade, her feet propped in the chair across from her. There was not a breath of wind.

"Do, sir, be seated," she said, her tone as if his arrival were expected.

"I stand very well here," he said.

"For heaven's sake," she cried, standing

up. "Please sit down."

She shaded her eyes as he crossed the garden and took the chair she offered.

"Sir, will you be so good as to tell me your business?"

"I am here to see De Sousa."

"I am Luisa, his daughter. Who are you?"

"I am Michael Coughlin," he said.

"An American."

"Yes, but my papers are British."

"Lysander, the man who answered the door, he is a witch," she said. "He claims to have killed many people with his art where he came from. He fled for fear of retribution and this is his sanctuary. He never leaves the villa."

Michael looked over his shoulder to see the man who answered the door passing in the shadows.

"He seems a pleasant enough fellow," he said, turning back to the woman.

"He has the power to change himself into a crocodile and devour people."

"I may have lost some men and dogs to him," Michael said, taking a second, more scrutinizing look when Lysander appeared with tea and crullers. The man was either handsome or ugly, he could not tell. His features were sharp and his eyes surrounded by scar tissue. One scar seemed to source from his forehead on one side and the other side from his jawline and the effect of his face seemed an illusion. His complexion was coal black and to look at him made one vaguely dizzy.

"I do not recognize his people," Michael said.

"No one does. That is what I am telling you."

When she went to see what was keeping her father she left him sitting there with a memory of something rare and beautiful. When she returned it was on the arm of De Sousa, her father.

He was a man short, slender, and pale, and though his face was soft and melancholy, he was a deliberate and self-concentrated man. He seemed guarded and distant like many businessmen. He told Michael they'd be leaving in a year.

"What will you do?" Michael asked.

"I would rest from business and its cares."

"You will stay for dinner," Luisa said.

The dining room was long and cool and kept in shadow. It opened onto the garden where the sun was bright. Servants arrived with trays of food. They ate beneath red, white, and pink bougainvillea, the platters of roast chicken and vegetable kabobs. There were glasses of sherbet and lemonade, raisins, prunes, and nuts.

Michael told De Sousa he'd been granted permission by the king of the Ndebele to shoot game anywhere in his kingdom. Thus far he'd taken 107 elephants and as many hippopotamuses, whose ivory was more dense than both elephant and walrus and highly prized for the making of dentures. He speculated on the number of royals and upper class whose mouths he'd filled with teeth and at this very moment were enjoying their mutton and beef.

"I like this boy," De Sousa said to his daughter. "He has something to him."

As the sun set an accident of light twinkled on the silver coffee service and the unlit candelabra. He'd been in her company from midday to twilight to setting sun and now full night. The glass of the sideboard glowed in gold and red. De Sousa had fallen asleep in his chair after agreeing to do business with him.

"Take my hand," Luisa said.

"What is it?"

"Whisper," she said, touching a finger to her lips.

"It's dark."

"We will feel our way."

They walked through the garden. The vegetables, refreshed by a shower of rain, sprawled from their ordered rows and the several kinds of fruit trees bore an abundance of peaches and apricots. The air was strong perfume, exquisite and balmy. It was cooler, but not by much, and a breeze was coming out of the darkness before them. Fireflies flashed among the slender leaf blades of the bamboo.

At path's end, they passed through a silk curtain and were inside the aviary. Sweet songbirds filled the air, moustache birds and long-tailed whydah finches. They were birds captured with birdlime spread on a branch twig where the bird might land, and these her father exported. This delicate work was done by slaves who'd been gathered on the coast awaiting transport.

That night they traveled out to the lanes of the plantations on a two-seated trolley lit with lanterns and running on a narrow track laid through the streets. The trolley was pushed by two boys and in no time they were flying down the rails. Soon they were outside the town and she held his hand as they rode through the dense groves of mangoes, baobab, banana, and palm trees. Through the branches they could see the flashing lights of other couples making the circuit though the plantations.

Whatever hesitancy there may have been

between them melted away. Luisa told him of their life in Portugal, their houses in Lisbon, Sintra, and Nazaré where they raised jet-black swine, seven hundred or more, and whose meat was flavored by eating the husks of grapes pressed for wine and left to dry in the sun, and there were dozens of bulls one, two, and three years old and still a few years away from being ready for the ring, their coats glossy in the sunlight, their legs thin, and their tails long. And there was a breeding stable where they raised gray Lusitanos whose lineage went back to the time Muslims invaded the peninsula.

After that night, each time he left for the interior, she'd say, I am coming with you, and they would ride to the river where they'd take their farewells. She'd wave to him after he crossed and he'd respond by lifting his hat. They were soon married and these were the brightest and happiest days of his life.

Then one day he returned from the fly country to the west, bringing with him a nice lot of ivory, when he learned that Lysander in a fit of jealousy had murdered Luisa with an axe. When Lysander was finally coaxed from his hiding place, her father shot him dead with a horse pistol.

And these were the darkest days of his life. He lived without hope or desire, without want of food or drink. He was as if stark and dead and come to an end.

He told Elizabeth how after Luisa's death he began a life of aimless wandering in the company of slavers, missionaries, merchants, hunters, and killers. He was filled with hatred and there was an infinite longing for what would never be again. His soul felt like a place cold and barren.

He mounted a new hunt into the interior and returned to the bush and there he stayed for three years. All the while, rising inside him was vibrating aggression and a desire for vengeance. In moments he thought, What reality am I passing through? And for that time he was like a lunatic escaped from Bedlam, wounded and wandering and lashing out.

He did not care if he'd died alone, far from home, among strangers, and during that time, he met the Métis and the Lord and together they hunted and there came a steady flow from the interior of ivory, honey and beeswax, specimens dead and alive and traveling back up the trails were cloth, beads, brass wire, powder, lead, and chains.

"I am so sorry," Elizabeth now said. "I am

so sorry," she repeated, and she could not help herself and began to cry her tears wetting his skin.

"I am better now," he said. "Better than I was before."

In his recuperation he ate when he was hungry and buried himself beneath blankets and slept whenever he was tired. As she kept her accounts, he'd leave the bed to stand with his back at the fire and then return. Or he'd lounge by the fire, wrapped in a blanket and drinking warm tea. With each day he was getting better by degrees, able to sit up and then stand and then walk, able to blanket and saddle Khyber and then lift himself into the saddle and ride the land. But as with times previous, the fever left him chastened and dependent and in a languor he could not analyze.

In camp he became wandering and friendly. It was more than being returned to life after a great trial. There was a lassitude, a profound lethargy, an inability in his being. He had the distinct sense of an identity divided and separated, one watching and the other behaving.

One cold morning with Khyber he saw John going off to milk the cows and went to the cowshed with him. John sat beside the first cow. He washed the teats with water, and then holding the pail between his knees so she wouldn't kick it over, he milked her out. It did not take long before he had a quart of fresh milk and then spread a little Vaseline on the teats to stop them from cracking.

He watched as the boy's head drooped with tiredness.

"Mind if I give it a try?" Michael said.

By way of answer John stood from the stool, wiped his palms on the seat of his trousers, and handed him the bucket.

Michael sat on the low stool, close to the warm and companionable cow. He leaned his forehead into her stifle. He drew a hand along her mammary vein to her fore udder. She made a step and he moved the stool forward. He sat down again and leaned his head into her again. Feeling the warm udder, he took a teat in each hand. He pressed and pulled the withered teats at the same time. She let down her milk and he began to draw forth the warm milk and it foamed in the pail.

The milking relieved her of the pressure in her udder and she stood peacefully, chewing her cud and swishing her tail.

With Michael doing the milking, John rationed corn and hay and a little salt to lick. Then he brushed their black and white coats. He brushed their necks and down their backs. He brushed their shoulders and barrels, their fore ribs and flanks, until they were glossy in the morning light.

When they finished with the milking John let the cows to water and Michael carried the two pails of milk suspended on a shoulder yoke to Aubuchon's fire. The milk sloshed over the rim, splashing his trousers as he stumbled along. In the evening, when all was quiet and the first stars were just visible, he'd return to the silence of the cowshed. He'd sit again close by on the milking side, his face transfigured and he'd draw the hissing white streams into the pail. He'd close his eyes and see green pastures and horses knee deep in the silky grass and the dews that fall when the shadows climb. He'd see pointed firs and a pond and a house with white clapboards. He'd breathe the cow-breath.

Chapter 31

The air was cold with a nip of frost, the wind in the south, and then for five days the weather held and winter was like summer and even the evenings ran hot and sultry.

Then the wind died. There was a perfect calm and it was as if they could hear for miles. The world was as if in suspension, poised on its axis, waiting, expecting, and a deep uneasiness set in. A big event was coming. They knew it down into their bones. Their voices dropped to whispers as they moved about cautiously and warily, their eyes on the horizons north, south, east, and west.

A strange fog began to drift in that early morning and Michael told Elizabeth how thin his blood had become as they rode quietly through the hollow air, following on the heels of the skinners the source of the rifle fire. They carried food and water and belts of cartridges for Matthew and Mark. The boys had received a letter from their mother addressed to Matthew, which Michael carried to him.

Matthew read quietly and then abruptly handed the letter to Mark. Their father had passed. There was a description of his last peaceful days in town, quotations of his last words. He wished for them a vineyard and fruit trees, straight fences, square barns, shade, an endless source of fresh water. "We will soon be drinking at the fountain," he'd said, and "Remember me with all love," and then he passed. Whatever sorrow they felt, the boys kept to themselves.

Elizabeth would have stayed with the boys, but both were so reserved in their grief that Michael suggested they leave them to be with each other.

"Beware," Michael said to them, in parting, "This day is a weather breeder."

Soon the storm clouds rolled in. The wind was slowly picking up in the north and in short time became strong enough to lift sand and flatten the grass. Beneath him, Khyber was nervous and twitchy, as if there were electricity in her legs, and even Granby, stolid and sure as iron, seemed edgy. It was getting blacker in the north and cooler and the wind picked up.

They were halfway back to camp when the sky darkened. A storm of biblical proportion was rising on the edge of the round world and was as if sourced in the undivided essence of terror. In the north, it rose up as if a great black wall. Michael tipped his head back to see its height and there was evidence of a great turbulence in the blackness overhead. Then everything shifted so fast. The temperature dropped and the wind began to make a hollow roar. Its fury increased. It moaned and it drove a cold that went through the blood and bones.

"What is it?" she said.

"It's going to break," he said. "We are in for some god-awful weather."

She held the hair that was blowing about her face with a gloved hand. The horses moved under them, stepping sideways away from the wind. She looked to the looming sky with fear-bright eyes. Her face flushed with the cold air.

"Ride to camp as fast as you can. Don't look back," he said, and then ominously: "Do not save the horse if you have to."

Michael spun Khyber around and lowered his head and they rode off into the maw of the storm. The cold piercing wind came down on him. The rain was laced with ice. He rode on, and by the time the gale exploded with paralyzing fury, the wind so fierce he could not breathe, he calculated Elizabeth in sight of the bluff. The storm screamed all around him, like artillery or a hundred locomotives.

When he found the skinners and butchers they were islanded as if shipwrecked. The green hides in the wagons were already frozen, as were the ones they'd wrapped around themselves. They thought they'd hunker down and wait and soon they would be dead and frozen.

Michael came down on them with his whip. "Move," he yelled, lashing and snapping the air about their backs and faces. He gave the whip to the hides they wore. "We've got to run," he said as he delivered cracking blows. The men aroused themselves from their torpor and they panicked to life, fought to free themselves from their frozen cocoons. Shivering they climbed onto their feet and found they could not stand upright against the wind. Their thighs quivered, their legs gave out, and they fell down. They tried to force the blood to their extremities, swinging their arms and stamping their feet. They took the rope he handed down and passed it along, tying on more lengths as they went from one wagon to the next. Every effort made their lungs wheeze and their hearts race.

Matthew and Mark rode in. They dismounted and heaved their bodies into the sides of the oxen. They twisted their tails and beat them on their flanks. The rest of the men joined in as the will to live surged up inside them. The wheels cracked free and there was the screech of frozen axles inside the moan of the wind as it tore through them. The boys remounted and dropped lariats over the horns of the lead oxen and stepped off east following Michael, the blinding, stinging rain slamming into them, the gusts staggering the horses as they moved heavily forward.

Drenched to the skin, Michael knew they had to shelter. They all had to shelter, but they could not stop. To stop was to die. They had to move faster.

"Keep on," he cried as the freezing rain encased them in icy shells. The exertion caused them to sweat and their sweat was freezing on their skin.

For hours they labored on. Their muscles ached with the buffeting, every nerve, fiber, body, and brain, and they all wondered if they would die. At times they slipped and fell or the wind flung them to the ground and they were dragged by the rope until they could struggle to their knees and crawl forward and find their feet.

Michael could not tell east from west, north from south. Tired and weak he rode by feel and they traveled on in the direction he thought true. His hands throbbed with pain until they became too numb to hold the reins. He let them slip from his fingers and left Khyber to go at will. Before them there was nothing to see, nothing to touch. Khyber held her pace and direction over the miles. Her flanks heaved and her breath was coming hard and at the last extreme she fell to a slower gait and they were going over the bluff and down the wagon road and desperate not to be run over by the grinding wheels. They skidded over the frozen creek and into the camp and down there the storm was somewhat less severe, although they could hear a roaring overhead and still feel the bite of the frozen rain.

They unhooked the chains and pulled the pins, dropping the yokes where they stood. They set free the oxen and then the men pale and haggard crowded into the cook tent where Aubuchon had a hot fire burning and pots of stew and kettles of coffee. Their lips were blue and their teeth chattering. The tent walls rippled and snapped and threatened to tear away at any second.

Nearly frozen, and weak, his hands

cracked and sore, Michael slipped from the saddle and fell from the horse and to the ground. His knees buckled and he dragged himself upright. He pointed in the direction of Elizabeth's tent and following his hand Khyber led him down the path. He untied the door to Elizabeth's, where a fire roared in the little stove and brought Khyber in with him. Granby was there as well. Stiff legged, icicles hanging from his coat and hat, he passed through the curtain and only then, when he saw her sitting on her bed wrapped in a blanket with Sabi beside her and flames in the stove cherry red, was he relieved.

"You're safe," he said. His throat was frozen and his voice was a raspy and scraping sound.

"Don't worry about me," she said, her eyes wide. "What about the men."

"I have brought them in," he said. "Everyone is accounted for." His hands and limbs numb and cold, he went for his quinine, and when he returned, the red dog slipped in behind him and took a place by the fire. Elizabeth poured out brandy, but shaking so badly, he spilled most of it in trying to drink.

She caught him by his shoulders and helped him into a chair beside the bed. He tried to kick off his boots, but he couldn't lift his leg. She reached down and took his boot by the toe and heel and worked it back and forth until it came off. It was full of water.

"I've made the fire hot," she said. "I didn't know what else to do."

In her parlor he peeled off his dripping clothes and his skin pinked and prickled in the warming air. He added more wood to the flames and found towels to wipe down the horse. Khyber had given so much and now he needed to save her. Elizabeth took up a towel and they both rubbed her vigorously and dried her limbs and flank, her neck, her back and head that she not become stiff and chilled.

Michael placed his hand over Khyber's heart. He waited for her to nuzzle him and she did.

"Go in there," Elizabeth said, and he slipped through the curtain to her bed and he collapsed onto the ticking.

Elizabeth banked the fires and tucked him in, bundled herself, and picked up her medical bag. In a momentary lull in the storm, she ran to the cook tent, where the rest of the men were.

The men — their faces were now wet where once icicles hung from their mustaches and beards. Many had frozen their feet and fingers, ears and noses.

She told Luke, Charlie, and John to tether themselves with ropes and fetch all the blankets they could from the other tents. The men stripped off their wet clothes and wrapped themselves in the blankets. She inspected their hands and feet and faces and applied cloths that they'd warmed by the fire. In the medical bag was tincture of iodine and this she applied to the feet and frozen limbs and hoped amputations would be averted.

She told the three boys it was their job to tend the cook fires all night long and they tied off and went out for wood. Everyone was to stay where they were and work to keep warm. Charlie came back shortly thereafter, a split of wood in one hand and carrying the axe in the other. He dropped the split and let go the axe, but it did not fall. He held it up with his hand, frozen to his palm as if a neat trick.

"Aren't you a smart monkey," she said. "Get yourself to the fire." Charlie joined the other men, another casualty of cold.

Outside the wind lashed the tents as if with heavy whips and at times was a scream, shrill and whistling. The men lit their cigarettes and let them sizzle close to their fingertips. They were not hungry until they tasted Aubuchon's stew and then they could not get enough.

"Mr. Gough," she said to Ike, and he offered his hands the way a dog would offer a paw. She turned them over in her own and then swabbed glycerine on his cheeks and nose and told him to gently rub it in, and for all of this, the men felt her heart was full of kindliness toward them. When she was through, she told them their bodies would soon be in agony. She then tethered herself to return to her tent. She bent her head to escape the rain that filled her eyes and nostrils and froze her cheeks.

Michael lay there and watched the fire in the stove while Elizabeth sat by brushing her tumbled hair. The tea boiled. At her feet was a basket of food she'd brought.

"Cold night," she said, and told him he'd saved many lives.

She poured herself a cup of tea and was to offer one to him, but his eyes had closed and he'd fallen asleep. She sat close to the fire and sipped her tea and in the basket she found a wedge of corn bread. Everyone was safe and accounted for, and however tired she was, she wanted this moment to last.

Chapter 32

While they slept, the temperature dropped fifty degrees. The rain turned to snow and the snow blew and fell in a blinding descent. It beat against the walls and swirled about the roof. It piled up on the south side of everything as the wind swept the north sides clear and left patches of blasted dirt and frozen grass.

When Michael awoke, the blanket held the outline of his body in hoarfrost. The bedding around his head was stiff from his frozen breath. Elizabeth was curled up beside him, down inside the bedcovers. Pulling the blankets back over her, he stood by the bed. There was wood and with the last embers he was able to renew the fire in the bedroom and parlor stoves. From beneath the bed he pulled a quilt from under the warm dogs and wrapped it around his shoulders.

The red dog lifted his head as he entered

the parlor. The horses were there as well and Khyber was no longer in danger. Outside the snow was drifted and banked high. The surround was heavy and dense and white and the light was silvery and frosty and the edge of all things was as if cut with a knife. From the cook tent there came a steady stream of gray smoke. Overhead the sky was vast and slate blue and the wind a sighing moan. The creek was reduced to a thin black channel soon to be frozen over. Everywhere were the huge snowdrifts and frost and sparkling ice.

All that day long, Aubuchon kept hot water for tea and the coffeepot boiling and there was bread and stew and there was meat thawing and grilling on the cook fire. The men went out on stout ropes, working furiously to stock as much wood as they could inside the cook tent.

In the afternoon the wind died down and the air cleared and became as if crystal. In places the wind had swept away the snow and the frost. By needful habit he ascended the bluff to witness a vast ocean of white, the ice cracking beneath his boots.

Cupping his hand, he blew warm air to his eyes and he could see again, but there was nothing to see because the snow was everywhere and unbroken. He walked the bluff west until he came to a place where he was able to see the buffalo, their immense black forms coated with hoarfrost and hung with icicles against the white landscape. They browsed the frozen earth, rooting through to the frosty grass and turning their noses bloody.

To the north an old bull was being harassed by wolves. They'd surrounded him and were taking turns assaulting his flank. His legs were shredded and there was blood streaming down his sides. His nose was torn to pieces, his tongue eaten out, and he'd lost his tail. But he braced and fought on, turning and turning as they moved in on him, and at his feet there were three he'd killed.

He wanted to feel something for the old bull, but he did not. To feel something was an idea in his mind that could not find its way to his heart. He was not naive. He'd been to the dangerous limit of the world. He was not innocent. Michael turned back east and made for the wagon road. He'd been out longer than he should have.

That night the darkness came on instantly and this time the storm struck from the south and ever more viciously and did not let up for the entire night and into the next day. Finally the moon rose and they could hear the coyotes. Their pealing cry was loud and harsh and then it softened, and when it came again it was a wild, lonely, mournful haunting. There came a piercing answer from across the valley sharp and staccato.

As the temperature continued to drop they could hear the freezing land boom all around them. From the creek there came sounds like gunshots. From the woods came the sound of trees exploding. Elizabeth, in her random thinking remembered, *How like a winter hath my absence been. From thee, the pleasure of the fleeting year! What freezings have I felt, what dark days seen!*

That night in his sleep Michael was troubled. Several times he stepped from the bed and walked the room, tending the stove, brushing the horses, smoking a cigarette, having a sip of brandy. As the night wore on the sorrow magnified. He feared the onset of his old black days, much like those his brother had had. He wondered if he wore the same mark as David. Maybe it was simply the end of the languor he experienced after his malaria days and he was himself again.

"Come back to bed," she said. "Keep me warm." She sat up tentatively, the room so cold she could see her breath. She wanted him to lie back down. "What is it?"

"I was thinking," he said. "Tonight we are as safe as we will ever be."

On the third day there was no wind, but it remained bitterly cold. Michael stepped from the tent. It was so cold he could hardly breathe. He collected a bucket of snow and washed his face and ate some. When Khyber stuck her head out after him jets of steam blew from her nostrils and she backed inside.

Then the morning sun broke through and there was scattered light, and with a sudden burst a flood of light poured onto the land. The tents whitened and glowed as the ice caught the light and sparkled and the creek ice mirrored. The wind had blown away the snow and the creek was a wide and sinuous avenue that disappeared to the east gray and silver. The ice was thick and clear and they could see through to the current running beneath its vitreous surface over the stream bed below. There were swimming fish and turtles under the glassy ice and suspended matter floating east.

Luke was the first onto the ice. He took two steps when suddenly both feet went out from under him. He fell onto his back and went skimming along. The others cheered him on. Mark ran forward, threw himself down, and was gliding the slick surface and did not stop until he reached the far bank. In this moment, spinning, sliding, skating, and falling, the four brothers were boys again.

Outside was the blue sky, and the shadows on her walls were red and blue. Elizabeth retrieved a bottle of ink from beside the fire and lit two more candles with a match and opened her ledger book. Her parlor smelled like a stable. She wondered what damage the storm had done. She picked up her pen.

Then John was at her door, calling her name. He told her they couldn't find Charlie. He must have gone out in the night and not returned and was he with her?

"We found him," someone cried, and John wheeled and was running.

Elizabeth pulled on an overcoat and stepped into the cold sunlight and made her way in the direction of the calling voices. Others were moving in the same direction, following a slack rope that lay in the snow on its way to the stone bathhouse. Something cold and gloomy floated out from the doorway. A long fringe of icicles depended from the roofline. Charlie had made it to the bathhouse where he tried to start a fire but was unable to. The rope was unknotted at his waist and his clothes were in a frozen pile. There was a stiff crackling coat of ice upon his naked body. He was blue and his eyelashes frosted. He sat against a wall with his legs spread before him, a fist on his chest and the other against his cheek.

She could not speak for the pain that was in her heart.

In the cold he died, cold and then warm in his mind, and naked, like being born or going to sleep forever. She touched the frosted stone and when she brought her hand away she was holding the crystals of his last breath, his warmth, his air.

"He was just impossible to dislike," someone said.

"I must wash and dress him," she said.

She felt tired and crazy and good for nothing. How many months ago had she told Michael she was prepared to take the risk? And how many deaths had they endured since that night in the garden? She felt shame and self-reproach. It was her fault Charlie was dead. It was because of her ambition and desire and she could see it in no other way.

The next morning was also very cold, but the next was less so, and so it went until it became warm again and there was a soft wind from the south and the sun and a warming and by noon the land was running with water. As the days went by, the vanished world reappeared. The blizzard and their escape from it, like so many experiences, was too much to remember and soon was disappearing from their minds.

CHAPTER 33

Spring was advancing and with it the force inside Michael came surging back. Each day his muscles repaired and his body took on mass and he found himself again and he was as if returned from the remotest part of the remotest world.

The cottonwoods were in bud and soon they would leaf. New shoots of prairie grass were sprung from the earth. During the days and weeks, the buffalo were beginning to shed their winter coats and seek the muddy wallows.

When Elizabeth found him that night the evening star was in the west and the climbing moon a cataract of light. Khyber was on her back with her feet in the air like a big dog and Michael was sitting on her belly. He wore an indigo blue shirt, the sleeves rolled to his elbows to reveal the sleeves of his red cotton underjersey. His hair was untied and his beard was down to his chest.

Against the keen crispness of the night air she watched as he pulled a blanket over his shoulders and returned his rifle to the hollow of his left arm. Where he sat he could see south, west, and north with the ravine of the creek behind him.

Michael turned and watched her as she came on in her waistcoat and her last good dress, a pearl-colored Irish poplin. Her hair was brushed smooth, pulled back, and tied with a ribbon.

She could not say when it started, but little by little, day by day, she'd walked in this direction. There were signs to be read everywhere if only she'd read them. Was it the time of the malaria when she stilled his shivering body or the blizzard when they slept together for warmth, or was it the first time she saw him, she did not know.

Why mustn't this be? she thought, and she was alive and tender and thinking about the future.

"Is it you or your ghost?" he said, standing to greet her.

"Are you going or coming?" she said, her eyes fixed on his face in the moonlight.

"We just came in. What are you doing up so late?"

She wanted to say, I was sleeping and I dreamed about you, but instead she said, "I just feel like visiting, Mr. Coughlin, and to say I hope you are enjoying this beautiful weather."

Her legs weary, she stood there, experiencing a sudden need to sit or lie down. She experienced a strangeness passing through her, a lonely spasm, as if she'd not waken from the dream. She felt like she was going to cry and was afraid to say anything more because the dream's wondering and yearning and ache had not disappeared.

Khyber was rolling in the grass, and when she looked up, her expression was as if she did not know why and then she rolled some more.

"She is truly quite a horse," Elizabeth said.

He thought he saw sadness in Elizabeth's eyes. She stood as if she'd hiked the wagon road for the sole reason of hearing a voice.

"The boys should be back home by Easter," he said. They now had a decent bank account in Fort Worth and Elizabeth asked that they consider property in the vicinity of Meadowlark to make a new start.

Matthew and Mark wanted to go to Africa with Michael and he liked the idea of it. He'd leave this damned country for good. Elephants were still plentiful and the shooting would be profitable. Maybe they'd head for the diamond fields or take the big nets and cages into the land and capture animals. There had yet to be a successful breeding program anywhere and the zoos of Europe and America would pay dearly.

"I'm going to walk out for a distance. Will you walk?" she said.

"When the next man on night watch arrives."

She wondered if he understood her feelings, the tenderness of her intentions.

When the next man arrived they walked along the bluff. He felt her touch at the small of his back as if to let him know where she was and then she took his arm and together they slipped away into the darkling silence. They walked out beneath the starlit vault and birds took flight before them. The night that lay before them was so quiet they could hear the sound of their own footsteps swishing through the grass.

"What if I keep going forward?" she said.

"You will be me."

"Is that so bad?"

"You could lose what you love the most," he said.

"My life?"

"Yes."

"Listen to me," she said. "I have made up my mind today. Our work is ended. I told the freighters when next they came we'd be gone. I told them we were done and in a few days we'd be going north. They will come collect whatever hides we leave."

"What made you change your mind?"

"We have enough."

"Whatever your reason, I am pleased to hear you say it."

"Now I worry we have stayed too long and it's too late for us."

"No," he said. "It's not too late."

"In the morning we will tell the rest of the men and tell Bonaire."

"Bonaire already left," he said, and he told her how he'd ridden into Bonaire's camp that afternoon and it was bare. There was no sign of them except the overwhelming smell of wolf carcasses, their flesh rotting in a ravine and a dozen wolves hanging in the trees.

"When did he do that?"

"I calculate three or four days ago."

"Oh," she said, and then she did worry they'd overstayed and were doomed and she went to speak, but instead she said, "He was a tough old spirit."

"You should sleep, then," he said. "We have a lot to do in the morning."

"You don't think we're too late, do you?"

"No," he said. "In the morning will be fine."

"There is more I have to say." She let go of his shirtsleeve, sighed. When she looked at him, a mist seemed to blur her sight.

"Close your eyes," he said, and she did and lifted her face to him.

When he kissed her a tremble ran through her. She reached up to take his face in her hands and when she did he reached his strong arms around her and gathered her into him. He felt her body respond more heavily. Her head dropped and her chest began to rise and fall.

"Is it too late?" she said. "Am I too old?"

He touched her cheeks and her forehead. She tried to slow her breathing. He pulled the ribbon and her hair fell over her face.

He kissed her again and she felt to be carried from all pain and suffering, from sadness and grief and she was sure he could hear her heart. He laid her down and she lifted her face to receive more of his kisses.

"Hold me," she said. "Wrap your arms around me."

When he did he kissed her lips and her forehead and her tired eyes. Her shiny eyes were liquid and for the moment there was nothing but the flutter of pulse, the beating of their hearts as they lay side by side. She blew a strand of hair out of her face and he kissed her again.

Afterward, she slowly came back to herself and it was strange and wonderful. The sighs and the murmurings and the moment broke something loose inside him and inside her like a burning angel. She reached inside his shirt and felt his warm skin. He took her in his arms and held her tight to his chest. That night they lay awake on the plain talking before sleep and it was a few hours after midnight when her hand upon his shoulder aroused him.

"You were having a dream," she said.

He sat up and tucked his legs beneath him. He dropped his face in his hands and was silent for some minutes, her hand still on his shoulder and then he lay back down beside her.

When he stirred awake again it was with some vague premonition. Slowly he opened his eyes, to see nothing but the grasses close to his face. He looked at her for a few moments without moving. He held his hand to her mouth and she placed a hand over his.

"Stay down," he whispered.

"What is it?"

"I don't know."

There were sounds in the night. It was too dark to see anything. Birds were being disturbed. They were calling out in patterned distress. They were calling to each other and making their replies. A coldness was stealing its way into his spine.

Chapter 34

He peered intently into the darkness. To the northeast, something in the night loomed up. There was a dark form on the sky, the dark shadow of a man. The muscles in Michael's legs twitched. A shiver of death passed through him.

In the next instant two more shadow figures loomed up to the north and east and something dark was noiselessly descending on the camp. They were the shapes of running men breaking the line of the horizon.

"What is it?" she whispered, terrified.

"Lie still. They cannot see us here. We do not know yet."

"When will we know?"

"When we do."

A common thought held them: they'd stayed out too long.

Between them and the wagon road four figures moved over the low bushes. In the moonlight they moved on, slowly and furtively, and at the bluff they dropped from sight.

Then there was another and another. Dark shapes of running men and it was as if the night was walking.

He felt in his veins his quickened blood.

"We must do something," she said.

"There is nothing we can do," he said, pressing her down on the ground. He knelt beside her below the sight line.

"Now," he said. "Stay close to me," and bent low, she ran behind him to Khyber.

"Look there," he said, and pointed to a star on the horizon and told her to fix on it. He told her to ride west and away for a mile or two and then turn to the star and ride into it.

"When the dawn comes keep the light on this hand," he said and he took her right hand by the wrist and held it up. "This hand," he said.

"No, I'm not going," she said.

"You will," he said, and it was clear there would be no argument she could make.

"Promise you will be careful," she said.

A cloud crossed over the moon and he made a kiss sound and Khyber stood up. He threw on the saddle, cinching it tight and set the bridle. Elizabeth stepped into the stirrup and lifted herself to the saddle.

The horse stiffened, raised her head and arched her tail. Michael roped Elizabeth to the saddle that she might ride long after her endurance could last. Her shoulders were already heavy with exhausting fear. She clung with both hands to the pommel. He told her there was a revolver in the saddle-bag and passed up the reins.

"Go before me and don't look back," he said, and he turned her facing west of north. "Ride for your safety. Ride steadily and do not stop. Khyber will get you through. She will go until she drops dead under you."

"How will you find me?"

"I will find you. Are you ready?"

"You will be careful of yourself?" she said.

"Let her go," he said.

She leaned forward in the saddle, touched her heels into the horse's sides and curving her neck, Khyber started on a full run along the bluff, penetrating the wall of pitchy darkness. The grass flew up behind her into the air. Elizabeth fixed on the star out the corner of her eye. She knew she could go west and then make a straight path in its direction for days. The mare flattened out and she pulled hard at the bit, showing she was capable of more speed and more speed as they buoyantly traveled beneath the starlit sky. The moon made her shadow long and black across the plain.

Michael dropped down on hands and knees and crawled toward a side ravine. He'd heard no commotion, no gunshots in the camp, and knew by experience that was not good. He looked at the ground in front of him and saw where something had stepped. It was a place where horses had stood. He knew they'd stood there looking over the bluff. He slid into the ravine and then ran through the thickets with the rifle slung and his revolver at half-arm. At the end of the ravine he waited and listened. There came to him the soft sound of men moving through the camp. There was a long, raw cry he heard and he knew what it was. He ran again, crouching behind every chance cover. He ran along the creek with all speed and reached the high curved bank. He worked along the bank of the creek and then without stopping he slipped quietly into the water and waded against the inky flow until he reached the camp shore.

There was a sound in front of him and then silence. The moon went under clouds and the night went very dark. He strained his eyes into the darkness where he could see black and uncertain shadows.

His only intentions were to secure a horse

and a Sharps and the belts of ammunition.

On the pathway he found Aubuchon and a spilled basket of sugar doughnuts. His throat had been cut and with one hand he clutched it in his grip. His eyes were still open and the blood seeped from between his fingers. His other hand, the outstretched fingers worked convulsively. He clasped and unclasped his hand. Michael took his hand and looked down into his face. He moved the hand, trying to point to Elizabeth's tent. His eyes spoke and then his eyes glassed and he was dead.

The walls of Elizabeth's tent were dimly illuminated by a lantern from within.

Inside was one of the hard boys from so many months ago. The boy was built compact and quick-motioned. He wore broadcloth trousers and a collarless flannel shirt. His hair was close-cropped. He wore two holsters on his belt and carried a revolver in each. He was holding Sabi by the scruff as she twisted and snapped at the air. He readied a knife to draw across her throat.

Michael wondered what spurs the boy wore and were his boots lace-up and did he wear the leather gaiters as he stepped up and slid his knife deep in the boy's side and into his kidney. He let the boy to the floor, the knife inside him. There was a look of horror in his eyes when he saw Michael's face.

"Let go the dog," Michael said, and when he did, Sabi ran away, disappearing in the blackness.

"You killed me," the boy said, his lips rimed with sugar from the doughnut in his mouth.

"Yes."

"What about my people?"

"I will tell them what happened to you."

"You will kill them too."

"If I can."

Michael was halfway round the tent when he saw someone coming stealthily toward him. He did not experience fear, but he understood that he could die. He let the man pass by and reaching through the darkness he caught the man's hair, jerked back his head, and with his knife hand drove the blade past his clavicle and into his heart. Just as quickly he drew back the knife and the blade swept the man's throat and his blood gushed from his neck. Another man came by, his arms full of goods. Like all thieves he could not help himself and clung to what he'd stolen. Michael clapped him fiercely on the sides of his head and burst the drums in his ears, then kicked out his legs and beat him to his knees. He pulled the man's own knife from its sheath and drove its blade into the man's heart.

He waited the slow passage of quiet time. Then a horse stamped and snorted. With the second Sharps, he squatted on his heels and let it slide beneath the waters of the creek and then he moved on to the peninsula.

The horses raised their heads, their ears pitched forward. From his stud, he picked out Kershaw, an exceptionally big and strong and biddable horse. His sides were sleek from good feed and with his strong hips and broad chest he needed a half mile of running to warm to his work.

The other horses were frantic, whirling and rearing and pulling at their pickets. He cut some free and others he pulled the pickets and let them drag. Then he mounted Kershaw. With the reins over his elbow, he patted Kershaw's neck to quiet him. He shortened his grip and leaned forward in the saddle, shifting his weight over the withers. He carried his Winchester in one boot and a .50-caliber Sharps in the other. Buckled around his waist was a belt with forty-two cartridges and another over his shoulder and dozens more loose in his coat pockets. He thought to go east down the creek, but Kershaw shied and balked, and from the east there came a gunshot and then another. He loosened the revolver in its holster and on direction Kershaw spun like a top. Again he shortened the reins in his hands and then he gave Kershaw his heels. With ears laid flat back, with a half turn, he got the horse into his stride. Kershaw stretched his head out and champed at the bit.

The first gallop lifted Michael and pushed him back and he returned himself forward again. To his right and left the horses ran with him, tossing their heads and needing to run with Kershaw. They came up from the peninsula and bore in the direction of the camp. They passed through it and were aimed for the crossing and the wagon road and the bluff beyond.

Drawn across the creek there was a brace of armed horsemen. He drew his revolver and when he came on them they behaved as surprised. He heard the wheep sound of an arrow, the shaft flying past his head. Then, coming off the bluff, was the red dog through the air and into their midst. The red dog latched onto a man's cheek and hung upon it and would not let go until it tore away when they splashed into the creek.

Michael touched with his knees and the horse whirled. He fired the revolver and shot one of the men through the forehead. He fired again and another man went down. A horse reared and the rider fell hard to the ground. Flash succeeded flash as Kershaw chafed at the bit. The red dog was a swirl of fury at the feet of the spooked and frightened horses. The men could not see the red dog bounding from side to side. They could not shoot as their horses reared and ran and they were dashed to the ground where the red dog did his savage work.

Michael dug in his heels. Kershaw sprang forward and went clattering across the creek and took the slope up the wagon road where they gained the level of the plain.

The men fired after him, but they were shooting uphill and their aim went over his head. The trailing horses were mixed in the chaos. The three-pound iron pickets snapped at the ends of their ropes and the horses slewed about and kicked in the air to rid themselves of the pickets. Their hooves kicked and scattered stones down the hillside as they made to escape the pickets flying behind them and follow the leader on the plain.

On level ground, Michael loosened the rein and Kershaw broke into a gallop. He threw his body to the off-side, hanging on by a leg, and Kershaw shot clear of the bluff and they were running west upon the plain that stretched for furlong upon furlong. Behind him he heard the panting and snorting of the other horses and they plunged on through the sea of darkness.

As the crow flies, they were four hundred miles from home and Elizabeth was out there somewhere and he had to find her.

Kershaw reeled suddenly and stepped stiff-legged into a hole with a sickening jar and was flung forward to the ground. Michael threw himself back and jerked up on the reins. The horse reared up his shoulders and struggled to find his footing. Michael slid to the ground into the flat dark silence to see Kershaw's left foreleg dangling below the knee. Michael took up the leg and felt the bone inside the skin. His cannon bone was shattered.

Head held high, the horse struggled once more to walk and it was painful to see the animal as it limped about in its crippled condition. The other horses, their nostrils distended, their ears pointed forward, came in close. They walked to surround Kershaw, nosing his flanks and sides. Kershaw pricked his ears and made a thrumming noise in his throat and it was if he knew his time was over. Michael held the horse's face against his own. He looked into his eyes. The horse nosed him and rubbed its head against him and made another muffled sound. Michael stepped away and looked to his back trail. He listened for the drum of hoof strokes on the hard plain. From the place of camp something was set afire and there was a red glow pulsing beneath the darkness. How many miles were they from camp, he wondered and figured it was three, four at the most and the carry of sound through the atmosphere. Michael removed the saddle from Kershaw and one last time the horse tried to walk.

Michael went to Starbuck. He spoke to the horse quietly, gently, and the horse stood for him as he bridled it and spread the blanket. He lifted up the saddle and cinched it tight. He knew he could not shoot Kershaw for the sound of the gunshot and he could not leave him to be dragged down by the wolves and disemboweled alive. He looked into the horse's trusting eyes and thanked him for his strength, courage, and speed.

"They can't hurt you now," he said, and he raised the point of his knife to Kershaw's throatlatch at the base of his jaw. With a sharp thrust he drove the knife blade deep. The horse made a stifled groan and Michael wrapped his arms around the horse's head as it collapsed and carried it to the ground. After that it did not take long.

He regained his seat and leaning along Starbuck's neck they veered north and broke into a gallop and were swept along as if by the darkness itself. The free horses ran with them and they entered the long and lonely hours of night.

Chapter 35

When he'd almost overtaken her, Starbuck drew down to a hand-gallop, twisting his head a little toward Khyber. He checked the horse and it broke into a trot. He called to her and the trot became very slow. As she reined Khyber to a halt to face him he heard the hammer drawn back on a revolver.

"Who comes there?" she cried, and she saw it was Michael. Running with him there were other horses: Concord, Boston, Worcester, Granby.

"How did you find us?"

He shook his head. He didn't know to explain. He just did.

"What did you see?" she said, her voice a hollow of sound.

"Do not ask me that," he said.

"Aubuchon?" she said, a terrible sadness clutching at her heart.

"They are gone," he said. His face was that of a man come from a bad dream.

"They are all gone. Every one of them."

Starbuck heaved a deep sigh, his returning self-possession. He blew his nostrils in a loud snort as he recovered his wind.

"We must ride," he said. "We must keep them at a long distance if they should come for us."

"Yes," she said. When she could she'd go down on her knees and bitterness in her heart she would remember the dead.

Starbuck lowered his head, laid his ears back, and bunched his mighty muscles. He smoothly lunged out ahead of Khyber and she let him run a stretch and then she followed, Elizabeth forward in the saddle. They put their horses at it and moved on in the night across the open country. The time was so vast, the horses laboring on. They kept on at a hard gallop, scattering the herds of antelope and buffalo that closed in behind them and crushed and ate the evidence of their route.

The horses tore through the cold air as if weightless. They trembled in every limb with danger and fear. They rode at a killing pace, the hooves thundering, the tails streaming on the wind, their broad chests flecked with white foam. Michael felt the horses' hearts beat quick and tremulous and he dared not spare them. They had to ride the heart out of them for the sake of their lives. They never once drew rein until the horses were at their extreme, panting and foaming and hundreds of miles yet to go.

The blackness of the night turned to gray and it was near daybreak when he slackened their pace and assumed a more collected canter. When they rode into the dawn world the wind rose with the sun and the day became warm and windy with cloud skeins of pure white drifting across the sky. They would halt to rest. He reined back the horse and brought out his field glass. Standing high in the stirrup irons, he turned in the saddle to look east where the brightness was. He looked west where the darkness was and then he looked south. Elizabeth turned in the saddle to look also, a hand on Khyber's rump and she gasped. Michael's shirt was as if a blouse of crimson with the blood that drenched him.

"It's not mine," he said, and she felt relief and thankfulness. In the thin white light she saw how tired his face, his look of concentrated thought and resolute determination. He patted the swelling veins in Starbuck's arched neck. Now that he could see, speed was nothing to him and he'd make no attempt to keep it up. For the next while they would husband the strength of the horses and hold them well within themselves, so they might run again with the onset of darkness. They dismounted to relieve Starbuck and Khyber. He brought the glasses to bear and scanned again, sweeping his eyes, inch by inch, along the line of the horizon, until the entire circuit had been completed.

"We should change horses," she said.

"Not yet," he said.

He stood with his back to her as he studied the south horizon. She pressed his shoulders gently and then held herself against him. The smell of the horse's blood was on him.

The sun was coming hot and the air was watery with evaporation. Three more horses came in to make seven: Bayard, Marengo, and Diamond. They'd lost their picket pins and he cut away the ropes they dragged.

"Who were they?" she said.

"Whitechurch," he said, and it was another lesson in business, a secret revealed. One way or another men like Whitechurch would get what they wanted.

"Do you think they are coming?" she said.

"Yes," he said.

Through the yellow haze of the morning they could see the line of a river. They walked on a little longer before they mounted again and rode toward it. He did not want to stay where they might be seen, and if they were seen, it was an imperative they not have the river at their back but to their front for the widest sight lines.

By now the whole country was bright with a white light. Between them and the river there was an undulation in the land. They descended, then rose on its other side, and then they could see for miles, the clear atmosphere shrinking the distance. It must have been thirty miles with no tree, no bush, no landmark, only swell after swell of the solitary plain.

They turned back to the river and from over the water came the breath of morning and the horses scented it. He checked Starbuck and scrutinized the crossing. He calculated it to be two hundred yards across. It was a shallow braided river meandering across sandbars where willows grew and driftwood snagged. He studied the contour of a bar, the ripples on the surface, the water gurgling as a subcurrent rose to the surface.

He watched the loose horses as they descended the gradual slope to the water and stood to their bellies in the eddies with footing that seemed firm, their noses buried beneath the surface.

"Keep both your feet out of the stirrups," Michael said. "She will not go down, but if she does, slide back and hang to her tail and let her swim you out."

Starbuck went forward at an angle to the current, testing the sand with each step and Khyber following closely. The air above the water was surprisingly cold. Midstream the current bore down on them with all its volume. Starbuck stumbled and regained his feet. They bumped onto a ragged island, crossed it, and entered the water again. They struggled on until finally, the crossing complete, the horses climbed over a sandbar and onto the far bank. She could not know how relieved he was with the river now between them and whoever might follow.

They left the cover of the bottom and climbed slowly to a grassy bench on the far bank where they commanded a view of the river as well as the trail. When Elizabeth dismounted Khyber walked up behind her and nuzzled her shoulder.

Two does started from the violet shadows of the brush in the bottom, one of which he shot with the Winchester. Trotting out behind them was the red dog. His face and jaws were bloodstained and the blood clotted his back and coat and the hair on his breast. He was cut four inches long across his back. It was a fresh wound and still bled.

Then came Sabi, her long coat mudded

and thick with cockleburs. One ear was pinned back and her feet were cut and hot. She lay down on her side, her panting tongue lolled on the ground. She could go no farther.

"Sabi," Elizabeth cried as Michael dismounted and went to her. He felt her heart and bones and let her drink water he spilled into the palm of his hand.

It was here they would off-saddle for a spell. Michael loosened the horses' girths and slid the saddles to the ground. The horses sighed deeply. The high bank was covered with grass and the horses cropped the blades, quietly whisking their long tails.

He washed out the red dog's wound and swabbed it with carbolic acid, all the while keeping ceaseless vigilance. He doubled one leg under and sat upon it while he concentrated on closing the wound with six neat stitches and then more carbolic acid. Occasionally the red dog looked into his face and seemed to understand what he was doing.

He then sharpened his knife and took Sabi in his lap. He shaved the worst knots and tangles from her tail and hide. He unpinned her ear and washed her face. He found her moccasins in the saddlebag. He carried her to the doe that she might lick the restorative blood.

They took turns going down to the river, drinking and bathing their faces and necks with the cool water. When Elizabeth touched the glittering water it was so cold and her skin so parched she was stung by it. Her face and hands were burned from the sun as if by fire. Slowly her parched and cracked lips cooled and her nose and eyes were soothed. She drank a little and when she climbed the bluff Michael fed her pieces of liver from the doe.

Down at the river, Michael let the water run through his fingers, his eyes roaming the barren land. He took one last drink and went back up the bank. Elizabeth shut her eyes and rested her head against Starbuck's saddle. She missed the ever-faithful Aubuchon and could only think his blood was on her hands. She understood he died because of her willfulness. So many had died because of her.

"Aubuchon?" she said.

"There was no torment to be seen. His face was at rest."

"Oh," she said, and the tears ran down her cheeks.

Michael looked across the river from under his shading hand. He knew soon enough would come the foaming horses and riders on their backs and then there was something out there.

When he saw them he could not count their numbers for the golden haze on the horizon. He knew he needed to keep a regular interval between them, but he wanted them closer and when they were he placed the big rifle in position across Khyber's saddle. He watched the figure of a horseman pacing back and forth. He looked like he was trying to decide whether to come on or stay back and at four hundred yards he decided to stay back.

In the blue distance another was working his way closer. He was behind a swell in the ground and coming on an oblique angle. He was lying flat down on his horse's back and then he slid to the offside. Michael dropped his right knee on the ground, took aim, and fired the Sharps, and the five-hundred-grain bullet struck the horse in its cervical vertebrae. Its shape collapsed in the air. Then came the loud boom and the smoke floating away in the air to the south and he saw that he'd killed the rider through the horse's neck.

Elizabeth started. She felt a shudder go through her. She'd just seen a man killed. Starbuck picked his head up and snorted.

Michael had already reloaded the rifle. The rider at four hundred yards brought his horse forward a few steps. Michael shot him and reloaded again.

Above, the sky was blue and cloudless. There was something sweet and balmy in the transparent air. The tears were welling up in her eyes again. She felt haunted by death and guilt and the fear of damnation.

"It's not your fault," he said in a voice faraway.

"These men are on my conscience," she said.

"What's done is done," he said.

"Can you see them?" she said. "Do you think they will stop?"

"I hope not," he said, and it was then she understood why he dallied. Down here there were no consequences for killing men. He'd kill them down here where nobody cared.

Water, earth, and sky glowed as if they had been set on fire. The river was cast red as if dyed with blood.

Michael and Elizabeth were on the move again galloping a little east of north, pushing on. Sabi rode in his lap and the red dog loped along beside. The strong-lunged horses had regained their wind and this time when they rode they settled into a never-tiring lope, the other horses running with them.

Michael kept vigil on their back trail and their flanks. Some were too quick and made off before he could get a shot, but not often. From time to time he turned and rode in their direction and watched them scatter and each time upon dismounting from Starbuck, he leveled the Sharps across the saddle. He permitted them to come close and then he fired and killed and they rode on again.

They crossed a dry periodic creek and paused to let the horses graze.

Charlie was so much in her mind. She thought how he'd never had a proper bringing up or at most the wrong kind. He was a boy, innocent and natural. She wondered if there'd ever be a future for boys like him born into such a violent world. Her eyes began to sting with tears. What rights did she have when she let this boy slip through her fingers?

They traveled on in the broad light where they could see for miles. She rode beside him, her limbs aching with tiredness.

While the horses took a bite of grass, he again picked out the foremost rider and shot him and it was the death of another man. The pattern repeated again and again and she became angry with them, they were so stupid to go against his rifle. The belts were more than full enough to get them home and to the center of care.

The day turned hot and unpleasant and the journey took its toll on the horses. The wind was dry and withering and blew stiff and strong in their faces.

"Is there immediate danger?" she said.

"Yes," he said, letting his hand to pet Sabi.

"Where?" she said, and then, "I see them."

They emerged from a fold and onto a swell and she could see them again, their dark figures through clouds of dust. Wheeling Starbuck about, he saw them too. They were coming over the edge of the world, but this time he did not dismount.

"Is there not danger this time?" she said.

"Everywhere," he said, smiling grimly.

"I am not overwhelmed," she said.

"Soon it will be done," he said.

"Maybe someday we will return," she said.

"Yes," he said. "If you'd like."

"Maybe. Probably not," she said, and they both laughed.

On the landscape ahead a whirl of dust arose and blew south. He placed his right hand at his breast pocket to feel for his matches, but his pocket had filled with blood when he killed Kershaw and the matches were soaked and dried and now the pocket was as hard and stiff as tree bark.

"Is there tobacco and matches in there?" he said, indicating his saddlebag.

She reached back and opened the flap where she found his tobacco and papers and matches. He spoke to Starbuck and the horse steadied. Swaying in the saddle, the reins in the crook of his left arm, he rolled a cigarette. He struck a match and lit his cigarette. The red dog came in, sat back on his haunches, watched him intently. In thought, Michael held the match and then he dropped its flame in the tinder field of grass. It was a waterless place and the grass tongued with pale yellow and soon there were little waves and spurting streaks of fire running south before the wind. The red dog barked and danced. In every moment the blaze increased as it made its destroying way.

"This is how it will end," he said.

Elizabeth watched the fire. She understood and soon the yellow was papering the sky and crackling and rising and spreading its way south as fast as a horse could run and east and west and the lighting and the smoke cloud were beautiful and fairylike to her eyes.

He made a curse and it was then he

dropped from the saddle to the ground. He inspected his girth and pulled the big rifle from its boot and this time he stood erect and held the Sharps in his hands, the butt plate tucked into his shoulder.

At considerable distance, he knew the horse, the rider, his peculiar slouching seat, the bedroll behind his saddle, the black runner. They were crossing a beautiful sparkling and delusive lake. There were cattails and nodding bulrushes. Above the rider and the black runner rode their superior image in the sky. The runner's legs appeared twenty feet long and the rider was as if another twenty feet over that. Elizabeth saw it too and tipped back her head to take in the sight. There was an anger burning inside him and this was the man he wanted to kill.

As the flames began to roar he took two steps forward into the ashy cradle of the fire and one step back. He let down the rifle and waited as if for some sign of relenting, but it did not come. There was no reason to think anymore. There was no reason to wait. He brought the rifle around in front, adjusted for elevation, steadied his eye and opened his mouth. All things hovered and he pulled the trigger and they changed. A fume of blood spewed from the man's head and he fell to the ground as the horse ran out from under him.

Michael reached for the bridle reins and mounted Starbuck. He secured Sabi in his lap and whistled up the red dog. He adjusted their direction a few degrees north-northeast.

"Is it over?" she said.

"That's the story," he said, and made a nicking sound. Starbuck stepped off and then Khyber and they dropped into an easy canter and they moved on. A great conflagration was building in their wake, fueling and racing on the pinions of the wind that came against them and was a terrific roar and already a quarter mile long and twelve feet high. Behind them were the currents of fierce heat, the suffocating smoke, the sky red with burning flags.

The fire burned everything in its path. It burned the earth and the air and the water. It burned memory and history and experience. It burned everything that came before and she wished on the flames roaring with all they consumed and what remained.

In this way, they rode out of a past forever gone and it was as if they'd never been and none of what happened ever took place. Behind them the land glowed with red teeth and a wall of smoke filled the sky. She looked back once as if searching for something she left behind. It would be dark soon and they still had a long way to go.

ABOUT THE AUTHOR

Robert Olmstead is the author of eight books. *The Coldest Night* was a finalist for the Dayton Literary Peace Prize, a *Publishers Weekly* Best Book of 2012, a *Kirkus Reviews* Top 25 Fiction Book of 2012, and an Amazon Best Book of 2012. *Coal Black Horse* was the winner of the Heartland Prize for Fiction and the Ohioana Award and was a #1 Book Sense pick. *Far Bright Star* was the winner of the Western Writers of America Spur Award. Olmstead is the recipient of a Guggenheim Fellowship and an NEA grant and is a professor at Ohio Wesleyan University.

The employees of Thorndike Press hope you have enjoyed this Large Print book. All our Thorndike, Wheeler, and Kennebec Large Print titles are designed for easy reading, and all our books are made to last. Other Thorndike Press Large Print books are available at your library, through selected bookstores, or directly from us.

For information about titles, please call:
(800) 223-1244

or visit our website at:
gale.com/thorndike

To share your comments, please write:
Publisher
Thorndike Press
10 Water St., Suite 310
Waterville, ME 04901